AGATES ARE FOREVER

AGATES ARE FOREVER

A NICK CAMERON Mystery

LOGAN TERRET

SPARKPRESS

Published by SparkPress, a BookSparks imprint,
A division of SparkPoint Studio, LLC
Phoenix, Arizona, USA, 85007
www.gosparkpress.com

Published 2025
Printed in the United States of America

Print ISBN: 978-1-68463-288-6
E-ISBN: 978-1-68463-289-3
Library of Congress Control Number: 2024917350

Inteior design and typeset by Katherine Lloyd, The DESK
Original artwork by Michael Patrick Bailey

Dedicated to those who love rocks,

Raymond Chandler,

Charles Portis,

Martín Luis Guzmán, Nellie Campobello,

and Clarence Clemens Clendenen

"Geologists have a saying—
rocks remember."

—*Neil Armstrong*

CONTENTS

1

AN ACE OF DAMES

Most guys go their whole lives without finding a corpse. I need to stop finding them. Usually, it's only a minor inconvenience. But I never know.

So sit down and join me for a late dinner in Quartzrock, Arizona. It's a desiccated dump in the flat Sonoran Desert near the California border. Imagine a hundred RV parks on the surface of Mercury, and you've got it. Somehow it became a rock show mecca, and swarms of lapidaries settled here. Two are about to depart the business. Permanently.

Not me, though. I'm a geologist, and I'm here for the rock show tomorrow. I'm eating my usual hot beef sandwich in a booth at the Flying Mulewhip under a local artist's masterpiece—*Exaltation of the Mule*—which shows the kind of mule you'd take home to meet your mother. I see this hot dame come in. Long, dark hair, olive skin, Southern Italian or Greek. She's wearing a windbreaker, so I know she's from up north. It's sixty degrees outside, and an Arizona dame would be wearing a puffy coat and Uggs.

She looks around, then starts my way. There's a suspicious bulge in her jacket. I keep eating and pretend to ignore it, but she walks right up to my booth.

"You're Nick Cameron, the consulting geologist?"

I shrug. She reaches for the jacket bulge, then throws a hand-ful of rocks onto my plate. Gravy splashes all over my shirt and the Formica table.

"Ural mins," I mumble, which is how you say, "You little minx!" with your mouth full of mashed potatoes.

Hold it. These are the best Lake Superior agates I've seen.

"More where those came from," she says, taking a seat at the opposite end of the booth and giving her raven hair a coquettish toss. She's on the petite side and a real dish, worth scorching your eyes on. From her emerald eyes to her marathoner thighs, with stratovolcano breasts in between, she's hotter than a Soviet drill bit at the bottom of the Kola Superdeep Borehole. She sears her eyes into me—her left elbow is on the table and her chin rests on her knuckles as she scans me like a pyrometer drone checking out hot spots on Stromboli.

Now, I know some lapidaries in Ashland, Wisconsin, on Chequamegon Bay, which is like the El Dorado of Lake Superior agates. And I know some yeggs opened Johnny Rocco's rock shop safe for fifty pounds of agates last Thursday. So I think the stuff's likely hot.

"How much is more?" I ask.

"I'm at the Truck Stop," she says, rising. "Ice cream truck. Come see me and find out."

But I don't follow her out. I let her go and finish my meal.

The Truck Stop is not a truck stop. It's a motel. Trucks converted to rooms, cabins, whatever you call them. Scattered around on a two-acre patch of gravel. One is an old ice cream truck.

I stay in the garbage truck. It has a steel door with two combination dead bolts. See, when I come to town, I have stuff people want to steal. And I have enemies. I broke the Flagstaff Archaeopteryx ring. You probably heard of that. I've exposed more counterfeit dinosaur eggs, claws, and teeth than you can imagine. And whenever a new Lost Dutchman's Mine scam comes along, which is about every month, I hand the case to the Feds on a relish tray. The grifters in that racket hate me. The last thing they want on their tail is a thirty-five-year-old PhD geologist who boxes for fun and packs a Colt Commander.

I ask Janie, the waitress, for a refill on my coffee, and she comes back with the pot.

"Hey, Janie, you know that dame?" I ask.

"No, you big mug," she says, feigning jealousy and tilting a hip. "What'd the little chippy want?"

I like Janie. She gets it.

"Got some rocks to sell." I show her the agates.

"Nice. You buying?" She gives me a wink as she coos, "buying."

"Nope. But I'll take a look. At the agates. Already had a good look at her."

Janie says a mug like me could get in big trouble with a floozy like that, but it doesn't matter because Sheriff Pershing will run her out of town within the hour anyway.

I've seen all my usual clients—I hold court at the Flying Mule-whip on rock show eve—so I pay my tab, leave Janie my usual 100 percent tip, and head for the Truck Stop. It's only a half mile, so I walk. Geologists do a lot of walking. Especially in the dirt, which I'm doing now because there's a dearth of sidewalks in this pigsty.

I unlock the garbage truck, settle in, and open my vintage Samsonite travel bar. I think Philip Marlowe had one. If not, he should have. I pour myself an Old Cornpone, which is my favorite bourbon. I own a dozen barrels of it, sitting in a Kentucky rack house somewhere. It's not for me—I only drink a few bottles per year. It's an alternative investment. It's like a zero-coupon bond that gets bottled when it matures.

Now, what do I do with the rock-throwing minx? First thing I do is call Johnny Rocco and get a description of the stolen agates. They sound mediocre, not worth cracking a safe for. Not even worth putting in a safe in the first place, to tell the truth. But he says there were a few good ones, and maybe those are the ones the dame threw on my plate. I wouldn't trust Johnny farther than I can throw the Cape York meteorite, but stealing is stealing, and if the agates are his, I'll get them back.

I look out the window. The garbage truck has only one, but it's big, barred with a wrought-iron grid, and eight feet off the ground, so totally secure. The ice cream truck is about twenty-five yards away, and there are no lights on. It's too early for her to be in bed. Unless she's turning a trick, as Janie would say. But I don't think that's her style, not that she'd have trouble finding customers. She's probably in the Truck Stop Clubhouse, a Western bar and restaurant next to the tank truck. The tank truck is for large families. No, I won't go and see. She knows where to find me.

Tomorrow afternoon, I'll be appraising at the fossil tent. It's tiring work, so I try to catch some shut-eye. For bedtime reading I have a copy of *Two Smart Dames* I found at a local junk store. Copyright 1949. The cover art is appropriately lurid for the genre but doesn't fit the title. The two smart dames are in negligees. Why not graduation gowns with thigh splits? I doze off as Shaun O'Malley, PI, finds his partner on a slab in the morgue. But around midnight, I hear the bell on the ice cream truck jingling. It's a little brass bell where you shake the clapper. Some cutesy ice cream truck thing. I go to the window. There she is, standing by the bell, looking my way. She knows I'm here, and she wants to talk. I go to her truck.

Some dames ask me to look at their rocks when they really want something else. Not this one. She wants to get right to it. The rocks, I mean.

She says her name is Theo and offers me a drink. Jägermeister, which is like a handful of black jelly beans with an Everclear chaser. I respectfully decline. Then she drags out some burlap bags and plops them on a table.

A geologist usually wears his loupe on a lanyard around his neck. For me, that's just a garroting waiting to happen. I keep mine in my jacket pocket. When I go for it, she leaps to the bed and grabs a roscoe from under the pillow. She points the gun at the floor with her finger off the trigger, using the two-handed Weaver hold, her eyes on my right hand and ready for instant response. This dame knows what she's doing. Her gun's a Smith & Wesson snub-nosed revolver. Five shots for sure, no jams, and especially good for a southpaw, which I see she is. I approve.

"Relax, sister," I say, slowly pulling the loupe from my pocket. She puts the gun away but doesn't apologize. She shouldn't. Her reaction was reasonable, under the circumstances.

Most agates are sold by the bushel, but not these. These are prime gemstones, expertly cut and shaped, mainly cabochons but some faceted, all with perfect banding and colors that are rich, rare, and varied. The pick of a thousand bushels. Obviously not from Johnny Rocco's safe. But here's the thing: they were highly polished once, but they've been underwater awhile. A long while.

Easy to restore the polish, but that's not the point. I think she may have stumbled on some old-timer's cache. But that's not my business. These have been in the drink so long the old-timer would be moldering in the boneyard by now.

"Nice rocks," I say. "So what's your game?"

She says she's selling them for her brother. Not sure I believe that, but I ask if he has more. Yes, he does. Lots more.

"It looks like these have been underwater a long time," I say.

She gives me that wide-eyed "what are you, a wizard?" look I get from devious lapidaries when I call out something that's blazingly obvious to any geologist.

"I think they have," she says.

And that's all she says. No explanation why. That's odd, and I'm not sure I want to get involved. I don't need clients, so I choose them carefully. They need to be frank with me. And not splash gravy on my shirts.

"It's late. Let's talk about it over breakfast," I say.

She can tell I'm suspicious, but I think she respects that. And she hasn't gazed into my eyes with breathless longing, so I say goodnight and hit the rack in the garbage truck.

2

A DEUCE OF STIFFS

I wake up at 06:00 and text Paco Madero. He's one of the two lapidaries in Quartzrock who could afford to buy the agates. The other is Joey Huerta, and I text him too. They're both early risers. Neither has seen a batch of gem-grade agates recently, and they're interested.

I'm shaving when I hear the ice cream truck bell tinkle. I look out. There she is. With a tight sweater over those stratovolcano breasts and tight jeans on those marathoner thighs, she's hotter than a uraninite vein at the Oklo natural fission reactor in the Statherian Period. But she doesn't come to my truck, just stands there looking at my window. I notice her car has Wisconsin plates. Lake Superior agates, tolerates the cold, Wisconsin plates—ten to one she's from far Northern Wisconsin.

I finish shaving but don't go to meet her. I pick up where I left off in *Two Smart Dames* and wait until she knocks. A few minutes later, she does.

We walk to the Flying Mulewhip. I order the Muleskinner's Snack, which is chicken-fried steak with three eggs, hash browns, toast, and fried apples. She orders the Yard Waste Special, which is an enormous salad, with the chicken option for protein.

Over breakfast, I give her my estimate. She grins like one of those ads for dental implants, showing off her alabaster chompers.

She must have a good dentist, which is unusual for Northern Wisconsin. I edge into asking her how much more her brother has. If he's sitting on a huge stash, he could break the market if he tries to dump it all. Not that I care, personally, but I'd like to tell my clients if there's a chance of that.

But she doesn't bite. For now, she just says he has a lot more. Whether he does and whether "he" even exists, I don't know.

Enough bullshit.

"I need to know the provenance," I say. "I don't touch swag, and I don't like lost-and-found. So where'd you get the agates?"

We stare into each other's eyes. Hers are green. Mine are blue. If we had kids, would their eyes be aqua?

"A relative collected them."

"And this relative stored them in a fish tank, or what?"

"He put them in a place where they got wet all the time."

"And why did he do that?"

"Because it was a good hiding place."

I think she's telling the truth, as far as it goes. She hasn't grabbed her nose, tugged on her ears, looked away, furrowed her brow, hidden her palms, or done any of the other things amateur detectives think signal lying but really do not. Truthful people give prompt, direct, and concise answers, and that's what she's doing.

"Okay," I say. "Two guys are interested. Paco Madero is free before ten, and Joey Huerta is free from ten to noon. Normally, I'd charge ten percent for brokering a deal like this, but I'm already in town, so I'll do it for five percent plus ten bucks to launder my gravy-stained shirt. Agreed?"

She smiles and nods. We shake on it. A warm glow pulses between our hands, like energy is passing between us. We both pretend we didn't notice.

It's 09:00 by the time we finish breakfast, and Paco said to be there before ten, so we saunter back to the ice cream truck and load the rocks into my two-year-old Porsche 911. I got it at a bargain price from a guy who wanted a Maserati sedan instead. He was an anesthesiologist, and he must have anesthetized his brain or he would not have made that choice.

I drive us to Paco's compound. He's got a dusty, barren acre fenced in chain-link with three double-wide trailers on it. Lives in one, store in another (appointment only), and his shop in the third. Normally, he'd buzz us in—there's a camera at the gate and it sends motion alerts, so he knows when someone arrives even before they push the buzzer. Today he doesn't buzz us in, so I figure he's working in the shop. I know the code, so I open the gate.

We pull up at the shop. Usually, it's noisy in there because of the tumblers, rock saws, and whatnot. Today, dead silence. And the door is ajar.

"Is something wrong?" Theo says.

Well, yeah, there is. I open the door and see the big vibratory rock tumbler knocked over with Paco's big body face down on the floor, his head stuffed inside the bowl. Half-tumbled Petoskey stones and dirty gray tumbling mud are all over the place.

Paco's not breathing. I feel his wrist. No pulse and he's already getting cold. No point trying CPR.

Most people would be screaming and running for the door and spewing all over the place. Not Theo.

"Is he dead?" she asks calmly.

"Yeah. Paco Madero has gone to the big gem show in the sky."

"What do we do now?" she says.

What we do is stand outside, roscoes out, backs to the wall. She watches left, I watch right. I call 911. My guess is that whoever did this is long gone, but who knows—somebody might be in the house or the store. The only odd thing I notice in the compound is a big pile of crushed stone by the gate. It wasn't there on my last visit, and it's topped with a sign that reads, redundantly, *Hermosos Paisajes Landscapes*. These redundancies are common in Arizona, like Table Mesa and Picacho Peak. California is no better. Check out the La Brea Tar Pits in LA.

Within ten minutes, we have an ambulance, two sheriff's patrol cars, the highway patrol, and the sheriff himself. If you think they're suspicious because we both have roscoes, you don't know Arizona. Here, cops think it's suspicious if you don't have a roscoe.

We spend the rest of the morning talking with cops. I know defense attorneys say this is a bad idea, but that's because all their clients are guilty. My attorney says if you're a clueless innocent bystander, go ahead and talk. Just don't lie and don't speculate. If you don't know, just say, "I dunno."

The cops interview us separately. They spend a lot of time with me because I know a lot about Paco, and they want to know everything about him. Yes, people said he was sometimes involved in dodgy dealings—for example, La Pierre de la Chienne, or Dogstone, which was a legendary Petoskey stone presented to Louis XIV by Jesuit missionaries from New France and set in the jeweled collar of his beloved dog Bonne. Paco claimed Charles de Gaulle carried it out of France in 1940 and entrusted it to the Mexican ambassador in London in 1944 as security for a secret Mexican loan to the Free French. Somehow, it ended up in Quartzrock after being pilfered from a diplomatic bag on its way to Mexico City. I think he stole the plot from a thriller he was reading. Nobody in Quartzrock believed it, though a shady French collector did, to the tune of 800 Gs. But I have no personal knowledge of those dealings, just hearsay. Paco was always strictly on the level with me. Somewhat eccentric, but most lapidaries are. A good friend, if not a close one, and I'll miss our poker games. Do I have any idea who might want to murder him? No. I tell them Paco worked the Dogstone scam with his buddy Joey Huerta, and they should talk with him.

As morning wears on, I get the feeling Theo and I are suspects. Later, I find out they checked with Leonard, owner of the Truck Stop, who verified that we were there until we left for breakfast, walking. And with Janie, who verified that we were having breakfast at about the time Paco cashed in. And with every jamoke along the way who saw us walking to the Flying Mulewhip and back and God knows who else. Our story checks out every which way.

You might think that would eliminate us as suspects, but no. Not with the Arizona Department of Public Safety and the DPS Sherlock who's joined the investigation. It does eliminate us with Sheriff Pershing, though. The county mountie knows me and knows that while I stumble on lots of corpses—hey, show me a consulting geologist who doesn't—I don't make corpses. Not usually, anyway. And I can tell he thinks Theo is just as surprised by the whole thing as he is. He says she's got no rap sheet either. Given her behavior at the Flying Mulewhip, I would have expected at least a few arrests for rock assault.

Around noon, Sherlock starts asking me why a PhD geologist hangs out with lapidaries and amateur paleontologists. I tell him I have enough dough to do what I like, and I'd rather deal with lapidaries and amateur paleontologists than blowhard Texans in the oil patch. And that I expect even more dough from my pending patents for hydrogen production by water oxidation of iron-bearing minerals *in situ*. Maybe enough to leave me playing poker with Elon Musk and calling his bluffs.

This shuts Sherlock up for the moment. He decides to give us a break and talk with Joey Huerta. After all, when one rock dealer is murdered, his buddy rock dealer might know the killer. If he isn't the killer himself. Didn't I tell him that two hours ago?

The sheriff brings us some KFC and leaves us alone to eat. Neither of us does.

Then I hear sirens. First one, then another, then another. Ten minutes later, the sheriff comes in shaking his head and rolling his eyes.

Joey Huerta is dead. The DPS Sherlock found him in his living room, squashed under a seven-hundred-pound amethyst geode.

Joey Huerta being murdered while we were talking with a gazillion cops might suggest we are not the perps in either case. But no! See, in Sherlock's mind, we could be part of a gang conspiracy to murder leading rock merchants.

What finally lifts the cloud are Paco's security cameras. They show a short, dumpy guy who looks like a hobo creeping under the fence at Paco's compound, going into the shop, emerging covered with tumbling mud, and creeping away under the fence again. Some poor CSI slobs are rooting around in the gravel like truffle pigs snouting a trail of tumbling mud, we are assured. Maybe they think the guy dropped his driver's license or something.

Security cameras also rule out the assistant medical examiner's theory that Paco committed suicide by plunging his head into the rock tumbler and drowning himself. And that Joey accidentally toppled the giant geode onto himself while dusting it.

So now the cops have two murders on their hands with nothing to go on but some low-resolution video showing a short, dumpy guy who looks like a hobo. The action plan? Run around town stopping every short, dumpy guy who looks like a hobo.

In Quartzrock, that's half the male population.

So Theo and I are free to go. She's tired and a little shaken up—not that she shows it, but I can tell. I take her back to the ice cream truck. Let her rest for a few hours and plan my seduction. And let Jeweler Jake cover for me at the fossil tent. I do the same for him sometimes. Right now, I have other plans.

Before leaving, I ask Leonard to keep an eye on the ice cream truck and tell him to repel boarders if he sees a short, dumpy guy who looks like a hobo. If some palooka is running around whacking rock dealers, Theo might be on the list.

Me, I'm always on the list.

Now, there's one guy in this town who really knows what's going on, but nobody really knows him aside from me, Sheriff Pershing, and maybe a couple high-end jewelers. That guy is Francesco Benally. But just Frankie to us. Navajo father and Italian mother.

Nobody in Quartzrock, except me, knows where Frankie gets his dough. He makes fine, and I mean fine, Navajo jewelry, the kind people commission, not the stuff you buy at gas stations. But he spends forever making each piece perfect, so he doesn't sell many. Of course, he knows a lot about gemstones. But whenever he has doubts or just wants to confirm his gut feel, he calls yours truly. And in return, he gives me information. And feeds me if it's lunchtime. Which it is. I can smell pancetta frying. *Una mano lava l'altra*, as Frankie says.

Frankie doesn't have a shop. His house (a double-wide) is his shop, with workspaces here and there. Every time I visit, he's moved stuff around. I see an original Modigliani drawing has switched places with a 1920s Navajo storm rug. No, you don't throw a rug like that on the floor.

"Hey, Frankie, it's Nick," I call through the screen door. "I got somethin' for ya."

"Door's open," he calls from the kitchen.

I lay a large *soppressata* on the kitchen counter. It's a Calabrian-style salami I get from Andretti's restaurant and market in Scottsdale.

He doesn't say anything, which for him is not unusual. Why bother? He knows I always bring him soppressata, and he knows I'm here for (1) the carbonara he's making and (2) a lead on who whacked Paco and Joey. He points to the kitchen table. Some turquoise there.

I take a gander at the rocks.

"It's all fake," I say. "You don't need me to tell you that."

"It's nicer if I tell the customer you say it's fake. He won't feel like a complete fool if he thinks it takes an expert to see that. The guy wants me to make a necklace for his girlfriend, but I'm not putting my name on that junk."

Frankie thumps down a bowl of carbonara in front of me. He's holding the bowl by the rim with his beefy fingers in a talon grip, and his palm completely covers the top. I'm not a small man, but Frankie could be a lineman for the Patriots. How he makes fine jewelry with those huge mitts escapes me. Maybe mass gives stability.

"He took the railroad," he says.

"Who took the railroad?"

"The short, dumpy guy who looks like a hobo, idiot. What you geniuses missed is that he *is* a hobo, so he likely hopped one of those short freights at Hope. He's probably caught an east-bound at Williams by now."

"So who the hell is he?"

3

A GREEK RADIOMAN STRIKES IT RICH

"They had it comin'," Frankie says.

Hmm. How do two rock-tumbling reprobates get on the wrong side of a homicidal hobo? No point asking. Vendettas are common among lapidaries, believe it or not. Now, the right thing to do is cut the cackle and eat. Frankie will spill when he's ready.

But he doesn't.

"My advice to you," he says after a few minutes, "is to get out of town and take your lady friend with you. I'll buy her agates. You can drop them off with Yazzie in Window Rock. He'll retail them for me."

"I'm not going to Window Rock," I say.

Silence for fifteen seconds. Seems like thirty.

"Okay, I'm going to Window Rock," I say.

Still silent. Now for about a minute.

"You know who your lady friend is?" Frankie asks.

Well, no, I don't. I only know she calls herself Theo. I'd assumed she didn't want to tell me more because she was wanted on rock assault charges or possibly morals charges or both in twenty or thirty states. But I was wrong about that.

"No," I say. "Who is she?"

"She's one of Metaxas's grandkids. She and her twin brother."

I put down my fork and lean back in my chair. Who has not heard of the Metaxas Agate Fortune? Well, you, for starters, so here's the story.

Miles Metaxas—radioman on a Greek freighter called *Paralos*—puts in at NYC in the 1930s. Back then, it took forever to unload and load a ship, with lighters and cranes and hooks and cargo nets and longshoremen looting stuff and so on. So he has a week or two of leave and decides to visit a cousin in Chicago.

He likes Chicago but doesn't have the money to open a restaurant. But he gets an idea. People in remote areas need vacuum tubes and radio repair, and he knows all about that. So he buys a used car, a stock of tubes and radio parts, and bums around Northern Wisconsin selling vacuum tubes and fixing anything with a vacuum tube in it. Screw that *Paralos* scow and her jerk of a second mate anyway.

Business is slow until he stops in Hurley, a slime pit in far Northern Wisconsin that was the vice capital of the Northwoods at the time. Jackpot! Hurley has more bars and bawdy houses than permanent residents. And they all have radios and phonographs and jukeboxes making a din at all hours of the day and night. And they all use vacuum tubes, and half don't even work because the drunken gormless oafs have no idea how to repair them. But Miles Metaxas does!

So Miles spends a month in Hurley fixing their stuff and sells out his whole inventory of vacuum tubes, not to mention capacitors and resistors and potentiometers and so on. Then he sets off for Duluth, which is the nearest place he can get more.

Now, about twenty miles outside of Ashland, which is on Lake Superior at the south end of Chequamegon Bay, his car gets a flat tire. His spare is flat, he's out of patches, and nobody comes along, so he spends the night in his car. In the morning, he goes down to a creek to get some water and sees these funny-looking rocks in the creek bed.

Agates!

You might think he'd go up the creek looking for a source, but he doesn't. He follows the creek down, and when he hits the Lake Superior shoreline, he finds a pebble beach that's like the Comstock Lode of agates.

Long story short, back then land up there was really cheap, so he buys the lower part of the creek and a quarter mile of shoreline. And that's where the Metaxas Agate Fortune comes from.

Miles hooks up with some Scandi dish in Ashland and proposes. She's Danish. People are a little wary of Greeks up there, but her father figures if the first modern king of Greece came from the Danish royal family, who is he to squirrel the deal? Besides, Miles is rich. So Miles marries Katrine or whatever her name is and gets his cousin from Chicago to come up to Ashland and open a restaurant so he can eat real food instead of the roadkill the locals eat. Miles never really understands Katrine, and she never understands him, but despite that, or because of it, they are very happy together and do many charitable works. Eventually, they have a son who marries a reputable local girl—that's relative, you understand. At that time, "reputable" in Ashland just meant more reputable than in Hurley.

Anyway, by then, Miles has cashed out of the agate business and has a bunch of commercial real estate, stocks, bonds, and so on. To memorialize himself, he founds and liberally endows the Metaxas Radio History Museum in Chicago, which gets about three visitors per year, not that he cares. He outlives his son and croaks at a ridiculously old age, so old that when it hits the news that he's croaked, everybody is surprised because they thought he croaked twenty years ago. Kinda like Doris Day.

Miles leaves a foreign trust for his two grandchildren. But here's the catch. Miles doesn't want his heirs messing around in the agate business. He knows his success was dumb luck and figures if his grandkids try it, they'll end up in bankruptcy court.

Or in jail, which is where he thinks most lapidaries and gem merchants belong anyway. So if any trust beneficiary traffics in gemstones of any kind, including, without limitation, agates, he or she is cut off without a cent. If they both get cut off, the corpus of the trust goes to the radio museum.

So now I know why Theo didn't tell me her surname. And her story about the relative stashing agates makes sense. But why is she taking a big risk selling them?

4

MAKE MINE A MONSOON

I mentally rejoin Frankie, not that he's missed me. He's opened the slider door that leads from the kitchen to his deck and is sitting at the kitchen table, looking out toward a line of saw-toothed, barren mountains about ten miles away. These are young mountains, uplifted by detachment faulting in the late Eocene. They're dark and rugged, with jagged peaks and deep canyons.

"I guess old Miles's wife must have been quite a dish, if his granddaughter is any indication," I say.

No reply.

"So, any ideas on who pushed the button on Paco? And Joey?" I say.

Frankie is absorbed in the desert and doesn't answer. Some fluffy clouds have rolled in. The monsoon usually doesn't start until late June, but this year it's early.

"Smell the creosote?" he says.

"No," I say. He's talking about the smell of the creosote shrubs that dot the desert here. They're scraggly, bad-hair shrubs. The botanical version of a coyote. But they have big root systems that snarf water from ground you'd think is totally dry, and they will outlive all of us. A specimen in California is 11,700 years old, and its appearance hasn't improved with age.

"Close your eyes, breathe in slowly through your nose, and fill your sinuses," Frankie says.

Is this a yoga class or something? But I do it and catch a whiff of creosote. It means rain is coming.

"I don't know who killed Paco and Joey, Nick," Frankie says. "I know he's a hobo, and he's short and dumpy, but he's a strong man and a smart one."

I don't ask him how he knows these things. He's looking at the clouds and isn't talking much. There's a long silence. The clouds are piling up.

"Nick, I've lived here for almost twenty years. I can think of a dozen people who might want to kill Paco and Joey. But this guy isn't one of them. Which means his motive must be something I don't know about. Something new. But also something very old. It's interesting."

We sit in silence for a few minutes. I hear thunder. I can see Frankie wants quiet time to think about this, and it may take awhile. Maybe he'll have it figured out after I deliver the agates to Yazzie. I get up, wave, and leave him staring out the doorway at the thunderheads.

The rain starts as I get in my car, a few huge drops falling on my dusty windshield. I'll wait it out. Loud thunder is followed by a weird green twilight, like you sometimes get up north before a tornado. The monsoon hits with a punch of wind that rocks the car and then dies down as the rain comes in torrents. In ten minutes, it's over, the sun is shining, and my car is clean. Monsoon rains are brief.

I've missed most of the day at the fossil tent. Being a witness in a murder investigation is probably a good excuse, but I should make an appearance, and I do.

Andrew's fossil tent is big enough to host a circus sideshow, and it's filled with long rows of sturdy folding tables heaped with low-end fossils of ammonites, trilobites, shark's teeth, corals, fish, and so on. Heavy pieces of petrified wood lie under the tables on the dirt floor. The high-end stuff is wisely placed in glass display cases. My appraisal table is to the left of the entrance. It's a plain eight-foot plastic folding table like you see in VFW halls, with a cheap but comfortable executive chair from Office Depot on a plywood sheet. A cooler filled with ice water, Mountain Dew, and a few sandwiches sits to my left. Jake is sitting in my chair, standing in for me like I said he would, and he gets up when I walk in. He's heard about Paco and Joey and asks me for details. I tell him what I know, but there's a line building, so I sit down and get started.

I do appraisals for free as a favor to Andrew—it draws in the customers, and Andrew is a fair dealer, so he deserves the traffic. There are four types of people seeking appraisals, and the amount of time I spend on clients depends on how appreciative they are.

Client knows what he has	Client knows what it's worth	Client profile	Time allowed
Yes	Yes	Dealer/collector	1 minute, wasting my time
Yes	No	Rockhound	3 minutes
No	Yes	Delusional	2 minutes for kindly letdown
No	No	Dilettante	5 minutes

If the person is a kid, I increase the time allowance and tell them about the geologic era and period, its biota, and so on.

A freckly ginger kid with a Diamondbacks cap has an ammonite he just bought. I tell him all about ammonites, assure him he got a good deal (true), and then let him talk about baseball.

Some old woman has a Psychopyge trilobite with black shell preservation, and, astoundingly, iron pyrite (fool's gold) eyes. It's rare to find pyritization in trilobite fossils, and I've never seen one where only the eyes were pyritized, clearly showing their compound structure. The piece is striking. I give her my estimate, which prompts an "Oh, my!" Then I refer her to a jeweler in Scottsdale who collects high-end fossils and tell her to say Nick Cameron sent her.

Another kid has a piece of granite, borderline pegmatitic, with very coarse and unusual crystals. It's not a fossil, but who cares? I talk about granite.

I'm just finishing up a digression on the mother of all feldspar crystals when my phone bings. It's an alert from Leonard at the Truck Stop: *Hobo on the port bow.*

I jump over the table, shout, "Don't take less than twenty bucks for it!" to the kid, plow through the crowd of rock people to my 911, and slam the pedal to the carpet. Within five minutes, I tear up to the ice cream truck like a dust devil. Leonard is standing there with his coach gun, a twelve-gauge double-barreled shotgun with twenty-inch barrels.

"What happened?" I say.

"He crawled under the west fence along the wash. I was in the office watchin' the cameras and ran out here. He was makin' for the ice cream truck but saw me with my scattergun and did a fast one-eighty and went under the fence again. Guess he's not stupid, anyway."

Frankie pulls up in his F-350.

"I called Frankie too," Leonard says.

"Did you call the cops?"

"Not yet."

"Don't," says Frankie as he walks up. "Later. So which way did he come from?"

Leonard points to the west fence, and Frankie goes to

investigate. There are some lemon trees along the fence, and the ground around them is soft and wet from the recent rain. Frankie squats down and takes a close look at the hobo tracks. After a few minutes, he comes back.

"Did you notice his shoes?" he asks Leonard.

"His shoes? No. Why?"

"Because he's wearing Brooks trail runners. That's not what he was wearing this morning, and it's pretty odd footgear for a hobo."

Leonard says Theo is in the truck, probably napping, so I offer to guard it while Leonard and Frankie look at the video and Frankie makes a copy. Ten minutes later, they return.

"The video is good, but he was far from the camera. But definitely the same guy as this morning," Frankie says.

"So why is he after Theo?" I ask.

"Maybe he isn't," Frankie says.

"He might have thought you was in there," Leonard says. "You parked your car by the door when you brought the girl back this afternoon, and you went inside with her." Leonard gives me his hillbilly grin. "Maybe he saw that."

"Okay," Frankie says, "but Nick's car wasn't there when Mr. Hobo made his dash." He walks over to the lemon trees and comes back. "He wouldn't have been able to see the car from that angle, so yes, if he didn't reconnoiter well, he may have thought Nick was still in there. So Theo, Nick, or both, impossible to say for sure who he's after. But Nick has a strong connection to Madero, and Theo doesn't, so Nick seems the more probable target. On the other hand, if he was outside Madero's compound when Nick and Theo arrived this morning, he would have seen them getting out of Nick's hot rod, and maybe he thinks they were both in on whatever beef he had with Madero. We don't know at this point. I'm going home. Nick, see you and Theo tomorrow morning early. I'll let you guys secure the perimeter here until then. Lenny, go ahead and call 911."

Frankie leaves, and Leonard and I talk about what to tell

Theo. We go through a half dozen ways to sugarcoat it but decide the plain truth is best, including Frankie's guess that the hobo was after me, not her.

We ring the ice cream truck bell a few times, and Theo cracks the door. First, I tell her that Frankie will buy her agates. That makes her happy. But she's furious when I tell her about the hobo.

"What did you get me into?" she says. "I just wanted to sell those agates, and now some maniacal hobo is trying to kill me?"

Well, yeah, I guess that's an accurate assessment of the situation.

Leonard tells her that he and his friend Leroy will watch our trucks until we leave tomorrow morning. Leroy is one of those lanky hillbilly types. He's tastefully tattooed with a longhorn skull, a human skull crossed with Colt Peacemakers, and, incongruously, a hammerhead shark. He's missing a few teeth and sometimes wears overalls without a shirt. He loves to fight, but only with reasonable provocation, and he'll relish a chance for some righteous ass-kicking. I'll sleep well with him on watch.

When the cops arrive, there's little to do but take notes, download the video, and look at the hobo tracks. Like Frankie, the cops think it's the same guy who whacked Madero and Huerta, but they think he's likely after me and Theo because we're possible witnesses. He might think we saw him as he was leaving Madero's compound, they say. Of course, Madero's cameras got a better look at him than we would have anyway, but he probably doesn't know they exist. Sheriff Pershing admits they're just guessing about his motive and admonishes us to be on high alert. He offers to have a deputy stand guard but seems delighted to let Leonard and Leroy do it instead. I tell him we're leaving town tomorrow and he highly approves.

To Leroy's disappointment, Mr. Hobo never shows up.

5

ALL ABOARD FOR MURDER (ALMOST)

In the morning, Frankie pays Theo in cash. I'll deliver the agates to Yazzie in Window Rock, as Frankie and I agreed yesterday, though *agreed* might not be the proper word to use here. But Frankie says he wants Theo to come along in case Yazzie has questions about the rocks. It's a nice, believable way to get her out of town. Not that she needs a big incentive.

Frankie looks at Theo and nods to me. "What about Nick's cut?" he says. "A deal's a deal, Theo."

Theo counts out my 5 percent onto the table and I take it.

"I want both of you to be very careful," Frankie says. "I don't know what's going on with this guy, and the cops know less than I do. I told them he was wearing Brooks trail runners, but they insist he was wearing Nikes."

And so we start off for Window Rock. Me in my Porsche, she in her Subaru. Yes, I know that lesbians are one of Subaru's market segments, which you might think elevates the probability of Theo being a lesbian. It doesn't matter. I've spent enough time with support vector machines and neural networks to know just how dubious binary classifiers can be.

It's a four-hundred-mile drive to Window Rock, and Theo thinks any long drive should be turned into an adventure. Eat, pray, stop at curiosity shops. She wants to shun the autobahn and take two-lane blacktop. I approve this decision for other reasons, mainly that on the freeway route there's a risk of long delays from accidents, wildfires, and so on. On back roads, you can just turn around and take another route.

We take Highway 60 and pass Hope, where Frankie said the hobo would hop a train. Here the highway follows the tracks for about thirty-five miles until you get to Aguila. But at Salome, which is just a few miles east of Hope and a good thirty miles before Aguila, I look in the rearview mirror and see Theo pulling into the parking lot of a Mexican pottery store. Or pottery yard, since it looks like half the inventory is scattered around in the dirt outside a big, corrugated steel shed. I hang a U-turn.

Some pretty Talavera planters and pots sit outside, but she walks right by them and goes into the shed, where a faint odor of dog urine rises from the dirt floor. That's good, tells me the place is on the up-and-up. If this were Scottsdale, the place would be a clip joint reeking of essential oils, and I'd hustle her out of there.

The shed is chock-full of rickety, free-standing shelves piled with heavy pottery. If one shelf topples, they'll all go like a string of dominoes. I almost trip over a "Sleeping Mexican" planter. It seems shameless for Mexicans to make such a thing, but it's probably some inside joke.

Eventually, I find Theo in the far corner. She's looking at a quartet of small tin figurines. A frog mariachi band.

Some guy, probably the owner, comes up.

"It is very . . . whimsical, *si*?"

"Indeed," I say. "Do you sell many of these?"

"*Este momento.* See?" He points to a vacant place on the shelf to the left of the frogs. "I sell to a man from the train, *un vagabundo.* He comes here sometimes. He is still here, I think," he says, nodding to the opposite end of the store.

Then it happens. I hear creaking, and a shelf at the far end of the store topples, then the whole next row, and on toward us in a wave. It sounds like Sheriff Pershing's parade posse galloping over a plank bridge in a thunderstorm.

As the last shelf topples, I grab Theo and throw her to the ground, me on top, though not in the way I'd like, if you get my drift.

Mr. Hobo doesn't know we're looking at the shelf against the outside wall. When the shelf behind us topples, it hits the wall, leaving us lying safely on the floor under a sort of lean-to. I have a lump on my head and turn to face the ceramic bear that did it. The bear seems to be grinning. I feel like I've been worked over by a flyweight from the rain of ceramic beasts, but nothing serious.

"You okay?" I ask, getting up. She is. The owner seems to be in shock. I hear the *vagabundo* running out the door.

"Stay here. I'm goin' after him," I say.

I stumble to the door through a sea of potsherds and see the hobo running toward the tracks.

"You break it, you buy it!" I shout.

For a short, dumpy guy, he runs fast. But I do my road work. I'm gaining on him a little, but he's clearly pacing himself, like a distance runner. Then I see a four-car train approaching from the west. It's slowed down for the town, doing about twenty.

I'm a hundred yards from the tracks when the hobo reaches the train. He turns to me and waves. Then he drops his bindle— yes, this guy was actually carrying an old-timey bindle on a stick over his shoulder—sprints alongside the train like a juiced-up jaguar, grabs the ladder of a gondola, and pulls himself up. He's obviously done this before.

Now, if this were the movies, I'd run up there and hop the train, creep from one car to the next, lose my balance a few times, and cling on desperately with one hand. Then we'd exchange a few hundred rounds of fire because of course we'd both have backpacks full of ammo. He'd still get away.

No dice. The gondola was the last car of the train, so I couldn't get there in time to hop it. If you think the last car would be a caboose, you haven't seen freight trains for forty years. Besides, my ammo backpack is in the Porsche.

But he dropped his bindle.

I think he dropped it for some particular reason, so I approach cautiously. I get about twenty yards away and stop. Someone's behind me.

"Nick?" I hear Theo say.

Then I see a wisp of smoke coming from the bindle. A fuse.

I whip around, grab her, and throw her to the ground. Again. And I'm on top of her. Again. Still not the way I'd like, though.

Ka-boom! And ka-whizz, shrapnel flying every which way. I feel one hunk of it hit the sole of my right boot. Good thing consulting geologists wear hiking boots.

I roll off her.

"Could you please stop throwing me on the ground and then mashing me?" she says.

"I'm trying to protect you," I say.

"I can protect myself. Can't you just say, 'Hit the dirt!' or something?"

Some thanks the hero gets.

I find the thing that hit my boot. It's part of a tin figurine, like the ones we were just looking at.

"That's the fiddler," she says. "See, that's his bow. The violin must have blown somewhere else."

For a second, I think she wants to scarf up all the pieces and make me glue them together for her, but she doesn't. We walk back to the shop.

Jesus (the store's proprietor, not the Son of God) is on the horn. I expect to hear the guy wailing, "Ruined! Ruined!" however you say that in Spanish. But no, he's talking to his insurance agent. He asks if we could wait and give a statement when the law comes. I don't think a 415B, pottery shop vandalism, is high priority, and it could be hours before the county bull rocks up. I give Jesus my card. The bull can call me if he wants a witness statement.

Theo buys the frog mariachi band.

And no, we're not singing to the county bull about the bindle bomb. It smelled like black powder and was a sorry excuse for a bomb. Probably a fireworks shell the hobo stole from a Fourth of July show. With tin frogs for shrapnel. It's almost insulting. And nobody in Salome paid any attention to the boom, far as we can tell. Because in outstate Arizona, explosions and gunfire pass without notice. Everybody's doing it!

And as for linking the hobo to the lapidary murders, the cops are still thinking the miscreant is local to Quartzrock. They have no clue he's a real hobo, not just a short, dumpy guy who looks like one. Frankie will noodle this out a long time before the cops do.

But I need to call Frankie. Mr. Hobo wasn't breaking pottery for fun. He went for me, Theo, or both of us. Why, I still don't know.

Theo thinks running into the hobo at the crock shop was a freakish coincidence. I disagree and say she is grossly underestimating the probability of this occurrence. I explain my reasoning, counting off the points on my right hand:

- Thumb: The highway follows the railroad track, and this was the railroad route Frankie said the hobo would take.
- Index finger: This highway was the only reasonable two-lane highway route for Theo and me to take.
- Middle finger: Jesus told us Mr. Hobo visits his joint now and then, and Theo obviously has a thing for oddball collectibles.
- Ring finger: It is therefore unsurprising that both Mr. Hobo and Theo would interrupt their journeys

to stop at Jesus's joint. More likely than not, in my opinion.

- Pinkie: Collectibles devotees spend hours browsing in places like this, so the probability of their visits overlapping is moderate, far higher than at a gas station, for example, where visits last only a few minutes.
- Continuing with thumb of my left hand: Therefore, the causal chain is clear, and the meeting, while less likely than not, is unsurprising.

"You're mansplaining," she says.

I let it go. If she wants to believe Mr. Hobo is mystically linked to her destiny, that's fine with me. In a way, I find it charming. A few years ago, I was seriously involved with a yoga instructor who would go to DEFCON 2 when Mercury was in retrograde. In romance, opposites often do attract. Sometimes this dialectic leads to a beautiful synthesis. More often, it leads to madness and woe.

We hit the road again, but with elevated situational awareness. Twenty miles and she stops for some slightly flavored seltzer water. You know, seltzer water with, like, one milligram of mango flavoring. Five dollars, please. I need to get in on this racket.

6

SHEER GRANDEUR
OF ROCKS

One thing about being a consulting geologist—you look at rocks in an esoteric way. I see their subtle nuances of light and shade, the cragginess of their youth, the mellow features of their old age. Each rock has its own story. Jonathan Edwards said that to understand nothingness, imagine what the sleeping rocks dream of. But I say that rocks dream. And in their dreams, they speak to me. They tell me how they arose from the molten globe of Hadean earth. How they once lay under the ocean, then above it. How they endured the weight of glaciers and the blows of unruly asteroids. How they watched as life spread, first in the sea, then on land. Then they look back into the abyss of time, before the sun and the earth, before galaxies, before stars, and tell me of darkness, and fire, and atoms rushing through the cosmic void.

Nah, that's nonsense. Rocks can't talk while they're sleeping. Had you going for a minute, didn't I?

Sedona is on our route, about two hundred miles from Quartzrock and halfway to Window Rock. Of course, Theo wants to stop there. It has pretty but geologically uninteresting rocks. What is red sandstone good for? Do you have any idea how much red sandstone there is on earth? Way too much, I'm telling you.

I know Sedona because the shops traffic in crystals and gemstones, and I get called in when storekeeps want to make sure they're not being ripped off. So I know a place Theo will like. Ramona's. It's a nice little shop run by, yes, Ramona, who looks like Stevie Nicks. Actually, all the dames in Sedona have the witchy look of Stevie Nicks, with hippie shawls and scarves and big gypsy hair. All the guys have the sand-in-the-shoes look of Jimmy Buffett. I think this explains the pervasive shag banditry. They can't tell each other apart and are actually having sex with total strangers.

Ramona is not Ramona's real name, obviously. Her real name is Doris. Try selling aura photographs if your name is Doris. Ramona is a certified mineral healer, and Theo wants some time with her. Apparently, she has something she needs to be healed of. Low sex drive is my guess.

Theo and Ramona click like a revolver. I leave them to their auras and oils and incense and step outside.

And make the call to Frankie.

"Whadda you want?" Frankie answers.

"You need anything?" I say.

"No. So where are you?"

I tell him Sedona. We haven't made good time, but he knows that with Theo in tow, I won't. Then I tell him about the crock shop.

Silence for a minute. He's thinking. Or maybe he's making a sandwich—how the hell do I know?

"He missed the train at Hope and walked the tracks to Salome," Frankie says. "But he sees that crock shop and naturally decides to pick up some collectibles."

"Naturally?"

"Sure. Hoboes collect stuff. Every one of 'em has a stash, usually several. Look around under railroad bridges. They're pretty good at hiding it, but even a white guy can find it if he's sharp. It used to be Pez dispensers and Hummel figurines, but

32

they dumped that junk before the market crashed. Then it was Pokémon cards. Now it's just stuff they like."

Silence for five seconds.

Then he says, "My gut tells me he's after you and doesn't mind a little collateral damage. But for now, we need to assume he's after both of you."

I'm waiting for Frankie to tell me what, if anything, I should do.

"Hit Window Rock tomorrow. Spend tonight in Winslow. Stay at La Piazza. You know the place, nice old hotel near the tracks and close to the railroad yard. He's on the run, but no heat so far. If he doesn't stop in Winslow, he's not a hobo. That place is like Stuckey's for hoboes."

"What do I do, watch the tracks all night?" I say.

"You have your night vision stuff?"

"Of course."

"Look around the yard at night. Not too late. Hoboes bed down early, unless they're out stealing stuff, and this one won't be. Don't try searching, just watch. After twilight, he'll bed down in a car. Get the number. I can trace it. Not a sure thing, but ten to one he'll stay there until the cars move out at daybreak. He'll have picked one that's going where he wants to go."

"You don't want me to take him?" I ask.

"Of course not, doofus. What would you do with him? Tell the Winslow cops you were wandering around the yard and bagged some grubby hobo that you, a consulting geologist, think whacked two lapidaries in Quartzrock? They'd hold you for evaluation. Besides, Sheriff Pershing says the DPS guys think T-Bone is the prime suspect."

T-Bone is a homeless guy who thinks he owns Quartzrock, or pretends to. He issues his own currency, and most local stores will accept it for small purchases.

"Well, T-Bone is short and dumpy and looks like a hobo," I say, "so he matches the description. But T-Bone is everywhere.

You can find physical evidence of T-Bone all over Quartzrock. It's totally nonspecific. Pershing will set them straight."

"No, Pershing will let them go down ratholes until they beg him for help. T-Bone is enjoying the attention. And thanks to you, the DPS has another team chasing down that Dogstone scam, which has absolutely nothing to do with this case, trust me. You never should have mentioned it."

"Sorry. I thought it might be important."

"Well, it's not," Frankie says. "But not to worry. I'll find a way to stop that fool's errand. But please take Mr. Hobo seriously. You've seen him run. How do you think he fights? Just because he's dumpy doesn't mean he's soft. Yeah, yeah, you're a pugilist. But I know butterballs who could beat the crap out of both of us. And he might have a gun. Stay clear of him for now."

"Okay. Recce and report. Got it."

"And make sure Theo's room is on the second floor. And tell her to drag a desk or something in front of the door."

Hmm. Seems like a good excuse to share a room.

I walk by Ramona's and see her and Theo playing around with selenite spheres. So I go for a cup of coffee.

After half an hour, Theo calls and says she's ready to go. She's loaded down with essential oils, healing rocks, and palo santo incense. Also a new name. Her spiritual name, revealed to her by Ramona. It's Siobhan.

7

BOTTOMS UP
TO HIS HOLINESS

I need to tell ya something. I don't fault these people for using astrology or tarot cards to conquer indecision. Why not? It's no worse than flipping a coin. Or watching which way a bird flies or a horny toad skitters. And surely no worse than taking advice from an intelligence analyst, a financial planner, or an economist. Or most lawyers, for that matter.

I tell Theo, aka Siobhan, that we should spend the night at La Piazza in Winslow and continue to Window Rock in the morning. I tell her La Piazza is a swell joint—nice, clean rooms and good grub. Somewhere in there, I mumble about it being near the tracks. You know, like when you're selling a used car, you sneak in "might need new injectors" while showing off the sound system. She's still recovering from her mystic interlude and doesn't seem to notice.

She wants an iced nutmeg cappuccino, so we head back to the coffee shop. It's my favorite in Sedona because it's independent and because the owner's auburn hair distinguishes her on sight from Stevie Nicks. Mandalas cover the walls, and Deva Premal is always playing softly in the background.

And there's a statue of Ganesh, the demi-elephant god so beloved in the Hindu pantheon. I can't take my eyes off it. Like I said before, I was seriously involved with a yoga instructor a few years ago, Jackie. She had a big Ganesh statue in the studio. She was planning a trip to India, where rabies is endemic, and asked me if I'd pay $1,200 for her rabies vaccine. I said sure, who wants a rabid girlfriend? And she beat me on the head with a yoga block. But I paid for the vaccine.

Jackie spent a year working in an orphanage south of Chennai. We both agreed to put the relationship on hold. When she returned to the States, I was out of the country, and she took up with some other guy. A year or two later, she was diagnosed with pancreatic cancer. Her boyfriend said he couldn't deal with it and dumped her. Worse, he did it by text message. Jackie put up a good fight but died nine months after the diagnosis, surrounded by friends and looking forward to her next incarnation. I expect the boyfriend will be reincarnated as a javelina. I have no desire to be reincarnated as a javelina and will not have another serious relationship until I can make a serious commitment. Grandpa Cameron said it's good to learn from your mistakes, but better to learn from the mistakes of others.

I see Theo is looking back and forth between me and the Ganesh statue, probably wondering what I am thinking about. "Interesting statue," I say.

Theo shows me her healing rocks. She's warming to conversation when my phone plays "We Will Rock You." It's Frankie.

"Whadda you want?" I answer.

"You need anything?"

"Yes, but nothing you can give me."

"Hey, Madero was a ham radio guy, right?"

"Yeah. Look at his compound—there's a crazy antenna on a big mast. He talked about it now and then, ten-meter band, twenty meters, forty meters. He showed me the stuff in his radio room, but I never saw him use any of it."

"Interesting. What about Huerta? He had the same mania?"

"He had all the equipment, but I never saw him use it. I don't think either one had a mania for it."

"Okay. That's all, just confirming."

"Okay, see ya."

And I hang up. You don't ask Frankie to explain himself.

"Who was that?" Theo asks.

I tell her Frankie. Then I ask her point-blank why she's selling agates when she stands to lose her trust by doing it.

She laughs.

"I could make more working at Walmart than I get from the trust."

"Really?"

"Well, no. I get about five times what I'd get working full-time at Walmart. But it's still not much."

"So what's the problem? I thought old Miles was loaded."

"He was. But about two years ago, our payments started going down. Now they're about a quarter of what they were. The trust was depleted by bad investments."

"What kind of bad investments?"

"Lots of them. The trustee gives us the financial statements."

I don't press for more information. But it sounds fishy. Miles wasn't a guy to make sucker bets. Frankie needs to hear about this.

And so, with Theo following close behind me, we head north to Flagstaff, where we can pick up Route 66 and I-40 to Winslow. To do that, you need to ascend the Mogollon Rim, which is one of the longest escarpments on earth, hundreds of miles long east to west, and easily one of the most beautiful. It takes you up to the southwestern end of the Colorado Plateau. I've seen a lot of escarpments, and let me tell you, if I had to decide, this would be my escarpment of choice. You leave the half-assed high desert of Sedona at the bottom and arrive in Flagstaff among ponderosa pines at the top.

But honestly, Flagstaff has too many trees. You can't see anything! What's the point of living in an alpine landscape if you're
hemmed in by a bunch of stupid trees? Give me an unobstructed
view of the mountains any day.

Of course, once you leave Flagstaff heading east, there are
no trees at all, just high plains with purple sage, and you can see
forever. Which is good because the railroad tracks mostly follow
the freeway. You could spot a stray hobo a mile off in this terrain.

Keeping bow watch for hoboes makes me think about hoboes
stashing collectibles under railroad bridges. Frankie said even
a white guy could find some. Well, I've spent more time in the
woods than Frankie has, and I want to try my luck. I bet they
choose isolated, stable bridges that are rarely visited or maintained. And I know one of those. It's northeast of the Rock Trail,
which is at the Meteor Crater Rest Area about twenty miles west
of Winslow, on the north side of the road. Yes, it's called that
because it's a trail among rocks. They didn't spend much time on
the name, but at least they didn't call it the La Roca Rock Trail.

I click on my turn signal a mile before we get to Meteor City
Road and see Theo does the same. We get off there, go north over
the freeway, and pull over. I get out and tell her to follow me, got
something interesting to look at.

We drive a few miles west on a crappy road and then north to
a spur track off the main line. It crosses a dry gulch on a bridge.
Not much of a bridge, just steel beams across the gulch. But lots
of room for hiding collectibles under it.

"What are we doing here?" she asks when we stop.

"Looking for something," I say.

"What?"

"Collectibles."

I can see she thinks I'm crazy, but she follows me down the gulch and up under the bridge. I pull a Celtic sock shiv from my toolkit for a probe. Picked it up doing reconnaissance in South Boston. I find a few places where the soil is loose and poke around a bit. I hear a clink and start digging.

Frankie was right. I find two shot glasses, hand them to Theo, and keep digging. I find two more and hand her those. She leans over me, letting her long hair provocatively brush my shoulder. Maybe Ramona's minerals are working.

"Nick," she says. "Pope shot glasses?"

Sure enough. She has brushed off the dirt, and the shot glasses have cameos of popes on them. Pius IX , Pius X, John Paul I, and Francis. Must be part of a series. Two conservatives and two liberals.

I'm not here to steal from a hobo, and stealing pope memorabilia must be bad luck anyway, so I put the booty back and fill the hole. But when I'm doing that, I find a piece of quartzite about the size of a martini olive. I push it aside and turn to Theo, looking down the gulch. She follows my gaze down the gulch, and I pocket the quartzite while she's looking away.

When she looks back, she appears confused, understandably. I tell her to go back to her car because I want to walk the track a little way. On the track bed, among the crushed stone ballast, I see a similar piece of quartzite, and another. Most people wouldn't see how these differ from the rest of the ballast, which is also quartzite, but I do. I pocket both and head back to the cars.

Theo is sitting in her car and rolls down the window when I arrive.

"What was that all about?" she says.

"Frankie told me hoboes collect stuff and hide it under railroad bridges."

"You bastard!" she shrieks, then starts hitting me. "What if that horrible hobo had been here? He might have killed me!"

"That seems highly improbable," I say.

"Improbable? Is that what you'd tell the police? 'Oh, yeah, Siobhan was killed by some hobo, but I thought that was highly improbable.'"

She grabs a hiking stick from the back seat and chases me down the gulch, madly flailing away and screaming she'll rip my heart out with a gaff hook and skin me alive with a potato peeler. Presumably not in that order, but she's agitated.

But what else could I say? Yes, the hobo could have been hiding in the sagebrush, crept up to her car, and bumped her off. That would have been far less likely than the meet-up at Jesus's crock shop, but for similar reasons, not as unlikely as most people might think. Honesty is the best policy, I say.

Now clearly, when a woman smacks you in the face, beats you with a stick, and threatens you with grave mutilations, it usually means she's lookin' for it. Happens every day, all over the world. So I have a feeling this will be a good night.

8

CHERCHEZ LE HOBEAU

Well, that feeling doesn't last long. Theo or Siobhan or whatever she's calling herself now stops chasing me, runs back to her car, and drives away as fast as a Subaru can go. Which isn't very fast, but fast enough so that she's checked in at La Piazza and holed up in her room when I arrive. Luckily, it's on the second floor like Frankie suggested.

Maybe it's just as well she's pouting in her room. If she impatiently demanded sex, I'd have to beg off because I need to case the rail yard for the hobo. And no woman wants to play second fiddle to a hobo.

Once I've checked in, it's close to sunset. I lay out my low-life casing outfit—runover boots, worn blue jeans (but not too dirty), plaid shirt, vintage Newark Bears baseball cap, and scraggly fake beard. I stuff the night vision goggles in a fanny pack along with a pepper spray grenade. Toss that in a boxcar and watch the hoboes spring forth. A chain wallet completes the effect.

I sneak out of the hotel. Nowadays there are surveillance cameras everywhere, so there's an art to this. You need to sneak without appearing to sneak. You carefully avoid people but take your time by pretending to look at the artwork, out a window, at a crack in the wall, whatever. And never show your full face to the cameras, but don't look away from them either. You know where the cameras are even if you can't see them because they're placed to minimize the number of cameras necessary, cheap bastards. Simple geometry.

Successful lurking follows the same principles.

I go to the lousiest dive I can find for dinner. I need to get in character. A greasy hamburger on chalk-white buns, fries, and beer. By the time I finish, it's dark. I pretend to stagger a little as I go out, and I can see the bartender is glad to get rid of me. Now I'm really feeling the part.

Before hitting the yard, I stop at a smoke shop and complete my ensemble with a pack of Camels and a lighter. And no, of course I don't smoke. I'd rather inhale stack fumes from the Port Pirie lead smelter.

The yard has that railroad smell. You could make an after-shave. I can see the ad. A gorgeous cowgirl walks into the roadhouse. A skinny, smooth-faced guy with hair parted on his right side is at the bar. She approaches, eyes him scornfully, then tilts her head back and inhales. Double take. The guy's chest and arms swell, buttons pop, sleeves burst, hair parts itself on the other side, and a five-o'clock shadow appears on the guy's chin. She smiles and sits next to him. Voice-over: "Steel. Grease. Creosote. *Hobo* by Versace."

I walk west and don't pay much attention to the cars on the inner siding because they're all intermodal cars. These are like flatbed cars but with a well that a shipping container fits into. The well lowers the center of gravity and gives more top clearance. Usually, they carry two containers stacked, as they're doing here. When they have open bottoms with just crossbeams supporting the containers, as these do, they're dangerous and uncomfortable to ride. There are two lines of cars on the outer sidings, but I'll need to check them later.

I wander to the yard's west end where there's a pile of scrap metal and a few shipping containers used for storage. I walk briskly by and turn as if I'm going to town. And now I'm out of sight from the yard. My plan is to find some gaps in the scrap pile so I can observe unseen.

But I feel like I'm being watched. So I look up at the moon and nonchalantly light a cigarette.

There's a bang like a boxcar door closing. I turn to look and come face-to-face with a railroad bull.

"Relax, bud, I always come here for a smoke," he says. "Here they can't see you from the yard." He has a Newark accent, like an NYC accent, but he says "heah" for "here" and "yahd" for "yard."

I offer him a doger and a light. In the light of the flame, I see he's a private security guy. Wilt-Garner Railroad Security. Never heard of it.

"You from Newark?" he says, with a hint of whiskey on his breath.

Oh, crap. Damn lighter. He saw my hat. I got it at Goodwill and wear it because nobody in Arizona knows what an angry bear clutching a baseball is about, especially when it's about a minor league team that folded years ago. But I run into the one guy in the state who does. And I don't know jack about Newark. Just the airport. And the Edison Museum in East Orange.

"East Orange, but that was a long time ago," I say.

"What part?"

"The shitty part. You could have guessed that."

He laughs, or rather chokes. He needs one of those smoking cessation classes. He's also drooling and spitting constantly. But he looks about sixty, so that may be normal for him.

"Those cars," he says, pointing to the middle siding. "They're going to Chicago. That'll put you closer to home. If that's where you're headed."

"That's good of you, man. Any suggestions for a car?"

"I'd say the boxcar. It's third from this end. Don't see many of them on this line, but it's best for travel. There's already a brother in there, goin' to Chicago, but he won't give you no trouble. Kind of a short, dumpy guy. Looks like he jumped in a mud puddle."

I've got a good poker face, but this bull must play a lot of poker.

"You know him?"

I say the first thing that comes into my head.

"Could be White Buns."

The bull chuckles. "He said Tucson Ted, but White Buns suits him better. How'd he get that handle?"

"I dunno for sure. Think he used to moon people at crossings."

The bull shakes his head. "Well, pardner, enjoy your trip with White Buns. I'm gonna tie up now. Give the new guy ten minutes to get down east a bit, then make your move."

And he leaves. He walks about fifty yards, then turns, waves, and nods in the direction of the boxcar. He seems like a helluva guy, but despite his exceptionally good poker face, I think he's hiding something.

For now, I'll assume I rolled a natural on this one. All I need to do is get the numbers on the boxcar. That takes five minutes, and then I'm outta there.

9

SHEER BEAUTY
OF SOLVENTS

*B*ack in my room, I call Frankie and report. We talk things over. The bull gave a good description, so he's probably seen our hobo. Or White Buns, as Frankie now calls him. Of course, he may have gotten the description from someone else, but that seems less likely, and regardless, the description is unlikely to fit anyone but our hobo, so his knowing the description is what's important.

Frankie's on a roll. He steps through seven scenarios:

1. The bull is on the level, doesn't know White Buns (other than maybe seeing him before), has no idea who I am, and has a soft spot for hoboes. (Possible.)
2. The bull is in cahoots with White Buns, who is really in another car or no car at all, and is trying to throw me off the scent. (Possible.)
3. The bull is in cahoots with White Buns, was warned to expect me, and wants to dispose of White Buns, who has served his purpose as hit man. He tells me where White Buns is, thinking I'll do the job. (Possible.)
4. The bull is in cahoots with White Buns, was warned to expect me, and is setting me up to be bumped

off in the boxcar and my stiff dumped on the rez. (Possible.)

5. The bull is in cahoots with White Buns, wants to get rid of us both, and doesn't care who whacks whom. He just wants to provoke a cage match in the boxcar. Hopefully, we whack each other. But if not, one down, one to go. (Possible.)

6. The bull is using the boxcar as an ant trap for hoboes and will have the cops raid it any minute. (Good idea, but unlikely. Cops don't like wasting time on hoboes.)

7. The bull is screwing with me and White Buns, and the train's really headed for Mexico. (Unlikely, pointless, risks hobo wrath.)

We strike off the last two but can't decide among the rest. Frankie says we need more information, and I agree. He's convinced White Buns has associates, but we have no reason to suspect the bull. Right now, anyway.

Then I tell him about Theo not getting crap from the trust.

"Interesting," he says. "She says this started about two years ago? That seems odd, but it would explain why she's selling agates. There's a rumor old Miles hid a big stash in the Apostle Islands."

"Really? Never heard that one."

"I'm not sure I believe it. There's also a rumor that a certain Apache chief was buried with a pot of gold. Like he was a leprechaun or something. That's nonsense, of course. Anything else?"

"Yeah. Inside Madero's compound, by the gate."

"Yes?"

"There's a pile of crushed stone. It's coarser than what you'd likely use for landscaping. Number three, I'd say, and it has a sign for Hermosos Paisajes Landscapes on it. I think that's a company Madero and Huerta set up for dealing in crushed stone. Could you take a look at that?"

Frankie hesitates. "It won't be easy. Cops are still all over the compound. But Chesney's the executor. I'll say I might be interested in buying the place. I won't get inside the buildings, but I can look around outside. What am I looking for?"

"You'll know if you see it. It's just a hunch, but for God's sake don't let anyone know what you find, if anything."

"Like I would?"

I apologize for the implied insult and we end the call.

I change into my Arizona lounge lizard outfit: white turtleneck, light gray sports coat, and white pants. This is consistent with the rule that a gentleman's clothing should leave no impression other than being appropriately dressed for the circumstances. For shoes, gray running shoes. Like the hobo, I prefer Brooks. The running shoes signal that I run and that I'm not the kind of guy who travels with five pairs of shoes.

It's only 21:00, and I expect there are lonely dames in the bar. Not many, though. I see a sizzling Asian dish. She's a bit overdressed for Winslow, but in a short cocktail dress revealing her bare shoulders, shield volcano breasts, and gams to die for, she's hotter than the Liuhuanggou mine fire. I don't know the barman, but he kinda knows me, so I take a seat, leaving one stool between me and her.

"Well, speak of the devil," the barman says. "Last time I saw you, the earth was only four point five billion and two years old."

It's a dumb joke he picked up from an old movie. Three years ago, I told him the earth was about 4.5 billion years old, and I haven't seen him in about a year. Who says vaudeville is dead?

I order an Old Cornpone neat and pretend like I'm not interested in the lady. Why does a Cameron drink bourbon instead of Scotch? Because I think Scotch tastes like formaldehyde. And yes, I've tasted formaldehyde, so I know whereof I speak.

The barman and I talk a little. I can tell the lady is bored. That's good. After a few minutes, she breaks the ice.

"Are you a geologist?" she says.

I introduce myself and give her my card. "And what about you?" I say.

She says her name's Jing and that she's a chemical engineer. That means she's smart. Getting a chemical engineering degree is a real ballbuster. That's why I'm a geologist.

Jing tells me she's a Chinese national doing some work here in the US. She launches into a tirade against the EPA, DOJ, and OSHA, mostly about how they limit the use of solvents, which makes it hard to apply films to things. Especially adhesive films. I forget the exact grievance, something about regs not making sense because you can recapture the solvents. She seems to like xylene. I say it's a great solvent, but I'm really more of an acetone fan.

Then she asks about my dissertation. I tell her it was about native hydrogen kitchens—natural geochemical reactors that produce hydrogen and can be exploited by drilling wells like natural gas wells. She wants to know more. Can output be increased? Yes. How?

A Klaxon horn goes off in my brain. Never discuss trade secrets with anyone, especially a chemical engineer. My patent applications are public, but some aspects are vague, and that's intentional. Ask any patent attorney. I tell her it's not worth discussing and ask what a nice girl like her is doing in a place like Winslow.

I've moved over next to her because the bar's getting noisy and it's hard to hear. I notice she's hardly touched her drink. She looks over my shoulder.

"A girl over there is staring at you." She giggles.

I turn and there's Theo, sitting in a booth alone. And she's glaring, not staring.

I tell Jing that Theo and I are strictly business. And that she drives a Subaru.

"Would you like to meet her?" I ask.

Jing looks surprised. "Yes, that would be nice," she says.

Jing, meet Theo. Theo, meet Jing. Let me get you drinks.

What's your pleasure? Amazingly, Theo doesn't want a Long Island iced tea or Jägermeister. Blow me down, she wants a Negroni. Jing left her martini at the bar and wants a gin and tonic. I get their drinks and say I'll be back in a few minutes.

This maneuver flummoxes them. But who cares. I can tell Jing isn't in the mood, despite my undoubted charms. And this is an opportunity to patch up with Theo.

I go to the lobby and check my emails and texts. As usual, this process starts with mass deletions followed by a careful reading of the remainder. One is an alumni email with a photo of Professor Bradford—he's an emeritus; more about him later—at the Boulders golf course in North Scottsdale, which is one of my favorites. But there's no word from Frankie, so I go back to the bar.

Jing is gone, but Theo is still there.

"May I?" I say. She nods and I sit down. She tells me Jing has a conference call with Beijing. I see Jing drank only a third of her gin and tonic.

Neither of us says anything for a minute.

Then, at the same time, we both say, "Sorry." She tells me she's sorry she overreacted, and yes, the danger was remote. Then I tell her I'm sorry I didn't keep a closer eye on her.

She says she's ready to hit the rack, and I walk her to her room. Surprisingly, she doesn't invite me in. I guess Ramona's minerals take time to produce decisive results. I tell her to pull the nightstand in front of the door, then I say goodnight.

In my room, I take my loupe to the quartzite I picked up at the railroad bridge. It's very light gray with a brownish cast, and only slightly heavier than normal quartzite. Because it's laced with gold. Some of the richest ore I've seen. Hundreds of ounces per ton. But the gold grains are very small, so you need a magnifier to see them. That's normal. But the crystalline structure is unusual, so I recognize the petrology. It's from a defunct mine in Mexico.

10

THE RAILROAD BULL
GETS A WOODEN KIMONO

Theo, Jing, and I are having breakfast in the hotel dining room. It's crowded. A decent menu, but skip the local color dishes featuring corn, beans, and squash. That's Native American stuff. The three sisters. Not terrible, but not great either. Beware of local dishes. They usually suck. If they were good, they'd be national dishes.

We've ordered, but before the food arrives, two cops come in. They talk to the hostess. Then the hostess rings a little handbell. Everybody pipes down.

The lead cop bellows, "Is there a geologist in the house?"

That happens all the time in Quartzrock, but I wasn't expecting it here.

Jing looks at me. I raise my hand, then walk up to the cops.

"We'd like you to take a look at something," the lead cop says. "You don't have to, but it would help us out."

Sure, why not?

They drive me to a small clapboard house about six blocks from the hotel. Houses in Winslow are mostly small because they were built as cottages for railroad workers. And they're usually neglected and run-down, like this one. "A cozy bungalow awaiting your personal touches" is how a Realtor would describe it.

Something must've happened here because it's crawling with cops and firemen.

"What's up?" I ask.

"Not for me to say it was homicide," the lead cop says as he parks the car. "But it looks like old Arley was speared with a ballast fork."

A ballast fork is a railroad tool, like a garden spading fork, but with eight or ten narrow but solid tines. You use it to move the crushed stone ballast on the track bed.

"Why do you need a geologist?"

"There's some stuff in Arley's shed out back, and we don't know what to make of it," the cop says.

They take me out back to a scabrous shed walled with chipboard. Old Arley obviously didn't have a building permit for this thing. Though in Winslow, maybe he did. They lead me to the door. It's hanging on loose hinges and has "2620" scrawled on it in white chalk. The lead cop opens the door but doesn't let me go inside.

I don't need to. A quick look-see tells me everything.

"That's a ball mill, an old one. You use it to powder ore. That red thing that looks like a turkey fryer is an electric furnace. You can buy them on Amazon. The rocks in that barrel and on the floor, they're ore. This is an amateur gold refinery. And that thing is a mercury retort. You stick your mercury-gold amalgam in there, heat it up, and the mercury boils off and collects in that flask so you can reuse it. What's left in the retort is mainly gold. It's a great way to poison yourself."

I point to a plastic barrel full of dirty water with an aquarium aerator bubbling away. "And leave that barrel alone. It's an even better way to poison yourself."

"Why?" the lead cop asks.

"Because it's a cyanide solution. He's trying to extract whatever gold is left in the tailings, after his mercury amalgamation run. Terrible idea. Get a hazmat team in here before Winslow becomes a Superfund site. Meantime, stay out of there and post a guard."

I get a whiff of something I don't like and add, "But no closer than five yards."

"Why no closer than five yards?"

"Because I can smell hydrogen cyanide. The jamoke didn't balance the pH right, and that barrel is gassing off. Maybe not enough to kill you, but I wouldn't take the chance." I could tell them to pull the plug on that damn aerator, but best if they don't go in there.

The cops back away and look at each other. They take me around to the front porch. The front door is slightly open, and they let me look in.

And there, on the floor of the tiny living room, is the corpse of the railroad bull. Eyes open. Ballast fork shoved up under his rib cage. And into his heart and lungs, I assume. Some dudes in CSI coveralls are slithering on the floor.

The police and fire chiefs are there on the front porch, which is just big enough to hold all of us. I tell them what I told the two cops.

"You think he might have died of cyanide poisoning?" the police chief asks, nodding to the corpse.

I look at the chief. "He's been harpooned with a ballast fork."

"Sure he has, but look again. There's almost no blood. If he'd been alive when this happened, there'd be blood all over the place."

He has a point. Maybe the killer poisoned him or strangled him but just wanted to make sure, testing him with a fork to see if he was done.

The chief thanks me, and the cops take me back to La Piazza. On the way, they tell me a neighbor described a possible suspect. Any guesses?

11

THE CELESTIAL EMPRESS
WOWS THE FIREDAWGS

*T*he cops are dropping me at La Piazza when I tell them about Jing. Why not ask her about the cyanide vat? Good idea, the cops agree.

Jing acts like this is an everyday thing for her. In China, maybe it is. Oh, ho-hum, a vat of sodium cyanide gassing off. Just dump some lye in there.

So Jing and I raid the hardware store. They have twenty cans of lye. Must be a lot of clogged drains in this town. I grab ten. As we run by the cashier, Jing hands him a C-note. He chases after us, threatening to call the cops, but stops dead when we jump into the cop car. He looks at the C-note, realizes Jing overpaid by a Grant, shrugs, and goes inside.

We rock up at the bull's house and the firedawgs act like Jing's the Celestial Empress. She's wearing a simple black dress and heels that display her gorgeous gams. Not exactly morning wear, but she's probably traveling light. You'd think these guys had never seen a class dame before. They try to avoid staring, turning to talk with each other, but it's no good. They just can't keep themselves from stealing glances at her.

While they're ogling, Jing and I talk with the police and fire chiefs. The police chief says he can't smell anything, but Jing explains that most people can't smell HCN, which is true. She can't smell it either, but the fire chief and I can. It's a genetic thing, like whether you hate cilantro.

Surprisingly, the police chief asks Jing to describe the reaction that's generating the gas and how the lye will stop it. He seems to understand her explanation perfectly and wants us to proceed. But the fire chief doubts the HCN level is dangerously high—he's used to seeing hydrogen cyanide as a combustion product in house fires—and wants to wait for an expert hazmat team instead. They argue, but the police chief paints a frightful fresco of mass casualties blamed entirely on the fire department, and he wins. A firedawg bring us a couple of respirators.

The police chief wants a sample of the liquid before we up the pH, which makes sense from an evidentiary viewpoint. But I doubt the railroad bull bobbed for apples in the vat or lingered over it, savoring the gas. He wouldn't have made it into the house. I saw a bottle of whiskey and a half-full glass on a lamp table in the living room next to a ratty Barcalounger. I'd test those. And of course, they will.

So the fire chief and I do the job while Jing directs the operation. She had a digital pH tester in her purse.

Back at the hotel, Jing and I find Theo waiting for us in the dining room. She looks at me like she thinks I was poking Jing against the cyanide barrel. Not a chance. I've had sex in a respirator, and it's no fun at all. Jing tells her what we did, and Theo calms down a little. Until Jing starts asking if I ever get to Chicago or Los Angeles, at which point Theo falls into a jealous snit and excuses herself to finish packing. This is promising.

Now, of course I knew that sodium hydroxide would raise the pH in the cyanide vat and stop the gassing. It's high school chemistry stuff. So why ask Jing? Because it was the polite thing to do. She's more of a chemist than I am, and I respect that. And she knows I respect that. And I can tell that makes her want me.

Unfortunately, we both need to hit the road. But she's invited me to visit her in Chicago, and that's what counts.

Before she leaves, I give her a piece of the gold-bearing quartzite I picked up on the track bed. I ask her to have someone run an analysis to identify the probable origin. She says she has a geologist friend at Tsinghua University. I bet the rock will be in Beijing within forty-eight hours.

12

WILL THE REAL YAZZIE PLEASE STAND UP?

It's time to bug out. Cops aren't stupid, and somebody in Quartzrock or Winslow may see some similarity between these three murders, including Nick Cameron's proximity when they happened. Not that they'll think I pushed the button. But they may think I have some connection to the guy who did. And I'm not interested in spending another half day talking with cops.

I hustle Theo into her car, and we head out for Window Rock. Cell service is good on I-40, so I call Frankie. I don't like talking while I'm driving but don't have much choice right now.

"Whadda you want?" he says.

"You need anything?"

"No. What's up?"

I tell Frankie about the railroad bull's demise.

"Well, that explains why he wanted you to whack White Buns," he says. "That was, let me see here, that was option number three, no, more likely number five. So White Buns sees you casing the boxcar and thinks he's been double-crossed. Correctly, I may add."

"And the mercury retort explains why the bull was slobbering like a schnauzer when I talked to him. The dude salivated himself."

"Yes. I can't wait to see the medical examiner's report. Mercury, cyanide, alcohol, nicotine. And I'd give twenty to one on opiates too. He's a toxicologist's dream. The ballast fork just iced the cake." After a brief pause, Frankie continues. "Oh yeah," he says, "I called Chesney, and he'll show me around Paco's compound. But you need to tell me what I'm looking for in that rock pile. I don't like this 'You'll know it when you see it' stuff."

"Sorry, I was getting to that. I think it's a pile of track ballast, by the gate. And you're looking for gold-bearing quartzite. Very gold-bearing. Mixed in with lots of other quartzite, so don't expect it to jump out at you. It will be a bit grayer than the rest, with a slight brownish cast."

Frankie whistles. Then I tell him about the pope shot glasses and finding the quartzite around the bridge.

"Look," I say, "nobody puts super high-grade in track ballast by accident. And it didn't fall out of a hopper car because you don't transport it in hopper cars. Something weird is going on here."

"Why didn't you tell me this last night?"

"It was just a hunch at that point. I hadn't had time to take a close look at the rocks from the bridge. Or seen the bull's shed, of course."

"The ore in the bull's shed, same stuff?"

"Sure looked like it, from what I could see."

"Yáadilá."

"It gets weirder. I could be wrong, but I think the ore's from Mexico."

"Yáadilá."

"Specifically, from the Emilio Rayón mine."

A brief pause.

"What did you say?" Frankie says.

"I said I think it's from the Emilio Rayón mine. That's near the Emilio Nylón mine."

"White man make funny. Red man no laugh."

"Heap big gold Emilio Rayón, but many moons since yellow metal flow from ground," I say.

This Tonto Talk goes on for a while. It ends with me asking where I ride my war pony after Window Rock. (Don't do Tonto Talk with strangers, or you might get a knuckle sandwich. If your Native American friend initiates it, it's okay to respond in kind.)

"Right now, beats me," says Frankie. "I need to noodle this. I'll text you."

"See ya."

There's no point yammering about Window Rock. It's a small town, and the only things it has going for it are a big rock with a hole in it and being the capital of the Navajo Nation. Oh, and the voice of the Navajo Nation, KTNN, which is worth listening to even if you're not Navajo. There's an app for it if you're out of range.

We find Yazzie's place, where I'm supposed to deliver the agates. It's a double-wide, kinda like Frankie's. Yazzie takes a quick gander at the agates, nods, then gives us that "now get outta here" look. And we do.

Theo seems bewildered. We stop at a Chevron for gas.

"So what do we do now?" she says.

The obvious answer is that she should go back to Bumfreezer Falls or wherever her igloo is. But if I say that, she'll think I'm trying to get rid of her. And I don't want to get rid of her. So I tell her I'm getting instructions from Frankie.

There's a low-end food mall nearby, and we agree to get a taco. She's pretty dark and might pass for a Latina. Me, I look like some heavily tanned white guy. Kind of a cross between Bill Gates and Dr. Roy Chapman Andrews, or his knockoff, Indiana Jones. Like a field geologist, in other words. So we're still conspicuous. Now she knows how a Navajo feels at the Scottsdale Fashion Mall.

Lots of people are in town visiting the tribal offices, so we wait in line to order. While we do, Frankie's text comes in.

Superior.

I reply, *?*

And he replies, *Wisconsin, idiot.*

kk

So I tell Theo, "Looks like I'm going to Superior."

If you don't know where Superior is, it's across the bay from Duluth. It's Duluth without the frills.

"That's on my way home," she says. "We could make the drive together. I enjoy your company, and you did save me from the bindle bomb."

And so, racked with longing, feverish with unquenched desire, Theo, aka Siobhan, follows me to Superior.

13

TRAGEDY STRIKES
THE RADIO MUSEUM

I don't know what you folks do on a cross-country drive, but I listen to local AM radio. Ag and livestock reports are especially interesting. What's the wheat outlook? What kind: hard red winter, hard red spring, soft red winter, white, durum? And then rye and oats and corn and soybeans and sorghum and so on. But lean hogs are my favorite. Trim and toned. No flabby hogs for me.

That's during the day. At night it's more fun to pick up distant AM radio stations, the fifty-kilowatt ones from the big cities far away. KMOX in St. Louis faded out when we passed Minneapolis, but now WLS in Chicago is coming in loud and clear. The news. Cardinal Whatsisname said something. Some festival at Navy Pier. And then, by the way, the Chicago Fire Department is fighting a three-alarm fire at the Metaxas Radio History Museum.

I bet 95 percent of Chicagoans are saying, "What the hell is the Metaxas Radio History Museum?" But I know what it is. Frankie needs to hear this.

"Whadda you want?" says Frankie.

"You need anything?"

"No. What's up?"

"The Chicago Fire Department is fighting a three-alarm fire

at the Metaxas Radio History Museum," I say. "It's expected to be a total loss."

"Source?"

"Radio. Listening to WLS."

"AM radio? How quaint. Don't you have satellite?"

"I dropped the subscription. Never used it."

Frankie is making noise with cooking utensils. There's a brief pause while he uses a can opener.

"Well, thanks for the info," he says. "I suppose you're thinking White Buns is behind this, right? Because he was in a boxcar headed for Chicago, and he seems to be slaying and laying waste to everything in his path?"

"Attila the Hobo. But I don't see his motive. It's connected remotely to Theo, but how could torching the museum hurt her? Besides, I bet it's grossly overinsured."

Frankie says something that sounds like "Baiee!" Whatever that means in Navajo, if anything. Maybe he cut himself. He's careful in his jewelry work but a little careless in the kitchen.

"What if I told you that Madero and Huerta were trustees of the museum?" he says.

"Huh? Where'd you get that?"

"Chesney. He's been working with a forensic accountant going through Madero's stuff. There are three trustees, appointed from the ranks of a ham radio organization, the Ancient and Respected Radio League. Madero and Huerta were two, and the third is some guy who's a ham radio celebrity because he can copy two hundred words per minute of Intercontinental Morse Code."

"That's very good," I say. I'm honestly impressed, in the way I'm impressed by that guy who did a marathon on a pogo stick.

"It's a rare skill. Anyway, Chesney says it's a good thing Madero was whacked—saved him languishing in the federal pen. He was getting, like, six hundred thousand dollars a year from the museum."

"Isn't that a lot for being trustee of some rinky-dink nonprofit?"

Frankie must have cut himself because I hear the medicine cabinet in his master bathroom opening. It has a distinctive clank because of its ridiculously strong magnetic closure.

"*Si*," he says. "But it wasn't a salary because the trustees are only paid reasonable expenses. He was getting it through some bogus radio maintenance company the museum contracted with. That's just one of many reasons for the federal pen, according to Chesney. He says there'll be nothing left in the estate after the IRS wets its beak."

"Still doesn't make sense. Madero and Huerta are dead, so why torch the radio museum? Spite? *Damnatio memoriae*?"

"Cut the Latin crap. I don't think White Buns took that box-car to Chicago, and I doubt he knows anything about the radio museum. It's possibly an accident, more likely insurance fraud, but most likely an attempt to destroy evidence of something. By whom, we could speculate all night, but it sure ain't White Buns. I need to find out more about the museum. Chesney has copies of the museum trust documents, and there might be a clue in there. But right now, I need to hit the rack."

I ring off. Frankie goes to bed between 20:00 and 21:00. He gets up at 04:00.

If you have gephyrophobia, you probably want to avoid the Blatnik Bridge from Duluth to Superior. That's all I've got to say about Duluth.

We arrive in Superior around 22:00 and check in at the Superior Agate Inn. That's where Frankie told me to stay. It's not a dive, but it's not the Four Seasons either. The bar is open, and we can still get bar food, so we order some sliders. The décor is nautical—ship's lanterns, binnacles, blocks, and ropes. Lots of rope draped on the walls. I could see White Buns hanging somebody in this place. He seems to use whatever's handy.

Now that she's close to home, Theo seems at ease. She talks about her boat and fishing. That's a big thing on Chequamegon Bay. We're sitting in one of those semicircular booths. She gradually snuggles next to me. I guess Ramona's minerals are finally working. She rests her head on my shoulder, and I put my arm around her. The bartender is an older guy, maybe in his sixties, and he smiles at us in a kindly way. Probably remembering his salad days. There's nobody else in the bar now, and he's getting ready to close. I take Theo in my arms, and we have a long, passionate kiss. She's hotter than a pyroclastic flow sizzling down the flanks of Mount Pelée.

"What's your room like?" she asks.

Now, if that isn't a come-on, I don't know what is. Especially since the rooms in this place are all pretty much alike. We walk up the stairs to mine, which overlooks the harbor.

"Your desk is different. Mine doesn't have a drawer," she says.

She opens the drawer, and there, staring us in the face, is a porno magazine. *Tennis Skirt Strumpets! Wimbledon Exposed!*

Well, that quenched her ardor. Her smile disappears, and she quietly closes the drawer. Obviously, she thinks I put it there. She still doesn't know me. I shun pornography. But if I liked it, I'd be ogling *Golf Skirt Strumpets! Daffing on the Links of St. Andrew's!*

"I'm tired," she says. "I may leave early, before you're up. Good night."

"Good night."

No use trying to convince her I didn't do it. If I find the son of a bitch who put that rag in my desk, I'll string him up from that stupid fake yardarm they have hanging over the bar.

But now that I look at it, it's pretty tasteful stuff. The tennis skirt is the leitmotif, with no nudity at all. Gorgeous babes posing seductively with tennis rackets fifty different ways, while a liveried waiter offers them Pimm's Cup. All viewed from the angle of a Prince William look-alike in the umpire chair. The English know how to do this right.

But I put it back in the drawer. See, in my opinion, pornography is stupid. It's like trying to sate your hunger by looking at pictures of food. What good does that do? None at all.

I pour myself a bourbon and google *metaxas radio museum*. Great website. Judging from the photos and descriptions, it was a pretty good museum. You'd think it would be boring displays of antique radio equipment—stuff the Ancient and Respected Radio League would drool over. Not at all. A replica of the Titanic's Marconi room, pitched at an odd angle, with a mannequin robot desperately keying *CQD CQD SOS SOS CQD DE MGY MGY*. I bet Miles demanded that. A big console radio from the 1930s playing FDR's fireside chats while a family of mannequins in period dress stares raptly at it. An interesting collection of small, early transistor radios that teenybopper mannequins are clutching to their ears, and so on. The social significance of radio in the twentieth century, really. Not the kind of stuff Madero or Huerta would think of, that's for sure.

A loud knock on the door. It's Theo.

She looks frightened. I let her in.

"This was in my nightstand," she says, holding out a magazine.

It's *Cambridge Coxswains*. English rowing pornography. I've heard of that. Studly guys in blue tank tops, muscles rippling as they strain at the oars. That's the cover. Inside, things I can't imagine doing in a racing shell, though the sliding seats probably help.

She says she can't stay here overnight. She thinks we've stumbled into an Anglophile fetish hotel. I tell her Episcopalians likely had a convention and left some stuff behind. Still, I can see why she's wary of the place.

I carry her bags down to her car and follow her to a Best

Western or Fairfield Inn or something like that—they're all the same to me. She checks in, I carry her bags to her room, and she closes the door behind us. I turn to leave, and she's blocking my path.

"Nick, could you please stay with me tonight?"

"Okay," I say. There are two queen beds. She immediately takes one, and it's obvious she wants me in the other because she has her suitcase on the other side of the bed. So not a come-on. She's still shaken by *Cambridge Coxswains* and wants a guard.

She spends ten minutes in the bathroom putting on her nightie and then turns out the lights. I strip down to my skivvies and turn in.

Around 01:00 I wake up to the seductive heat of Theo's soft hands stroking my bare shoulders. She leans close, her warm breath on my forehead, her long, scented hair caressing my chest with a velvet touch. In the dim light filtering through the drapes, her emerald eyes have turned dark and deep, like the green water turns abyssal black when night falls on the lagoon at Midway.

"You were snoring," she says.

14

BORROW MY WATCH,
TELL ME THE TIME

*T*heo gets up at 04:30 and leaves when I'm barely awake. She'd get on fine with Frankie. Me, I'm an 06:00 guy.

I go back to my room at the Agate Inn. After a shower and breakfast, I get an email from Frankie. He wants me to engage Bilkson Consulting to come up with a mission statement and slogan for my consulting company. It's Lochaber Consulting, if you want to steer some business my way.

There's no explanation, but for Frankie, that's not unusual. He includes the address and phone number. It's in Superior, but the firm also has a Chicago office. That's obviously odd, like "Offices in Los Angeles and Youngstown."

So why does a guy from Arizona need to use a consulting firm in Superior? Frankie says to tell them I'm thinking of spending the summers up north and will be expanding my business here, and I need something that will appeal to the local market.

Bilkson Consulting is located in a "professional building" along with Realtors, lawyers, counselors, and a psychic. The receptionist looks me over with unveiled lust, scanning me up and down like the lidar on a self-driving car. I introduce myself and tell her what I'm after. She excuses herself for a minute. She's quite a dish but not my type, unfortunately. It's not the stripper heels and the huge hoop earrings. They could be whimsy. But if I took her for drinks, I just know she would order a piña colada.

I look at the walls. They're festooned with award plaques. Like Best of the Year 2018. If you check it out, you usually find that somebody puts the locals on the Best of the Year list in rotation. So every few years you end up with a plaque. It keeps the funds flowing to the Elks, Kiwanis, or whoever is doing the rating. I see no harm in this. It's a good scam. Everybody's happy.

But on the other wall, I'm gobsmacked to see framed photos captioned *Metaxas Radio History Museum*. They look like what I saw on the website. If that's the quality of work these guys do, I won't mind talking to them.

The receptionist returns with a nerdy-looking guy who has a receding chin and introduces him as Phil Farkey, vice president. His shoes are not shined, his pants are not ironed, his sports coat has shiny elbows, his shirt looks like he slept in it, he parts his hair on the right side, and his glasses are crooked. He must be the brains of the outfit.

And he is. We adjourn to his office, where there are even better photos of the radio museum exhibits. I look at them, then take a seat.

I see sketches on his desk.

"The radio museum burned down last night," he says, nodding to the photos.

"I'm very sorry to hear that. Looks like it was a class joint."

"It was. I spent a lot of time on it. Two years ago, we got a big contract to redo all the exhibits. You should have seen it before that. It looked like a rummage sale for the Ancient and Respected Radio League. Except for the Titanic Marconi room, which was pretty good. But," he says, gesturing to the sketches on his desk, "*if* it is rebuilt, I can make it even better."

"I'd give strong odds on that."

"Let's hope. Now, Amber says you want a mission statement. Is that correct?"

I can tell he thinks mission statements are stupid.

"Yes. And a catchy slogan for the website."

He almost rolls his eyes. Now he thinks I'm a complete idiot. "And your line of business?"

"I'm a geologist. I'm in the rocks racket."

Snap, just like that he thinks I'm a smart scientist who's doing this just because some doofus told me I should.

"That's cool. We've never worked with a rocks guy. Anyway, I just do the radio museum. John Corsnaed—he's our president— he and Melanie Clusterratio do the business consulting stuff. I'll introduce you."

John Corsnaed is a tall, silver-haired, well-frocked, pompous airhead, and his sidekick cutie Melanie unconvincingly feigns marketing expertise. They don't have anything cooking, so we go to a conference room with a nice teak table and teak chairs. They ask questions and take notes.

"I keep people from doing stupid things," I tell them. Could I elaborate? Sure, I keep people from paying too much or selling for too little. I keep them from buying fakes. I tell them what they have. I tell them where to buy and where to sell. I broker deals and, rarely, I dabble on the rock exchange myself, but never for high stakes.

"So you're kind of like *Antiques Road Show* for rocks?" Melanie asks. That's very good. She's not as dumb as her boss. He thinks I'm a paleontologist.

"Kinda, yes."

This goes on longer than you want to know. Then they say they'll present their ideas to me tomorrow.

On the way out, I pass Phil's office. The door is open and I knock to get his attention.

"How'd it go?"

"Great. Say, I've got a question. These exhibits for the thirties and forties. The families are all staring at the radio. I've seen that in old ads. Did people really do that?"

Phil smiles. "I've talked with a lot of old-timers, and the answer is yes, they did, at least when they were really listening."

"Why? Not like there's anything to see."

"True. But I can tell you what one old-timer told me."

"Okay."

"What else was there to look at?"

15

MAN ON THE MOON WAS ONCE A DREAM

*T*here's not a lot to do in Superior at night, so I retire to my room and read *Structural Geology Algorithms*. It's pretty good, and I can run the scripts on my laptop. Keeps my mind off *Tennis Skirt Strumpets*.

I'm screwing around with MATLAB, and all of a sudden I have a burst of insight. At that disgusting cyanide shed, I saw "2620" chalked on the chipboard door. I thought it was something the cops did. You know, marking locations or something. But now I see what it meant. It's the hexadecimal value for the death's head symbol (☠) in Unicode.

So hoboes have stopped scrawling crude glyphs on unpainted fences and taken to Unicode. Why not? It's the twenty-first century, right?

But why not have a Unicode block for the old hobo symbols? If they can allocate hex 2620 for the death's head (☠) and 534D and 5350 for the swastika (卍) and (卐), what's wrong with having a Hobo block for stuff like this?

Not a damn thing, right? When this is all over, I'm going to Mountain View to pitch this to the Unicode Consortium.

I'm ready to turn in when Frankie sends me an encrypted email. He's using "one-time pad" encryption software I wrote myself. Frankie insisted on something provably unbreakable, and OTP is provably unbreakable if you do it right. The hard part is generating your own truly random numbers. The rest is trivial. We encrypt and decrypt offline using cheap tablets, and the keys are on cheap flash drives we crush after use. Frankie inserts incomprehensible Navajo phrases here and there, even though he knows that OTP is unbreakable and message padding is not needed. If Code Talker Grandpa did it, so will Frankie,

I guess. Anyway, the text is an offender profile. Frankie's brief intro says it's something "they" put together. I'm not sure who "they" are—FBI, DPS, or somebody else. It seems cagily vague, like something Nostradamus would have come up with. It's not worth reproducing in full, but here's an excerpt:

> *The lethal use of objects related to the victim's occupation—rock tumbler and geode, in these cases—may be a signature. Alternatively, or in addition, it may suggest an animus against the occupation of the victims, probably resulting from prior lapidary dealings with the victims, or other lapidaries, or childhood disappointment in rock collecting. However, the offender belongs to the organized type and therefore may simply use materials he knows will be at hand, which are related to the victim's occupation. . . . While the offender's dress is shabby and his appearance unkempt, this may be a disguise. . . . The offender is probably much stronger than he appears, though the poor physical condition of the victims and an element of surprise may have permitted a person of ordinary or even inferior strength to overpower them. . . . The offender is likely unemployed, perhaps recently, but may be employed, likely in a skilled or unskilled trade or occupation. Regardless, he has a strong need for people to like and respect him, and he has found some of his ambitions thwarted, or simply unrealized. He may also feel that, at times, his efforts are unappreciated, or not fully appreciated. He may have invented a novel lapidary technique credited to others, for example. . . . Likely this offender will kill again, though given the uncertainty of his signature and undistinctive MO, subsequent offenses may not be attributed to him, and in any case, a period of dormancy is possible, or even likely.*

The next day, I hit the Bilkson offices at 13:00, the appointed hour when my mission statement and slogan will be revealed in glory. Amber gives me her lascivious grin and escorts me to the conference room where John Corsnaed and Melanie Clusterratio await.

There's a relish tray on the table. Somebody spent a lot of time on this. Baby corn, pickled pearl onions, pepperoncini, Castelvetrano olives, pickled beets, and so on. Quite a variety. Then some Triscuits and a mild cheese dyed a shocking yellow. It tastes okay, though. Hey, it's Wisconsin. I haven't eaten lunch, so I dig in.

John Corsnaed fires up the big screen and kicks things off with, "Looks like we've got the right people in the room." Duh. I'm the sole customer. I look under the table to see if anyone's hiding there. They don't get the joke.

Justice makes me want to describe every single page of the horrible PowerPoint and make you suffer as I do. I won't. It's longer than a doubleheader with ten rain delays, a gusher of bilgewater like McKinsey or Deloitte would come up with. It leads off with the general theory of mission statements, then a bunch of boring geology stuff. This is to "level set" us. As you can probably guess, "level set" is code for padding a presentation with stuff everybody in the meeting already knows, usually lifted from other presentations.

But the weirdest thing is the leprechaun. Every page has a leprechaun pointing at something, lurking in the background, grinning, touching his nose knowingly, grabbing his crotch (nah, I made that up), and so on. What does it mean? It's distracting. I lose track of what they're saying and concentrate on this Lucky Charms dude. Is there some hidden message here?

Just when I'm about to say I need to go feed my dog, we come to a slide showing the leprechaun with a pot of gold. And on the next slide, my mission statement:

To be Earth's most customer-centric geological consultants, telling customers anything and everything about their rocks.

And then the slogan for my website:

Man on the moon was once a dream. So was Lochaber Consulting.

Wow. This is like when my college girlfriend gave me a mustache spoon. You know, you want to say, "Are you out of your mind?" but you can't. Not her fault she's a dingbat. And not John Corsnaed's fault either.

Of course, there's a difference. My college girlfriend *gave* me the mustache spoon. But Corsnaed wants $4,800 for this stupid PowerPoint.

16

PAY UP, FRANKIE

I forgot to mention that Melanie Clusterratio was wearing a tasteful suit with a short, pleated skirt kinda like a tennis skirt.

I text Frankie and tell him I'm back from Bilkson. He calls.

"Whadda you want?" I say.

"You need anything?"

"Yeah, I need forty-eight hundred dollars wired to my primary DDA account, asshole."

I tell Frankie about the PowerPoint. I can tell he's muted his phone so I don't hear him guffaw. I am not amused.

"Red man think heap big funny. White man no laugh," I say when I'm done.

There's a pause. "I just submitted the wire. Now I've got something else for you."

"Oh, let me guess. You want me to put on a dog suit and play the fiddle on Main Street?"

"Wasn't my plan, but a good idea's a good idea. After you're done fiddling, how about making an offer on the Superior Agate Inn?"

"How about no? Is there a Diné word for that?"

"Several, actually. Just trust me on this. You don't need to pretend you care about the place. You're just acting as an agent for a group of investors. You've seen it and made favorable reports.

They're interested. You're doing it as a favor to me. If you need a convincer, call and put me on speaker."

"I haven't made any favorable reports," I say. "The clientele is a bunch of tow-headed Scandinavians who look like cave fish. And Anglophile fetishists."

"You in or out?"

"Okay, I'm in. After this can I go to Ashland? Theo is craving."

"Up to you."

It's pretty obvious something weird is going on at Bilkson. They can't possibly survive on Phil Farkey and his radio museum business, and nobody would hire them for anything else. But what, if anything, does that have to do with the hotel?

"Oh, by the way," Frankie says, "if you're wondering, and if I were you, I would be, police and the DPS think the railroad bull's death is unrelated to the Madero and Huerta murders."

"Huh?"

"Nick, they don't know what we know, and until ten minutes ago I didn't know what they know. So here it is. The neighbor in Winslow who described the suspect gets vaguer the more he talks. Now he isn't sure about much of anything, other than the guy being middle height or shorter with a medium or heavy build. The cops think—correctly—that lapidaries and amateur gold refiners have little in common, besides rocks. And the railroad bull has no discernible connection to Madero and Huerta. But mainly, the railroad bull had a large supply of oxycodone and hydrocodone in his house and was obviously dealing the stuff, so the cops reasonably think it's drug-related. The only drugs found in Madero's and Huerta's pits were acetaminophen and beer."

Early evening my phone bings. It's a message from Jing. *PCM*. So I call her. And record the conversation.

"A friend was going to Beijing, and I had her take your sample to the geology department at Tsinghua University."

"What do they say?"

"They say, I have it here, they extracted and assayed the native gold, which is present in very fine grains. They say it's 92.44 percent gold, 6.90 percent silver, 0.62 percent copper, and 0.04 percent iron and other metals. It's extremely rich ore, ten kilograms of gold per metric ton, but they think it would be highly unlikely to find it in large quantities. The silver and copper percentages and their isotope ratios, the composition of the gangue, and the fine grain texture suggest it is from the Ocotillo Mines in Arizona. Do you know where they are?"

"Sure. They were worked out a long time ago. The guy I got it from said it comes from a mine in Mexico—a mine people think petered out but really didn't."

"Really? What mine?"

"I don't remember. He says he can lease the mine for peanuts and wants me to bankroll him. Must be a scam of some sort. He probably got the sample at a rock show."

"See, it pays to check. So when are you coming to Chicago, Nick?"

"Well, Jing, I'm a little busy up here in Superior at the moment, but let me see . . . I expect probably end of next week. Will you be in town?"

"I can be," she coos.

Yeah, let them play me for a sucker. That quartzite is from the Emilio Rayón mine. Nothing like it ever came from the Ocotillo Mines. The guys at Tsinghua know that. They're lying. Trying to send me on a snipe hunt. So I send them on a snipe hunt. Gnaw on this bone, Ministry of State Security foo dogs.

Now, Jing might be a dupe who believes the guys at Tsinghua are telling the truth. Doubtful. I think she's a spook, which is why I asked her for the analysis in the first place. A spook of the industrial sort, which is what most MSS spooks are, though I doubt she'd turn up her nose at state secrets if they came her way. Probably a sparrow too. Which is fine with me. I've never nested with a sparrow before. She's expecting a hawk, but she's gonna get a pterodactyl.

17

NICE JOINT YOU GOT HERE,
I'M HANKERIN' TO BUY IT

Chanda Bhatt manages the Superior Agate Inn. The desk clerk tells me she's gone for the evening but will be in tomorrow morning around 08:30. So another boring evening. Who needs Ambien when you have *Structural Geology Algorithms* at your fingertips?

The next morning, I hit the main desk around 09:00. It's a little busy with people checking out. The clerk calls Chanda, tells her a Mr. Nick Cameron would like to discuss a business proposal, then has the housekeeping manager take me to her office.

And it's like stepping into Indira Gandhi's drawing room, which I saw at the Indira Gandhi Memorial in New Delhi when I was tracing the Nakshatra Opal, so I know what I'm talking about. But this suite has a wall of windows overlooking Lake Superior. And instead of an elder docent in a sari, I'm greeted by a young woman in Lululemon who would turn heads at the best yoga studio in Scottsdale. Take my word for it, she's a barn burner. Long, dark hair, big dark-brown eyes, and a yoga body hotter than flood basalt at the Deccan Traps at the end of the Cretaceous. Bhatt is usually a Brahmin name, as I know from the several Bhatts I've worked with, so I think she is likely Brahmin too.

Chanda rises at her desk, giving me namaste. That's unusual in this country, but I return it. I eye a large bronze statue of Ganesh. Not the kind made for tourists either. This one cost many lakhs of rupees.

And then another of Hanuman. I view it appreciatively. "Is he the guy who threw all those navigation hazards into the Palk Strait?" I ask. You learn this stuff when you're dating yoga women.

Chanda laughs. "You must be English."

"Scottish, lassie, but American first."

"Well enough, Mr. Cameron. Please sit down," she says, gesturing to a pair of Eames chairs facing the bay. "Would you like some tea?"

We settle down. I say, "Please call me Nick," and she says, "Call me Chanda." After some initial pleasantries—how long have I been staying at the hotel, have I enjoyed it, and so on—she comes to the point.

"So, Nick, you say you have a business proposal?"

Right now I'm thinking more of a proposition, but that'll have to wait.

"I do. I told a friend of mine this is a swell joint. Nice rooms, great views, good grub, high occupancy. A friendly, efficient, and courteous staff. He and his cronies are always on the lookout for, whadda they say, 'unique and well-established hotels.'"

I can tell she's interested. "And?" she says, flipping her hair.

"They wonder if you would consider an offer."

"My mother would need to decide, but I think yes, we would. That is, my family would. Clearly, the offer must be suitable."

"Of course."

I ask about the hotel's apparently high occupancy rate. She says it's popular because of the location and the harbor views, and the meeting rooms ensure a regular stream of guests for group meetings, business and fraternal. I ask if they had any overnights a few days ago. Yes, the Esteemed Brotherhood of St.

George. Episcopal? Yes. So that's where *Tennis Skirt Strumpets* and *Cambridge Coxswains* came from.

Then she drops the bomb.

"You know that we have the inn on a long-term lease, right?"

"No, I didn't. I assumed you, or should I say your family, owned it."

"Almost. It's a fifteen-year lease with thirteen years left to run."

"Who is the owner?"

"The Metaxas Trust. It's an old family in this area."

Frankie, you bastard, I'm gonna break your head with your stupid rain stick, tie you up in one of those rugs your auntie makes, and give you to White Buns.

"Have you heard of them?" Chanda says.

"Old Metaxas was in the agate racket, right?"

"Yes. You seem well-informed."

"I'm a consulting geologist. Agate barons, monkey gods throwing rocks around, you need to know these things."

I can tell she's impressed. Good. My friend Atul says smart guys are catnip to Brahmin women. Of course, other things being equal, smart guys are catnip to most women.

"Well, then. How would you like to proceed?" she says. "Surely your investors would like to see something. An income statement, cash flow?"

I'd rather have obsidian needles shoved under my fingernails than pore over income and cash flow statements. But I promised Frankie, so I have no choice.

"It's all in this PowerPoint," she says, walking to her desk and pulling a document from the file drawer. "But first you need to sign an NDA."

Chanda is really on top of things. After spending two minutes at her computer, she prints the NDA, I sign, and we look at the PowerPoint.

There's the damn leprechaun. Gee, I wonder who put this together.

"What's with the leprechaun?" I ask.

Chanda shrugs. "It's some sort of mascot for the consulting firm that did this. They did the PowerPoint. Our CPA gave them the numbers. He double-checked them."

"I see a big line item here for 'consulting services.' Same people?"

"Yes."

"That's a hell of a lot of money for a PowerPoint. What gives?"

Chanda hesitates.

"When we did the lease, we were required to engage Bilkson Consulting. The trustee said it was to ensure that the hotel is managed properly and its value as a going concern is preserved."

I understand the Metaxas Trust doesn't want its hotel turned into a flophouse or a meth lab, but this stinks. I doubt John Corsnaed could manage a toll booth on the Kansas Turnpike. And what they're paying Bilkson isn't much less than the hotel rent.

But it looks like the place is doing well. Occupancy rate is 85 percent. They're turning a handy profit. Eventually I get to the "consultant's recommendations."

"Hmm. Chanda, how is it possible to increase the occupancy rate by fifty percent when the occupancy rate is already eighty-five percent? Am I missing something? I'm a rocks guy, not a hotelier."

Chanda hesitates again. "I think he means to cut the vacancy rate by fifty percent and increase the occupancy rate to nine-ty-two point five percent. Of course, that's not what he said, but we don't pay much attention to Bilkson. We just view the consult-ing as an expense. But you won't be able to get the lease without agreeing to the same thing."

"Well, so be it," I say, smiling. "When in Rome. But you seem to be raking in the dough. Why cash out?"

"Two things. We can't find good people to manage the place,

so I've been doing it for more than a year. And my mother wants me to find a husband. I'd like that. We women have needs too, you know," she says, smiling. "And Mother wants to retire. We have all the money we need."

"Sound like good reasons to me." Especially the "needs" part, I'm thinkin'.

I tell her she should get Frankie to sign an NDA and email him the PowerPoint. She's okay with that.

Then we look ahead. The trustee of the Metaxas Trust is Hermes Scrool, an attorney with offices in Ashland. She calls his office and gets patched through to the guy. He babbles pompously for a few minutes about his duties as trustee. Then says he's not opposed, and I should meet him in Ashland day after tomorrow. He's out of town now.

Business out of the way, we start talking about other stuff. She has an MS in computer science from Berkeley. She thinks American yoga is good exercise. She thinks Sanskrit is a needlessly complex language that's better off dead. I agree, worse than Latin by a long shot. You yoga fanatics who think learning names of things in the nominative case is learning Sanskrit, you're crazy. Try conjugating some Sanskrit verbs.

I'm talking and notice Chanda's gazing into my eyes, her pupils dilated. I bet mine are too.

On and off I've been hearing this strange noise. Sometimes like an old-time dot matrix printer. Sometimes like a high-speed dentist's drill. It's faint but seems to be coming from a door at the end of the suite.

"What's that noise?" I finally ask.

She rises, takes me by the hand, and leads me toward the door. My internal seismograph is thrashing. Her hand emits strong compressional waves, coinciding with some thrust faulting on my side, if you get my drift. The sound gets louder. Then she opens the door, and it's piercing.

A big 3D printer is making a very detailed model of the Car of Juggernaut.

Right now, it's starting on the roof. She moves closer to me, gently grasping my forearm. I see she's looking at a twin bed in the corner. A jar of disposable earplugs sits on the nightstand. Yes, she sleeps with this contraption. So is she turned on by me or the 3D printer? It's hard to tell. Geek girls have weird fetishes.

Just then a fire alarm goes off.

18

THANK GOD FOR AAA

An Episcopalian brought a toaster into his room and incinerated his daily bread. Just as well—I wasn't really in the mood.

I go back to my room and brief Frankie on the meeting. The discussion is long and meandering and includes local news from Quartzrock you don't care about, so I'll summarize my conclusions.

Clearly, somebody is looting the Metaxas Trust and laundering the money through Bilkson Consulting. You charge a low rent for trust properties and then insist on big fees to Bilkson for their worthless advice. I bet this is happening at other trust properties too. But who would complain? The lessees aren't getting gouged because the low rent plus the consulting fees equals the fair market value of the rent alone. Chanda assures me this is true for the Superior Agate Inn. Lessees probably think the Metaxas Trust just wants to keep them from running its properties into the dirt and believes the gomerils at Bilkson Consulting can do that. Running properties into the dirt, especially resorts, seems to be a regional pastime up here, so it's believable.

And it's not likely this gets picked up on cursory audits. The way this fraud is structured, the books of the Metaxas Trust will be perfectly clean, and so will the hotel's and those of Bilkson

Consulting. The rent payments are low and the consulting fees are high, but all transactions can be verified and appear legitimate.

Now, because this fraud requires artificially low rents to compensate lessees for the fees they pay to Bilkson, it reduces the rental income to the Metaxas Trust and therefore reduces the trust distributions to Theo and her brother. Curiously, these reductions seem to coincide with the big contract Bilkson got from the radio museum two years ago. If this is just coincidence, Grandpa Cameron was a maypole dancer.

Who is running this scam? If you look under that fake oriental rug in the Bilkson lobby, I bet you'll find a cockroach named Hermes Scrool.

Frankie agrees with my reasoning and conclusions. For once, he doesn't have anything to add but says he wants to reserve final judgment until I meet with Scrool. He says "good work" and then says he has a silver melt going and needs to run. He has a shed out back where he keeps a furnace and his casting stuff.

And now I'm ready to leave for Ashland. I tell Chanda I'll be back. Then I check out and wheel my suitcase to the 911. It's parked by a hedge at the east end of the lot.

I'm by the trunk, which is in front on a 911, and my thumb is on the remote's trunk release when I look up and see "2620" scrawled on the windshield in grease pen. I jump back. I know there's nobody close because I looked around, as I always do. But this is bad. I'm thinking the car is wired with a bomb.

What to do? I can't call the police and tell them a homicidal hobo scrawled Unicode for the death's head on my windshield and I suspect a car bomb.

I could call AAA, which is what Scrotelli did when he suspected a car bomb. That's typical Scrotelli behavior for you. More about him later. He's quite the psychopath. He handed the AAA guy the keys and excused himself to take a leak. Fortunately for the AAA guy, there was no bomb.

But I don't need to call anyone. See, what White Buns doesn't know is that I have remote start on the 911. It didn't have that originally—something about German anti-idling laws—but I installed an easy aftermarket add-on. You press the lock button three times on the key fob to start, same to stop. It can cool the car down a little when it's been baking in the Arizona sun.

No cars are near mine, but there's a big maple tree about ten yards away by the hedge, well within range for the remote starter. I get behind that, hands over my ears, and press the lock button on the key fob three times. No explosion. The car starts. Then stops. I try again. Same thing. I can't look under it because it has almost no ground clearance, but I can snap photos of the under-carriage with my phone. Nothing there. I get in and try starting it. It stalls after a few seconds.

I'm thinking White Buns didn't have time to finish his dem-olition exercise and just disconnected something. So now is the time to call AAA. I watch the car until the tech arrives, then meet him by the hotel lobby, explain the problem, and give him the key. Then I go inside and ask the desk clerk about reliable mechanics in the area. She gives me the name and number of a shop that works on German cars. I head back to the car.

"Started right up, but then it stalled," the AAA guy says. "Somebody shoved a potato up the tailpipe. I know that trick, so it's the first thing I checked."

"It has two tailpipes."

"There were two potatoes. Russets, big Idaho bakers. Red potatoes wouldn't work for this car."

"That's weird. Who would do that?"

"Dunno. There was a guy crouched by it when I went over there, probably the culprit. But he ran away. He had a baseball bat, a DeMarini. Probably used the handle to shove the potatoes in there."

"DeMarini is a good bat."

"Yeah, that's what I thought. He probably stole it. It's usually kids who do this, but this guy was not a kid."

"What'd he look like?"

"Short, dumpy guy. Sure ran fast, though."

"Did he look like a hobo?"

"Kinda, I guess."

I see White Buns's plan. I start the car, it stalls, I try again, no dice, then I get out, left foot on the pavement, left hand on the door sill, head down because that's how I get out of the 911. And White Buns, who has crept around to the driver's side rear fender, whacks me with the baseball bat. How does he know I play baseball? This guy is devious.

I tip the AAA guy a double sawbuck and head east toward Ashland. After a few miles, I stop behind a CVS. Clearly, there's a GPS tracker on the car, one that reports over the cell network. And clearly, White Buns put it there when my car was parked overnight at La Piazza in Winslow. He knew I was going somewhere; the question was where. But he wasn't tailing me—the guy travels by train—and didn't need real-time position updates. So, to conserve power, he would have set the tracker to transmit only occasionally, maybe every hour or two. But I bet he wanted the positions sampled more often to know the route. Like, how near are the railroad tracks? So it would be receiving and storing positions at more frequent intervals, say, every few minutes, then transmitting them later in a batch. Of course, the bug needs an internal clock oscillator for the processor and the GPS receiver and probably another so it knows when to wake up, and they'll generate RF emissions even when it's not transmitting. And when it's receiving it will generate other RF emissions too. If you don't believe me, look up heterodyne.

Cheap GPS bug sweepers don't detect those emissions, just transmissions. Luckily, I have an excellent bug sweeper I got from a friend in Alamogordo who really knows this stuff. He makes them himself. He's one of those guys who can't talk about his work for national security reasons. For real, not like somebody who has security clearance because he writes articles for the Congressional Budget Office. Anyway, his sweeper should find the thing even if it's not transmitting, and probably even if its battery is dead, because it has a nonlinear junction detector besides its spectrum analyzer. I honestly don't know in detail how the thing works. It's mathematically trenchant. But I fire it up, and there's the bug, up inside the front bumper by the left radiator. I pull it off, using my clean handkerchief. What do you do with it? Obviously, you put it on another car. Before GPS trackers, White Buns would have had to tail me, and I would have needed to swap cars with somebody to give him the slip. Now you just foist the tracker on somebody else.

And praise the Lord, just then a UPS delivery truck pulls up and parks next to me. The driver goes into a pet grooming joint next to CVS. I stash the tracker in his rear fender. Now chase this guy all over hell, White Buns.

The next question is whether White Buns put a tracker on Theo's car. I text her and ask her to give me a call. I don't get a callback right away. She's probably running around in the woods somewhere or fishing or passed out on Jägermeister or whatever people drink up here.

It's a short drive to Ashland, a little over an hour, and I check in at the best hotel I can find, which at least has delusions of grandeur, if lacking it. The Ashland Cabana, on the waterfront.

There's a bulletin board in the lobby with ads for local stuff. Are hotel guests really looking for a drywall guy? But Trixie's Fishing Charters catches my eye. I don't care about fishing, but there's a photo of Trixie, and she's quite a dish. I scan the QR code, add her to my contacts list, and call. It's a bad connection because she's out on a charter, but she says tomorrow at noon would work for her. Meet her at the Troutfish Marina. Ask the marina guy, she says, and he'll direct me to her boat. She says $600 for four hours of fishing. That seems pricey, but I'm okay with it.

Posted next to the bulletin board is NOAA Nautical Chart 14973, which shows Chequamegon Bay and the islands north of it. I've been up here before but spend a few minutes refreshing my memory. Then I decide to drive up to Bayfield—about twenty miles—and find the marina. Which isn't hard. It's on the water! I park by the marina store, then take a walk down to the docks.

And there is Theo's Subaru. She probably keeps her boat here. I go back to my car and get the sweeper. And sure enough, there's a tracker, in the rear bumper.

There's no UPS truck handy, but there are lots of boats. So who gets the honor of being the decoy for a homicidal hobo? Easy. The big boat that says "Isle Royale Charters." Figure this out, Barnacle Bill the Hobo.

Now I decide to look around the joint. It has slips for about a hundred boats and transient moorage for a few dozen. I go to the gas dock and ask the attendant where Theo Metaxas moors her boat. He points.

"Over there. I forget the number." He pulls out his phone and checks something. "B33."

From where he pointed, B33 must be near the end of the long east-west dock that has slips for the larger boats. I thank him, return to shore, and walk to the B dock. It has no slips for the first fifty yards—probably space for transients, but none are tied up here now. Past that stretch are slips with some nice sailboats, thirty-five to fifty feet, and some high-buck motor yachts. I'm looking side to side but catch some motion dead ahead, toward the end of the dock by Theo's boat. A hand on the dock. Another hand. Somebody is pulling himself up from a dinghy or a canoe.

It's White Buns. How did he get here so fast? There are no trains to Bayfield. A stolen car? Uber?

"You break it, you buy it!" I shout, then sprint down the dock.

I'd love to see the expression on his face, but he's a hundred yards away. He jumps onto a fifty-foot Sea Ray, and I lose sight of him. Ten seconds later, I'm at the Sea Ray. He must be in the cockpit or the salon. "Permission to come aboard?" I shout, then jump on the foredeck. I hear an engine start—not the main engines, something else. Then I see White Buns taking off on a Jet Ski from the swim platform at the stern. A fully clothed hobo on a Jet Ski is something you don't see every day, so that's pretty cool. But son of a bitch, I thought I had him. Now he's heading around the south breakwater and out to sea.

Theo and some dame are watching all this from the cockpit of her boat. I wave toward the dock, and Theo jumps up and starts that way. I run down and meet her at her boat. Unfortunately, it's a trawler. Nice boat, but not a planing hull.

"Where's a fast boat?" I say.

She runs to the end of the dock and there, dwarfed by the cruisers, is an old Yamaha jet boat. It's maybe sixteen feet, twin engines, and 220 horsepower, so good enough.

"It's Cynthia's," she says. "We can take it."

"You drive," I say. "I'm an ocean sailor, not a jet boater."

I cast us off and barely make it into the boat as Theo pulls away. I fall into the forward passenger seat as she gives full throttle and we start to plane.

We round the breakwater and see White Buns is heading south. This kind of boat is hard to control in anything but flat seas, and we're skipping over the waves. It's yawing and she slows down.

"Can we catch him?" I shout over the din of the stinking two-cycle engines.

"I don't know. It feels like we're in the air half the time at full throttle."

I'd give anything for a fast V-hull, not this almost-flat-bottomed toy boat. Still, we seem to be gaining on him. We're doing about forty miles per hour, throttled back, and he's doing about the same. White Buns must have a good gut to take the pounding he's getting from this wave action.

On the port bow, a five-mile-long sandspit extends from the mainland almost to Madeline Island, a big island about two miles east of Bayfield. At the end of the spit is the Chequamegon Point Lighthouse. Three miles southwest of that is Houghton Point on the Bayfield Peninsula. These enclose the inner Chequamegon Bay. White Buns is in the middle of the strait, heading south.

"He's going to Ashland," Theo says.

Once we pass the lighthouse we get less wave action, and Theo throttles up. But so does White Buns.

"Flank speed!" I shout, pushing the throttle all the way forward. The engines scream like tortured loons, and we start closing on White Buns.

"He's heading for the ore dock," Theo says. This is a long derelict pier, a concrete foundation for a steel superstructure that was removed years ago. West of the dock, across a channel about a hundred feet wide, there's a spit of land where a tugboat is tied to a concrete dock. White Buns heads in there, and we follow.

He lands his Jet Ski on the riprap near the tugboat, jumps ashore, and takes off like a cheetah on crack. Theo jams the throttle full astern, and we pull up at the Jet Ski. Then she jumps out and runs after him, brandishing her little revolver and threatening to cut out his liver with a filleting knife and skin him alive with a fish scaler. Does she have the hots for this guy?

I grab a line, jump ashore, loop it around a rock, and follow Theo. She runs well, especially for being five four. But she's not catching the hobo. I shout, "Put the gun away!" But she keeps running. "You won't catch him," I say as I pull up beside her. "Follow me if you want, but put the gun away." White Buns is already two hundred yards ahead and has disappeared into a crowd in the lakefront park. They're having a band concert. I get near the bandstand and realize it's hopeless. There are a gazillion people here, all packed together. If White Buns were six foot eight, I might see him, but as we know, he's short and dumpy. And a lot of guys here are short and dumpy, same as in Quartzrock.

I stop and Theo catches up. I shake my head. If I wade into the crowd and find him (unlikely), he'll fight and people will break up the fight and he'll get away. If I pull my roscoe, I'll likely be shot by some off-duty cop or citizen with a concealed carry permit, and reasonably so. If I call the cops and try to convince them there's a homicidal hobo in the crowd, they'll think I'm crazy. If I tell the cops some guy stole a Jet Ski, I might get a reaction, but when they hear he abandoned the Jet Ski, they'll lose interest and say no harm done, just another case of Jet Ski joyriding. I decide we need to catch him after the crowd breaks up. Even if we can't hold him, getting a good look and some photos will be a huge help to Frankie.

But it doesn't matter, because I see him clinging to the back of a taco truck that's driving away down Seventh Avenue toward town. This crowd doesn't like tacos, I guess.

At least we gave him a good scare.

Theo and I walk back toward the boat. She takes my hand and presses close, looking up at me. There's a poplar thicket at the end of the little peninsula, and she steers me into it. We're out of sight, and we embrace for a long, sensual kiss. I think she wants me to take her right here, right now. Is woodland sex a thing in Northern Wisconsin? I don't find out.

Some guy shouts, "Hey, you, in the trees! Harbormaster says to get your toys outta here!"

So under the glaring eye of the water bailiff, Theo and I tow the Jet Ski back to the marina. I insist on gassing it up, along with the jet boat. Then I thank Cynthia for the use of her boat—Cynthia, who's lounging in the cockpit of Theo's boat and is quite a dish. Theo says she'll tell the owner of the Jet Ski what happened.

I tell her about removing the tracker from her car, and she thinks White Buns has been scared off for now. I'm not sure of that, but she says her house is well alarmed, and if White Buns tries invading, she'll blow him in half with her ten-gauge goose gun. I expect her to invite me over, but she says she needs to drive Cynthia home and is doing something with her brother tomorrow. She leaves with Cynthia.

I don't know how to read Theo. She reminds me of a girl I knew in college, a civil engineering student. One minute she would paw me in the grips of uncontrollable sexual craving and then, ten seconds later, she'd be sitting cross-legged across the room talking about storm drains. It's like her sexuality was controlled by unknown random variables. A friend gave me an elaborate explanation of how this might work, and how I could influence it. It made sense at the time—I was nodding and saying, "Ahhh! I get it!"—but in retrospect, I have no idea what he was talking about. I doubt he did either.

19

A HOOKER, OF SORTS

The next day, I get to the marina a little early. The Isle Royale Charters boat is gone, presumably to Isle Royale. I find a guy at the gas dock who points me to Trixie's boat and gives me a knowing grin.

It's an old steel-hulled fishing trawler, the dull maroon paint blistered and peeling, leprous with rust, a random length of electrical conduit for a radio mast, a naked red light bulb dangling from a wire on the port bow for a running light. The pilot house ports are yellowed plexiglass, nearly opaque, except one on the port side, by the helm, where the plexiglass has fallen out and lies on the deck. This allows the pilot, a scurvy oaf smoking a cigarette, to poke his head out and see where he's going. Dense white exhaust smoke issues from the stern. The wind blows the smoke into the pilothouse, where it emerges from the open port, making the boat look like it's on fire.

Just kidding. That's not Trixie's boat; it's just one that's passing by outside the marina.

Trixie's boat is a nice, clean, thirty-foot fiberglass cruiser with a flybridge, a polished hull blindingly white in the sunlight, downriggers, rod holders, and a Simrad radar dome on a mast above the flybridge. I can't wait to see the salon.

So that's the boat. What about Trixie?

Most fishing guides have greasy hair, scraggly beards, and whiskey breath and wear dirty jeans and flannel shirts. Trixie ties her blonde hair in a ponytail. She doesn't have a beard and smells of Marc Jacobs perfume. She wears cutoff jeans and a cropped tank top, both very clean, and believe me, her outfit leaves little to the imagination. She's hotter than the Central Skåne Volcanic Province during the early Jurassic.

And that's just what I can tell from the dock.

We introduce ourselves and shake hands over the gunwale. I cast us off and hop aboard. I can tell she likes me. I'm not some nauseating snob who expects her to do all the work. I join her on the flybridge, and she navigates out of the marina.

Bayfield is on the Bayfield Peninsula, which is shaped kinda like the horn of an anvil, with the flat top of the anvil extending over to Duluth/Superior and the curve of the anvil under the horn being Chequamegon Bay. Bayfield is on the lower side of the horn more than halfway to the tip. A cluster of islands, mostly small, are scattered all over below the end of the horn. These are called the Apostle Islands. They were named by somebody who didn't know how to count because there are more than twelve. More than reasonably necessary, in my opinion. And they're covered with an excessive number of trees.

I'm telling you this because Trixie says she's taking the West Channel, which runs north-northeast of Bayfield, hemmed in against the peninsula by a long, uninteresting island. I forget its name. Probably Long Island or something equally dumb. She says we can get some king salmon there.

We come down from the flybridge, and she has me steer at trolling speed from the main bridge while she messes around with the tackle. Eventually, she has two lines in the water and adjusts the downriggers to where the fish finder is showing big fish. The downriggers, for you city folk, are ten-pound (approximately) weights on thin stainless steel cables. You lower them to the depth where you want to fish. Right now, it's eighty feet. The fishing line clips onto the weight and drags a shiny spinning bait behind the downrigger. When a fish strikes, the line disengages from the clip, and then the fun starts. These fish are really stupid. They'd bite on a toy submarine if it were shiny enough.

We catch a couple of salmon, a fish I detest unless smoked, or better, loxed. She throws them in a live well.

This goes on for a while, and frankly, it's not that interesting. We pass one island, then another, and then Trixie says she's going to put in at Raspberry Island for a break and a snack. It's one of the smaller islands, but she says it has a lighthouse that's preserved as part of the National Lakeshore, and there are a couple of docks where we can tie up. And we do.

Trixie has me sit down in the salon and brings me a beer. Then she sits down next to me and stretches out her arms, arching her back and giving me a lubricious smirk. The guy at the gas dock, Trixie's attire, and the $600 tariff make me wonder if I paid for more than a few fish.

A boat pulls up at the second dock. I look out a port to see what's going on.

Holy crap. It's Theo and some guy. Her brother, or I miss my guess.

"What is it?" says Trixie.

"Oh, nothing. Just a boat pulling up."

Theo and her brother aren't wasting time. They tramp down the dock and climb the hill up to the lighthouse. I see they're carrying burlap bags.

"Say, Trixie," I say, "I really need to go ashore for a few minutes. I promised a friend I'd get him a sample of the sandstone here. He collects Neoproterozoic sandstone. I'll be right back."

I jump onto the dock, then peek around the boat. When Theo and her brother are out of sight, I follow.

I crest the hill just in time to see them disappear into the woods to the north of the lighthouse. I give them a little time, then run across the two or three acres of grass that surround the lighthouse to where they entered the woods.

There's a path, which they obviously followed given there's a dense barrier of poison ivy, burdock, and nettles at the edge of the grass. See, this is why I like Arizona. You have prickly things in the desert, but there's plenty of space between them, and you can walk wherever you please. You can't do that up here.

I follow the path cautiously, pausing to listen. They're talking in the distance. A quarter mile and I see a sunlit opening ahead. The path ends at an abandoned quarry, so they're obviously after something there. No other reason to go there with burlap bags. I sneak off into the woods and hunker down. I can see the path, but they can't see me.

The woods smell nice. Mainly tamarack, cedar, and birch. The canopy is dense, so it's dark and cool, and there's little undergrowth. While I'm waiting for them to return from the quarry, I think about the geology of these islands. The sea cliffs and exposed rock formations inland are Neoproterozoic sandstone, close to a billion years old. That may sound old, but if you go inland and east of Ashland you can get into Archean shield rocks, igneous and metamorphosed stuff, that's 3.6 billion years old. That's respectably old, but you can find Hadean stuff in Northern Canada that's over 4 billion. The oldest exposed rocks on earth, in fact. Sure they're old, but they're out in the middle of nowhere and not really good for anything, so it's a wasted trip.

Here they come. Each has two bags, moderately heavy, probably twenty-five pounds each for the brother, maybe fifteen each for Theo. You can guess the weight by how they're walking.

So that's where the agates come from. Old Miles really did hide a stash, and it's somewhere in the quarry. The bags are wet, so the agates must be hidden underwater, just like I thought when Theo showed them to me in Quartzrock.

When they're beyond a bend in the path, I go to the quarry and follow their tracks. The bottom of the quarry is flooded, and the water could be fifty feet deep for all I know. Their tracks end by a large tamarack that overhangs the water. The stash must be submerged here.

Pieces of sandstone litter the quarry floor, and I pick up a nice one for my friend. Yes, I really know a guy who collects Neoproterozoic sandstone.

I head back and watch from the woods as they cross the lighthouse yard. They go down the hill, and when they're out of sight, I follow. Their boat starts up. I give them ten minutes to get underway, then saunter down to the dock.

Trixie's soaking up rays in the cockpit. "What were the Metaxas twins doing?" she asks. "Picking up rocks?"

Yeah, I know, some sleuth I am, you say. But I am. Trixie thinks the Metaxas twins have a thing for rocks. As do other locals, she says, who think them eccentric. Indeed, in most thesauri you'll find *eccentric, crank,* and *rockhound* listed as synonyms. And a polyglot friend assures me that the words for *eccentric* and *rockhound* are the same in many languages. But when you're scions of a fine local family, people excuse eccentricity. In my experience, they almost expect it. (I personally see nothing wrong with rockhounding. I don't do it, but at least its practitioners get exercise and sunshine, which is more than you can say for practitioners of most hobbies.)

Now, collecting rocks, buying rocks, giving away rocks—that's fine and won't disqualify the twins as trust beneficiaries. Selling gemstones will. So what Trixie and the locals don't know is that the twins are tapping and selling off a valuable stash of prime agates, not collecting stupid Lake Superior beach stones for their flower garden. But I know it.

I tell Trixie I love her company and the fishing has been great, but I need to get back to the hotel and prepare for tomorrow's meeting. She can tell I'm sincere and would love a dalliance with her but just don't have the time. That makes her want me even more.

When we get back to the marina, she wants to refund $300 of the $600 she charged me. I tell her to keep it.

20

NICE PINKIE RING, RODOLFO

I call Frankie to tell him about the agate stash and the chase across the bay.

"Whadda you want?" says Frankie.

"You need anything?"

"Yes. I need you to take someone with you to the Scrool meeting tomorrow. Rodolfo Graziani."

"The Fascist guy? I thought he was dead."

"Ha ha. Different Rodolfo. He's a Democrat from Melrose Park. As far as you're concerned, he's the money man behind the offer, and you're leaving all negotiations to him."

"What does he look like?"

"What do you think someone named Rodolfo Graziani from Melrose Park looks like? And don't be surprised if he hints he's representing an Indian tribe that wants to turn the place into a casino. Let him do the talking. He'll meet you at your hotel at nine tomorrow morning."

Fine with me. I wasn't looking forward to the meeting anyway. "Okay," I say, "got it. Rodolfo is the money man, and he does the talking. He may hint he wants to set up a carpet joint with an Indian tribe. Now I've got something for you. I found old Miles's agate stash."

I tell Frankie the story, and he's impressed. He spends time speculating about how the twins might be fishing the agates out of the deep water, then gets back on track.

"That's good work," he says. "It's nice to have a buried treasure legend be true for once. And talk of treasure, I finally got into Paco's compound. You were right for once. There is gold-bearing quartzite mixed in that pile of crushed stone. I've got a piece right here, and it's damn rich stuff. You need a magnifier to see that, though."

"That's how gold ore usually is, even when it's very rich. People think it looks like those gold-encrusted quartz specimens you see at rock shows. To most people, it just looks like a rock. Remember that scene in *Treasure of the Sierra Madre* where the old fart is jumping up and down, telling them they're dumber than the dumbest jackass because they don't even see the riches they're standing on?"

"I remember it well. But he's not jumping up and down, he's doing a jig. Do they teach you to do that in the geosciences department?"

"It's an interdisciplinary program. Geosciences and performing arts."

Silence for ten seconds.

"So, you're sure this stuff is from the Emilio Rayón mine?" Frankie says.

"Sure I'm sure. It has unique petrological oddities. I know because I had an old prof who combed that place over doing his master's thesis fifty years ago. He lectured on it for a week. I think I was the only one who stayed awake. The mine petered out in the 1920s and was totally worked out by the late 1930s. So the stuff we're seeing must have been mined a long time ago, a century ago, probably. That's what's so weird about it."

"I would say finding it mixed in with railroad ballast in Arizona is weird too. And I'm sure that pile at Madero's compound is railroad ballast. It's been washed, but it still has that railroad smell. You know what I mean?"

"Yes, it's quite distinctive," I say. Frankie has an exceptionally good sense of smell. Not quite on the canine level, but about as close to that as a human can get. I once took a book from one of his bookshelves—a Navajo dictionary—leafed through it, and put it back. He didn't see me do that. Two days later, he asked me if I was interested in learning Navajo. He could tell I had handled the dictionary just from the smell. But my night vision is better than his. We all have our gifts.

"Anything else?" Frankie asks.

I tell him about the trackers on the cars and White Buns trying to whack me in Superior, and Theo in Bayfield.

"That's more good work, laddie," he says. "So White Buns got a good look at your cars when you were at that Mexican crock shop and put on the trackers when you were parked overnight at La Piazza. I wouldn't worry, though. I'll give high odds he's on his way back to Arizona right now."

"How do you know that?"

"Well, first off, you got rid of the trackers and foiled his attacks. I give you high marks for foiling his attempt at the hotel and for deducing the Unicode connection. It would take a hardcore geek like you to see that one. I think you were just lucky at the marina, but you're a lucky guy. So he's been foiled five times now, if you include the bindle bomb as a separate attempt from the crock shop. Not that he's one to give up, but there's a good reason for him wanting to get back to Arizona. Specifically, gold."

Frankie stops talking. He might expect me to say something, but who knows what. "Got it. Gold. Go on," I say.

"Okay. I have some reliable guys walking the tracks between Gallup and Flagstaff looking for the gold-bearing quartzite. And they've found five places where it's mixed in with ballast. All on spur tracks, none on the main line."

"Huh. Five different places? That's weird."

"It is, and I have an idea why. But that's not why White Buns is heading back home. The guys also found a cache of the quartzite northwest of Two Guns that must have taken a long time to collect. And it had one of those cellular trail cameras set up to watch it. You know, the kind lazy hunters use. Solar powered. That seemed high-tech for a hobo. But now that you told me about the trackers, it's not surprising at all. He's not your grandpa's hobo."

Since finding the trackers, I've been reading up on hoboes. In the 1930s, it sounds like they were mostly "internally displaced persons." *Grapes of Wrath* stuff. Or what Grandpa Cameron told me he saw in Europe in 1945. But some people just joined in for the hell of it.

"Your grandpa's hobo was not your grandpa's hobo," I say. "Did you know that William O. Douglas hoboed for a spell, or claimed he had?"

"The Supreme Court Justice? The penumbral rights guy?"

"The same. Maybe he picked up that emanations and penumbras stuff from a defrocked astronomer in a hobo jungle. Now that I think of it, most of the Supreme Court's scientific analogies sound like they came from a hobo jungle. So, how'd your guys find the stash?"

"Ambrose—you don't know him—went off following some antelope tracks and saw the camera from the back. Then he circled around so the camera could see him and played like he found the stash by accident and wasn't sure what it was. He picked up a couple of pieces, then just walked away. Exactly what I would have done. Now White Buns will try to get it out of there pronto. He may want to whack you, and maybe Theo, but I bet he cares more about his gold."

I'm not totally sure about that, but Frankie is usually right about these things. I ask if he has someone watching the stash.

"Duh," he says. "One other thing. They found some around

the site of that big derailment that happened last March. Remember that? The Rabid Horse Gulch derailment. On a Cholla Railroad spur."

"Really?"

"Honest Injun. An engineer was killed in that derailment. It's what you call a clue."

I don't see how it's a clue but leave it at that.

The next morning, I meet Rodolfo in the hotel lobby. He's a big boy with dark hair graying a bit at the temples, olive skin, an expensive suit, and a hint of menace in his face. He intentionally plays up the stereotype with a diamond pinkie ring. That's an old mafia thing. Bling that substitutes for brass knucks. It's unnecessary. You wouldn't mess with this guy anyway. Not that appearances tell everything. You wouldn't want to mess with White Buns either, but you'd never guess it to look at him.

"Rodolfo?" I say.

He nods, then motions with his head to the parking lot. I'm riding with him. In a black Cadillac Escalade.

I have the address, so I navigate, giving him instructions. He doesn't say a word.

And he doesn't say a word when we get to the offices of Hermes Scrool. Which are in the same kind of dreary office building as Bilkson Consulting. But the furniture is nicer. And there is a fine oriental rug, recent manufacture from India but handmade, in the reception area.

I introduce us to the receptionist, an old sourpuss, and say we've arrived for a meeting with Mr. Scrool. Her phone doesn't ring during the forty-five minutes we're waiting. This makes me wonder how many clients Scrool has, aside from the Metaxas Trust.

Eventually, Sourpuss takes us back to Scrool's office.

Scrool rises from his executive chair behind his enormous mahogany desk. He's not much taller standing than sitting. He's in his sixties, I'd say. His face looks like a plate of pig intestines, contorted by long years of envy and malice.

He motions us to the conference table and takes a seat. His feet barely touch the floor.

"No lease," says Rodolfo. "We want to buy."

Scrool shakes his head. "That's not possible, I'm afraid."

Rodolfo shrugs and rises. Scrool raises his hands and Rodolfo sits down.

"It's possible, but we normally don't sell the trust properties. What's wrong with a lease? We can go longer."

"No. My people need complete and total ownership. Title in fee simple absolute, or nothing."

I can see Scrool's evil little mind churning.

"And why is that?"

"Because they can't do what they want to do without it."

Scrool grins. "I understand. I think I know what you're talking about," he says, glancing deliberately at a ceremonial Indian drum on the wall. It's a nice drum. The head has some deer-men with big antlers painted in black on a red background. What it means, I have no idea. I don't ask Indians what Antler Men mean, and Indians don't ask me what the Celtic Triangle means. Which is good because I have no idea what it means.

Rodolfo pretends not to notice that Scrool's looking at the drum.

"We deal here or not?"

"I think so, yes. The other trustee will need to agree, but he usually follows my advice."

Rodolfo nods.

"One thing," Scrool continues. "The current contract with Bilkson Consulting will need to be continued for, shall we say, ten years?"

"Don't need 'em. We run things our way. Anyway, I've seen the hotel financials, and their rates are ridiculous."

"I'm sorry, but it's not negotiable."

"Then you cut the price to make up for their fees."

Scrool pretends to consider this thoughtfully for a moment. "I think that can be done."

Rodolfo rips a page from the tablet Scrool set in front of him and tears it in half. So far, he hasn't taken any notes.

"I'll write our offer on this, and you write yours on that," Rodolfo says, handing Scrool a half sheet. Then he turns to me. "Nick, I love you like a brother, but I'll take things from here. Wait for me in that dive of a sports bar across the street."

I'm not going to argue with Rodolfo. Besides, I have no idea how to negotiate a hotel purchase. Rocks, yes, hotels, no. I leave and go to the bar. Which really is a dive. How did Rodolfo know? A quick look at Ashland, a knowledge of sports bars, and he gives short odds the joint is a dive.

They've got wrestling on one screen, stock car racing on another, and motocross racing on another. Three strikes and they're out, for me, anyway. I'll read *Journal of Metamorphic Geology* on my phone instead.

Some serious negotiating must be going on because it's an hour before Rodolfo strides in. He looks around, sizing everyone up, then comes to my corner table, sitting back to the wall. He orders a martini.

"Learned counsel is working up the papers," he says. "He'll email them to me tomorrow."

"Ehi, Rodolfo. This stinks. I know it stinks. You know it stinks. I recorded the whole thing. At least until I left. We should talk to the Bunghole County attorney or district attorney or whatever they call it up here."

Rodolfo eyes the waiter approaching with his martini. "The Ashland County district attorney. And I recorded it too. Audio and video. You just go do your rock stuff. Wait for a call from Frankie."

He throws a Grant on the table and drains the martini in one gulp. He must weigh 280, so he won't even notice it.

21

IF SHE WEIGHS THE SAME AS A DUCK, INDICT HER

I text Frankie to tell him the meeting's done.

Then I upload the audio to Hunnypaht, which is a hash-chained immutable repository. Good luck arguing recent fabrication against that.

It's about lunchtime, so I figure I'll drive up to Bayfield to see if Theo is at the marina. As a rule, people with boats in a marina spend a lot more time in the marina than at sea. But first I need to change clothes. I made a big concession for the Scrool meeting by wearing a sports coat, dress khakis, and loafers.

When I get to my hotel room, I notice Frankie has sent another encrypted email. Decrypted, it says to call a number I don't recognize after 13:00 CDT.

It's almost 13:00. I'm not sure what's going on, but I don't want to make the call on my cell, and I don't have a burner phone with me, so I go down to the hotel's "business center." It's a neglected cubbyhole with nothing but a desk, a phone, and a beige antediluvian printer with a serial cable dangling from it. Only the cleaning staff goes there. But the phone works. And to my surprise, the call goes through.

"Hello," Sheriff Pershing answers.

"What's up?" I say.

The conversation is long and convoluted, so I'll summarize.

The Arizona DPS thinks Theo hired the hobo to whack Madero and Huerta. Why? The radio museum trust provides that if a trustee dies and the death is not shown by clear and convincing evidence to be from natural causes, Miles's surviving issue—Theo and her brother, at this time—must appoint the replacement, which may be themselves. Miles was worried Chicago gangsters would massacre the trustees, take over the museum, and plunder its assets. This provision, and others, were intended to thwart that. Since there are only three trustees, this means that with Madero and Huerta whacked, Theo and her brother can take control of the museum for sixteen years, which is the maximum term trustees can serve. Miles loved FDR and didn't like short term limits. And yes, Theo and her brother are members in good standing of the Ancient and Respected Radio League. Miles paid for their life memberships.

From this, the DPS concludes that Theo knew she and her brother might be disqualified as beneficiaries of the Metaxas Trust because of their agate dealings, at which point the corpus of the trust would go to the radio museum. With Madero and Huerta dead, she and her brother would appoint themselves trustees of the radio museum, and plunder the museum just as Madero and Huerta were doing, but with a much bigger pot to plunder.

"Okay," I say. "Let's say she hired the hobo. Why would she risk showing up at Madero's right after he was whacked? That seems pretty stupid."

"Nick, in my long career, I have never once seen the 'Why would I do something that stupid?' defense work. The obvious answer is, 'Because you *are* that stupid.' And do you know how often a murderer pretends to discover the body of his victim? 'Great Scott, officer, I just walked in and there he was, skull stove in with a crowbar. Burglar must have done it.' The same thing happens in contract killings, but then it's the employer, not the killer."

"Sure, but . . ."

"Hold on, I'm not done," Pershing says. "I think the timing was just chance. But the DPS sees it differently."

He explains. The DPS has Madero's and Huerta's phones. They know I texted Madero, who responded, *free before ten*, and Huerta, who responded, *free ten to noon*. In the interview, I said I told Theo those times at breakfast. They speculate that as we were finishing breakfast, Theo texted the assassin and told him to push the button on Madero, then on Huerta. We arrived at Madero's thirty minutes later, and Theo saw the job was done. I called 911 and every cop within miles descended on Madero's compound. While that brouhaha was going on, the assassin went to whack Huerta.

"You said in your interview Theo seemed calm and unshaken at Madero's, right?" Pershing says.

This pisses me off. "Yes, she was calm and unshaken, and so was I. Is this jackass astounded because a dame wasn't screaming and fainting at the sight of a corpse?"

I hear a hint of a chuckle on Pershing's end. "There's some of that. To me she seemed surprised, though not upset. People confuse the two. But she has an incontestable alibi at the time Madero was killed—eating breakfast with fifty people at the Flying Mulewhip, now that we know the timeline—and of course ditto at the time Huerta was killed. It's hard to have a better alibi than being in an interview room with cops. The detective finds this suspicious."

This pisses me off even more. If she has a good alibi, that means she hired the killer? That implies that if she didn't hire the killer, she wouldn't have a good alibi, which is an absurd premise nobody would accept. Is this Bizarro World? It's not even worth arguing.

"Okay," I say. "But what about the hobo trying to whack her at the Truck Stop?"

"He wasn't trying to whack her. He was coming for a final payoff. That's what the DPS thinks. And they think they have evidence of an earlier payoff. And evidence of Theo casing Madero's place."

"Wow."

"Woe? Woe indeed. By the way, the guy who interviewed you is not the guy assigned to the case. He was just in town investigating some lemon truck hijackings. The new guy is very sharp. He's the one who developed this theory of the case."

I need a minute to digest all this. I look at the ancient printer with its dangling serial cable and yellowed tractor feed paper lying limply on the top. Cleaning people have been dusting that thing for ten years, probably.

"You there?" Pershing says.

"Yes. The theory is superficially ingenious. Too bad it's wrong. Besides, they keep trying to pin it on T-Bone, but they can't, so they don't even know the killer's identity, right?"

"True. But that doesn't matter. In a conspiracy, and I quote from memory, 'A conspirator may be indicted and convicted despite the names of his co-conspirators remaining unknown, as long as the government presents evidence to establish an agreement between two or more persons.'"

This really is Bizarro World. "Oh, man," I say. "How could they prove an agreement? Who's the county attorney now? Campbell? This is hooey."

"I'd use a different word, but I agree," says Pershing. "And despite your grudge against his clan, I think Campbell agrees. The evidence is weak and ambiguous. He won't put his ass on the line by filing the complaint. He's stalled as long as he can, but now he says he'll take it to a grand jury and let them decide. That'll keep the assistant AG—who is in a lapidary club and is fixated on this case, by the way—off his back. If they don't indict, Campbell says, 'Sorry, the grand jury is not buying this.' And if they indict and the case blows up, as it likely would, he just says, 'Hey, the grand jury thought this baroque conspiracy theory made sense. I had my doubts, but I bowed to the will of sixteen citizens good and true. Vote Campbell, man of the people.'"

"Never trust a Campbell," I say, quoting Grandpa Cameron. "And what if the case doesn't blow up?"

"It wouldn't be the first wrongful conviction I've seen. They're rare, fortunately."

It's true wrongful convictions are rare, mainly because a prosecuting attorney doesn't want to lose. Normally, he won't bring a case to trial unless he thinks he has very strong evidence of guilt. For the Bayesians here, this means that if a prosecutor goes to trial, there's a high prior probability of guilt, maybe 90 percent, so if the jury is right only 90 percent of the time, a conviction will be right about 99 percent of the time. And no, I won't explain the math. Do it yourself or take it on faith. Of course, if the prosecuting attorney is stupid, a psycho, a political hack, or under pressure, as Campbell is here, the prior filtering fails, and you have a serious problem.

"So this doesn't bother you?" I say.

There's a Frankie-like silence for five seconds.

"Nick, the only perfect justice is God's justice. Man's justice is like a filthy rag, *quasi pannus menstruatæ*, as Isaiah says."

"Amen, Father Pershing. But the grand jury will indict. You know what they say about grand juries indicting ham sandwiches."

"Yes. But our Navajo friend says he'll have the case wrapped up in two weeks. I believe him, but you know how he is. He won't tell me what he's got, and he wouldn't talk to the DPS or the county attorney if you dangled him over a slot canyon full of starving javelinas."

"So what do you want me to do about this?" I say.

"Nothing you can do. Just giving you a heads-up."

"But if the Metaxas dame disappeared for a few weeks, it might save everybody some serious embarrassment for arresting and extraditing the wrong person?"

"Nick, I'm ashamed of you for even thinking such a thing. I am telling you to avoid a hot potato. You must tell her nothing. Take no action that might make you an accessory after the fact, if the charges turned out to be true."

22

ON THE LAM
AT DAMP LAKE

Of course, Sheriff Pershing means exactly the opposite of what he said. So where can I hide Theo and her brother? I know a couple of lapidaries here, but I wouldn't trust either to keep his mouth shut. Besides, everybody here knows the Metaxas twins, so I need to get them out of town.

I set out for Bayfield noodling on this. And it comes to me. Trixie. She's likely involved in dicey stuff like everybody else up here and won't sing to the cops. I bet she knows a hideout somewhere.

Theo's Subaru is at the marina, but her boat is gone. Trixie's boat is there. And there's Trixie, messing around with lures in the cockpit. She's tickled to see me and gives me a big hug.

I tell her I have some friends who need to get away for a spell, to a nice, quiet, isolated place where nobody will bug them. She can tell there's something fishy about this—she flutter-blinks one eye while pretending to rub it with her index finger—but it doesn't seem to bother her.

"I have a cabin on Damp Lake," she says.

"Where's that?"

"About thirty miles south, on the Beaucoup de Lacs chain. It's not fancy, but it's out of the way. Nobody around. Good fishing, though."

"What do you mean by 'not fancy?'" I say. I have a bad feeling about what that might mean up here. "No running water, no electricity, what?"

"It has all that, but it's just old and not very big. It's twenty-four by twenty-four, all one room except for a little bedroom." She smiles at me when she says "bedroom."

"Will it sleep two people, in different beds?"

"Sure. It has a hide-a-bed and then the full-size bed in the bedroom." (Grins again.)

"Okay, good enough. Could I rent it for three weeks?"

Well of course I can, she says, and for me, special deal, $350 a week. We go into the salon and she draws a map of how to get there, "because to this place, navigation is useless." She says there's a key under the third rock to the left of the front door and another under the chopping block in the back. There's a small, stacked washer/dryer in the kitchen area. It kinda works. The refrigerator is turned up; you need to turn it down. The water heater is turned down; you need to turn it up. It makes strange bubbling noises, but it won't explode. The stove igniters don't work. You need to use a match; they're in the knife drawer. The window AC unit works as a fan, but not for AC. Don't need AC anyway. You may need to kick the space heater. Do not, repeat, do not, use the woodstove. No squirrels in the cabin as of two weeks ago. No cell signal there. And no telephone in the house. There's an old ATV if you need to get to the nearest store, which is a gas station five miles away. Propane tank is full. The water tastes like iron, and that's where the sink and toilet stains come from.

It sounds like a perfect hideout. I bet there are a gazillion cabins like that up here, full of snarling dogs and surly survivalists, so nobody will search for the one that has the twins in it. Theo may find the accommodations a bit rough, but when you're on the lam from a murder conspiracy indictment, you can't be choosy. And many young dames are a tad anemic, so iron in the water may do her good.

"You aren't going with them, are you?" Trixie says.

"Oh, hell no. I've done my share of fieldwork. I like a soft bed and good food. Speaking of food, how about lunch?"

She accepts. I'm liking this beetle. Not sure what her game is. But she's pretty and smart, enterprising, and fun to be around, so who cares.

I can't drive the twins to the cabin in my 911. Aside from having a rear seat suitable only for small children and elves, a red 911 will be noticed and remembered for years around Damp Lake. And I can't use Theo's car or her brother's car because somebody might recognize the bumper stickers, a camera might capture the license plate, and so on.

Over lunch, I ask Trixie if she has a four-seater car I can borrow. Preferably a junky one. She doesn't—she drives a Mercedes SL, of all things—but her brother is a crane operator working a gig down in Louisiana and he left his PT Cruiser up here. She makes a point of mentioning that her brother drove his Charger to Louisiana and the PT Cruiser is just his hunting and fishing clunker. He won it in a poker game. It's in the garage at his house, key on the workbench. She gives me the garage code.

A PT Cruiser is the ideal car for this. People look away when they see one, and nobody will confess to having seen one if they fail to avert their eyes. It's the perfect stealth vehicle.

After lunch, we return to the marina. I amuse myself by looking at boats for sale. A dozen are on the hard by the end of the docks and close to a fish cleaning station, which smells really bad and is surrounded by a cloud of ravenous flies.

It's nearly 16:00 when Theo's boat puts in. She and a couple of girlfriends had gone fishing. They take the fish to the cleaning station but don't notice me. She'll take her knives and whatnot back to the boat, so I position myself on that route.

I'm out of sight between a Catalina 27 and a Beneteau 31 when Theo passes.

"Hey, Theo," I whisper.

She flips around like a snagged salmon.

"Nick, what are you doing here?" she says.

"Shh. Come here."

She does.

"Okay, this is serious," I say. "The cops think you hired that hobo to kill Madero and Huerta."

Her jaw drops. First time I've seen that out of her.

"Why do they think that?" she says.

I tell her what Sheriff Pershing told me about the trust and radio museum.

"I didn't even know about that stuff with the radio museum," she says.

"Maybe not, but the cops think you did."

"But even if I did know about it, isn't that all just speculation?"

"If that's all they have, yes," I say. "But think. What did you do in Quartzrock? The day you showed me the agates."

"I had an early dinner at the Truck Stop Tavern."

"By yourself?"

She looks offended, like I'm suggesting she picked up a shagman or something.

"Yes, by myself," she says.

"And what then?"

"I drove around. Took a look at the town."

"Let me guess, you drove by Madero's place."

"I did, but I didn't know it was his place."

I look at her. She's getting the drift.

"And I stopped in front of it to look at the big antenna thing," she says.

Now it's starting to sink in.

"Okay. And after you drove around, then what?" I say.

"I went to that Flying Mulewhip place for a cup of coffee."

"Talk to anybody?"

"The hostess and the waitress."

"Anybody else?"

"When I left there was a homeless guy outside."

I nod.

"He asked if I could spare some money for food," she says. "I had seven dollars left in the envelope I got from the bank, so I gave it to him."

"What do you mean, the envelope you got from the bank?"

"I got some cash for the trip home at Wells Fargo. I put the hundreds and fifties in the zip pocket of my jeans and just left two twenties in the envelope in my purse. After the dinner at the Truck Stop and the coffee and pie at the Flying Mulewhip, the seven dollars was all that was left. Along with a few coins."

"You handed him the envelope? A Wells Fargo envelope with the red-and-gold logo?"

She nods. Now she's getting nervous.

"He was kind of short and dumpy," she says. "I don't think he was the hobo. I guess he might have been. But he tried to kill me at the Truck Stop, remember?"

"They think he came to get the final payoff for a job well done."

Her breathing is fast and shallow. I give her a hug.

"Don't worry," I say. "Frankie says he'll have this all tied up in two weeks. Meantime, you and your brother need to lie low. I've found a cabin on Damp Lake. Nobody will find you there."

"Good fishing there." She sniffs.

I'm glad I can give Theo a safe house for a few weeks. But it's damn inconvenient for me. She was ready to "take the relation-ship to the next level," as dames so charmingly say, and so was I. Now I need to wait weeks for that. I can't hang in the cabin with her because Frankie will be giving me orders at any minute. And besides, her brother will be there, and having a brother present is one of the strongest known anaphrodisiacs.

It's dark when I arrive at a woodlot on a washboard gravel road to pick up Theo and her brother, who looks like a taller and fairer version of old Miles Metaxas. It's a few miles from her house on the outskirts of Ashland. They've got a ton of stuff—clothing, fishing gear, and most of the pantry, including a twenty-pound bag of potatoes. I brought nitrile gloves, shoe protectors, a plas-tic sheet to cover the rear floor and seat, and garbage bags to put their stuff in. They can burn it all in the firepit at the cabin. Fibers? This huntin' and fishin' car is so filthy you could get a fiber match to any mammal in Wisconsin. Ah-ha! You think those fibers could tie them to the car. You're wrong. You could get a fiber match to any mammal in Wisconsin in Trixie's cabin too. And half the cars in Ashland.

But it doesn't matter. The first thing they say when I pick them up is, "This is Mel's car!" They went ice fishing with him a few months ago. Theo finds one of her lures on the floor. Every-body in this town knows everybody else, I guess.

I head east a mile, then have them turn off their phones and put them in Faraday bags designed for cell phones. My friend in Albuquerque makes them. They're tested and highly effective. Then we head south toward Damp Lake. I left my phone in the hotel, of course.

It was easy getting the PT Cruiser out of the garage. I always consider what can go wrong, like Trixie giving me the wrong keypad code, a dead battery in the keypad, a dead battery in the car, deflated tires, a nosy neighbor, and so on. But Trixie assured me all would go well, and she was right. Leaving my car at the hotel and walking a long, circuitous route to the house, I wore my low-life casing outfit, a fake chin, and a fake mustache. Partly because I don't want to be ID'd, but mainly because I don't want to be seen driving a PT Cruiser. A neighbor saw me but waved and turned away, apparently thinking I was one of Mel's buddies. Good old Mel had the foresight to hook the car to a trickle charger before he left for Louisiana, so the battery was topped up.

Trixie's map is great, and we hit the cabin around 23:00. If you're thinking it's odd to pull up to the cabin at 23:00, you don't know Northern Wisconsin. In June, you can read a book outdoors until 22:00, at least, and astronomical twilight ends soon before midnight. If anything, 23:00 is early. Most people are out whooping it up at bars and supper clubs and usually don't get back to their cabins until 01:00.

Theo is obviously a bit disappointed by the cabin. I told her it was "rustic," which is a Realtor code word for "shithole." I guess she doesn't know the code. But she understands her predicament and can't complain. She pretends not to notice the pile of romance novels in the bedroom, but I can tell she's drooling over them. That doesn't mean she's stupid. I knew a med student who devoured them. But they have an effect. She looks at the novels, then at the bed, and then at me, and we have another passionate kiss while her brother is fiddling with the water heater.

There's a TV and a large collection of VHS tapes. I haven't seen those since I was a kid. Mainly rom-coms, thrillers, and some soft porn. Astoundingly, one is *Cambridge Coxswains: The Movie.*

23

GRAB YOUR PENCILS, MEN, WE'RE GOING ON AN AUDIT

'm in Ashland. Frankie must be up to something because I haven't heard from him for two days. In the meantime, I've been hanging out with Trixie. She's a great friend and I like her a lot, but it's no more than that. Of course her bawdy hints aren't lost on me, but something always gets in the way.

I've been thinking about Theo, though. Maybe it's time for me to settle down. What would be wrong with little Mycenaeans chiseling Linear B on the nursery walls? But then I think about Chanda. What would be wrong with little Brahmins scrawling Devanagari on the nursery walls? Or Jing, little Mandarins inking logograms on the nursery walls? Or Trixie, little Vikings carving runes on the nursery walls?

Nothing. Four smart dames, each hotter than the nickel irruptive gushing into the Sudbury crater after the asteroid hit. In choices like this, it just boils down to which dame is your type. I think Theo is my type. Why? Because she's not the other types. Maybe one of them is your type, and that's fine. *De gustibus non est disputandum*, as Sheriff Pershing says.

Trixie wants to watch a Brewers game, and I suggest the dive bar where I waited for Rodolfo. I like baseball. I played in college and still have my first baseman's mitt. The girlfriend who gave me the mustache spoon autographed it for luck.

The game starts at 13:10 Milwaukee time, which is also our time, so I head over there at about 12:30 and wait for Trixie. It's Tuesday, and it's a small crowd. Some people in Ashland actually work for a living. One of the three TVs has the Brewers pregame, and the others have drag racing and a lumberjack competition. I take a booth. The bar tables are closer to the screens, but the booth is quieter and more comfortable. The bar is farthest of all from the screens, but it looks like most people there are more interested in the "bar" thing than the "sports" thing. I see the bar has a Jägermeister dispenser. This looks like a miniature refrigerator with three inverted Jägermeister bottles plugged into the top and "Ice Cold Shots" lettered on the sides.

Trixie arrives at 13:00 in a T-shirt and cutoffs, wearing a Brewers cap with her blonde ponytail sticking out the back. She turns lots of heads. The Brewers are playing at home and the Cubs go three up, three down in the top of the first. Trixie jumps up and down with joy.

Some guy walks in, goes to the bar, and talks with one of the barflies, who motions to other barflies, and then five guys get up and walk out the door. Then another guy walks in, stops, shouts, "Hey, Rick!" and motions *c'mon*. Rick (whoever he is) and two dames leave a bar table and exit.

Now the dive is emptying fast. I throw a double sawbuck on the table to cover our beers. "Let's see what's shakin'," I say.

What's shakin' is two white vans and three state police cars parked outside the office building across the street. A cop in a yellow vest keeps traffic moving. Other cops guard the building entrance and the vehicles. Some have shotguns.

We walk to the crowd, and I ask a guy in a sports coat and tie what's going on. "I don't know, but it must be a big deal because the guys who came out of the van had FBI vests," he says.

"Any ideas?" I ask Trixie. She seems to know everyone in town, but she's stumped on this one.

"Look, they're bringing someone out," she says.

It's Old Sourpuss, Scrool's secretary. They've cuffed the grizzled old carp. I know that's common, but it seems ungentlemanly.

"It's Ona Gleet," Trixie says. "My mom knows her. They're in Altar Guild."

"What church?" I ask. Pointless question, of course, but Trixie answers, "St. Olaf Lutheran. Scrool is a member too." Figures. Ona and Scrool probably thought they were worshipping Lex Luthor.

We wait ten minutes. I expect to see Scrool being carried out kicking and screaming. That doesn't happen, but the evidence stevedores start carrying out white boxes and stashing them in a van. Search all day on a drink o' rum. Stack evidence boxes 'til the evening come. Some poor bastards will root through that crap. Junior attorneys banging their heads on their desks wondering why they went to law school.

But I think Scrool gave them the slip. "This is boring," I say. "Let's go watch the game."

It looks like our fellow barflies agree. And not only them. Many concerned citizens have noticed there's a watering hole across the street, and soon the bar fills up.

Now I see why Rodolfo told me to stick with my rocks instead of running to the DA. A bust like this was already in the works, and Rodolfo knew that. Tax fraud, wire fraud, money laundering, who knows. And there'll be a ton of other charges too, just for the hell of it. Everything is against federal law nowadays. Use too much weed killer and they can put you in the federal pen.

And I give a hundred to one they're raiding the Bilkson Consulting offices too. Not that I think Phil Farkey and Melanie Clusterratio knew anything nefarious was going on. John

Corsnaed, that's another matter. But he seemed dumb enough to think people were willingly paying for his worthless advice, so maybe he was in the dark too. If his defense attorney needs someone to testify he was a clueless dumbass, I'll volunteer.

The Brewers win. This drives Trixie into a sexual frenzy. She's three sheets to the wind. She paws me and demands we go to my hotel immediately.

We get to my room and Frankie calls.

"Whadda you want?" I say. We've got a bad connection. He must be out in the desert.

"You [inaudible] thing?"

"No. Speak up. Lots of wind noise."

"Anything happening up there?"

I start to brief him on the Scrool raid, but he says Rodolfo already told him about it. He says Rodolfo really does represent an Indian tribe, and the tribe is seriously interested in acquiring the Superior Agate Inn. I say it will make a great carpet joint. Then he gets to the point.

"I want you to meet Sordo at Topawa," he says. Sordo is a guy we both know who lives on a reservation along the Mexican border. Or very near the reservation, I'm not sure which.

"Hold on a second," I say, then check Google Maps. Topawa is a tiny settlement about seventy miles southwest of Tucson, and about two thousand miles by road from Ashland. "That's three days if I drive. I'll get there a lot sooner if I fly Duluth to Tucson."

Trixie is on all fours, crawling around the bed.

"Fly to Tucson. Rodolfo will meet you at the Duluth airport and take your 911. He'll have someone meet you at the Tucson airport. And he'll get your car to Tucson so it'll be there when you get back."

"Get back from where?"

"Mexico."

Trixie pounces.

24

NICK RIDES

*T*rixie passes out immediately after pouncing on the bed. Lust is strong, but alcohol is stronger. I lift her up and transfer her to the sofa. I take off her shoes, Nikes, turn down the bed, carry her back there, position her in the recovery position, as you should when someone is unconscious, and support the position with pillows so she won't roll over on her back. She looks like a Viking princess, or what a sleeping Viking princess would look like wearing cutoff jeans and a tight T-shirt. I pull the covers over her.

I write a note apologizing that I've been called away on urgent business. Believe me, it's a sincere apology. I hang out the Do Not Disturb sign and leave the room keys and a big tip for housekeeping. I tell the desk clerk I'll be leaving very early tomorrow morning and want to settle up now, and do.

On the way to the Duluth airport, I call Frankie to give him my ETA. When I arrive, Rodolfo is waiting, as Frankie said, at departures. He gives me an in-the-know grin, wishes me *buon viaggio*, and drives off in my 911.

After switching planes in Minneapolis, I spend my time on the Phoenix flight reviewing the baroque case of Madero, Huerta, Scrool, the Metaxas Trust, the radio museum, and the Metaxas twins. Here's the summary of what Frankie and I have worked out:

1. Madero and Huerta were trustees of the radio museum.
2. Scrool is trustee of the Metaxas Trust.
3. Theo and her brother are the sole beneficiaries of the Metaxas Trust. They are also the sole surviving descendants of Miles Metaxas, who created the trust.
4. The Metaxas Trust provides that any beneficiary who traffics in gemstones of any sort whatsoever is disqualified.
5. The radio museum trust provides that if a trustee dies and the death is not shown by clear and convincing evidence to be from natural causes, Miles's surviving issue—Theo and her brother, at this time—must appoint the replacement, which may be themselves.

So that's the setup. Then comes the conspiracy.

6. The radio museum contract with Bilkson Consulting began two years ago.
7. Cutbacks of Metaxas Trust distributions to Theo and her brother began two years ago.
8. Scrool controls Bilkson Consulting, regardless of who the legal owners are.
9. The radio museum contract with Bilkson Consulting was obviously a bribe to Scrool. Improving the museum was an unintended consequence, thanks to Farkey.
10. The contract bribed Scrool to cut back trust distributions to Theo and her brother. Scrool arranged this partly by reducing trust income through the scheme of charging low rents for trust properties while requiring large consulting payments to Bilkson.
11. The distributions cutback would pressure Theo and her brother to sell off the agate stash.

12. Trafficking in agates would disqualify them as trust beneficiaries.
13. Once both were disqualified, the Metaxas Trust would be dissolved, and the corpus of the trust would go to the radio museum.
14. Madero, Huerta, and Scrool would merrily plunder the hugely expanded museum endowment.
15. But Madero and Huerta got whacked, which squirreled the whole plan because now Theo and her brother can take over the museum by appointing themselves trustees.

And that's it. The neat thing about this conspiracy is that it doesn't need to succeed completely. If it failed at step eleven and the Metaxas twins didn't sell off the agate stash, Scrool would still be happily embezzling, the radio museum would have gotten its makeover, and Madero and Huerta would still be plundering it.

Frankie had me engage Bilkson Consulting for the mission statement to satisfy himself that Bilkson wasn't a serious consulting firm but just Scrool's tool. Hey, I like that. Scrool's tool. Next, he wanted me to make an offer on the Superior Agate Inn to verify how the scam worked and to confirm Scrool's corruption. But Frankie thought the hotel sounded like something Rodolfo would be interested in, and sure enough, he was. In fact, Rodolfo had his eye on the place because a friend told him Scrool was being investigated, and he figured once Scrool was out of the picture, a new trustee would be glad to make a deal on the joint. There's much more to it, but don't ask me about it, ask Rodolfo, or consult the Indian Gaming Regulatory Act of 1988.

I've gone through all this in my head two or three times and made an outline when an attractive dame on my right, maybe a decade my senior, introduces herself as Lou and says she's from Winnipeg. She asks me about Scottsdale restaurants, the Frank

Lloyd Wright store at Taliesin West, and other things she obviously doesn't care about. Then, with obvious relish, she raises the subject she really does care about. She says Steve Jobs had a Greek island populated entirely by Greek prostitutes, except of course for himself and his sinister visitors.

I have no evidence for or against the existence of Prostitute Island, so I can't express an informed opinion, but Lou isn't looking for my opinion. I try to avoid remembering anything she says, but I recall octopuses, Fibonacci numbers, and, of course, Bill Gates, who seems to show up in every conspiracy, kinda like Punch in a Punch and Judy show. Hillary Clinton would be Judy. Eventually, Lou starts hinting she knows a lot more than she's letting on and just might let me in on the arcanum arcanorum, but my nods and one-word answers seem to convince her I'm just a stupid sheeple who doesn't care, and she lets me get back to thinking about the radio museum.

Now, the DPS thinks Theo conspired with a John Doe assassin to murder Madero and Huerta, then gain control of the radio museum and—after dissolution of the Metaxas Trust—all the Metaxas fortune plus the museum endowment. *Nothing we know contradicts that theory.*

And it gets worse. Right now, the DPS doesn't know that Madero and Huerta bribed Scrool to cut the trust payouts, enticing Theo and her brother to sell off old Miles's agate stash. But the Feds will know that soon when they follow the data trail they got from raiding Scrool's office and Bilkson Consulting, and the DPS will find out, depend on it. And that just gives Theo another reason, specifically revenge, for wanting Madero and Huerta whacked, right? Right.

And not only that. Remember that Wells Fargo envelope Theo said she handed to a homeless guy outside the Flying Mulewhip? Frankie says security camera video shows with high confidence that the homeless guy was, yes, White Buns.

So Theo had the means, motive, and opportunity to hire an assassin, and there's an expanding pile of weak but oddly consistent and somewhat persuasive circumstantial evidence suggesting she did. And nothing to refute it. Nothing the DPS knows about, anyway. But they don't know that Madero, Huerta, the railroad bull, and White Buns are all linked by the insanely rich gold-bearing quartzite. The real motive has something to do with that, not with some dorky radio museum.

This means we can forget all about the radio museum. It's done. Outta here. Let the DPS swim after that red herring. We'll find the real answer to this murder mystery.

But there's a lesson here for all of us. Beware of trying to prove a theory by just looking for supporting evidence. That's cherry-picking and half-assed Bayesian nonsense. If you're serious, you need to test your theory by trying to refute it. Refutation can be decisive. To paraphrase Einstein, a theory can never be proved true, but it can be proved false.

At the Tucson airport, a well-dressed wise guy type, smaller than Rodolfo and lacking a pinkie ring, meets me at baggage claim and drives me to the Palazzi Mobili RV dealership. We pull into the garage, which is roughly the size of the nave of St. Peter's Basilica. He gives me the keys to a Toyota Camry that's also in the garage and says Frankie will tell me what to do with it when I'm done. I check the glove box and see the car is registered to the RV dealer, and the paperwork looks in order, including the insurance card.

I spend the night in an overpriced Tucson resort designed for northerners who want sunny winter vacations in the land of the conquistadors. In the morning, I hit the continental breakfast at 07:00. It's early June, but there are still a lot of pale northerners hanging out here. I'm fascinated by a hopper of Froot Loops on the breakfast bar, but I assume the hotel understands its clientele. It does. I spend an hour reading the news, during which time the Froot Loops hopper is tapped down to Froot Loop dust.

I have a little time to kill because Topawa is only an hour and a half southwest of Tucson, so I drive around downtown and stop at the bronze equestrian statue of Pancho Villa. It's the one must-see in Tucson. Whining rotters want it removed because Villa wasn't Mother Teresa, but the city tells them to bugger off.

Some people never give up, though. A very white guy in camouflage pants and a Miller Lite T-shirt hands me a screed against Pancho Villa. Cleverly, he has included Mexican criticisms of General Villa, including one from Alvaro Obregón, who would later become president of Mexico:

Mexicans, that monster of treason and crime called Pancho Villa rises up to devour the cause that has cost us so many lives. He is united in a trinity of hate with Maytorena and Angeles. The three are deformed creatures. . . . It is time for Mexico's good sons to know that the devotees of waste, revelry, and licentiousness are with Pancho Villa and that we, the devotees of sorrow and privation, are with Carranza.

Got it, Alvaro. Villa and his merry men want Burning Man; you and Carranza want a procession of flagellants.

And then a long tirade from Salvador Alvarado. I had to look him up. He was a noted Carrancista. Excerpt:

Pancho Villa's mind seethes with perverse thoughts. His evil conscience makes him an eternal robber, eternal traitor, eternal assassin. Mexicans, if Pancho Villa triumphs in this war, think of what that will mean for our native land. Brave men and patriots will die; women will be

dishonored; children will never know the light of goodness;
and all for the sake of Pancho Villa's orgies and robberies
and assassinations.

Which sounds like a *New York Times* editorial about Donald Trump. Or a *New York Post* editorial about Joe Biden, take your pick. I'm not making this stuff up, by the way—a history prof at U of A told me these are good translations from a reliable source.

After paying my respects to Pancho, I get coffee and a snack and head out on Highway 86 to Topawa. I went to complete radio silence when I left Duluth. I'm absolutely sure my wise guy loaner car lacks OnStar or Safety Connect or anything like it, and I swept it for GPS trackers this morning, so nobody is tracking me. Obviously, people could find out I flew to Tucson and stayed overnight in the Froot Loops Inn, but nothing more.

This is saguaro country. Three years ago, on this road and at about the same time of year, I learned a little about harvesting saguaro fruit. I'd stopped to help a family who had a flat tire on their trailer. It was a small stake trailer, maybe twelve feet, with removable wooden sides. They didn't have a jack or a spare. A guy in a Jeep also stopped, and we lifted the starboard side enough so the father could get the wheel off. Then the Jeep guy and the father went to get the tire fixed. They left me as a guard.

The family was Tohono O'odham, and they were moving to a new house in Sells, which is the capital of the Tohono O'odham Nation. While the father and the Jeep guy were gone, the mother and a couple of the older kids decided to harvest some saguaro fruit. These fruits grow at the top of the branches, which can be twenty feet or more off the ground. First there's a ring of flowers that looks like a crown of daisies, then the flowers wilt and the fruits grow. I don't have a good analogy for what that looks like. The fruits are shaped kinda like shallots, so maybe a crown of shallots.

When the fruits start turning from green to scarlet, you harvest them. So how do you do that if they're twenty feet in the air? The Tohono O'odham have it all figured out. They make a long pole by lashing together saguaro ribs, which are the long, light sticks of the saguaro skeleton, and they tie a little crosspiece on the end to help with snagging and prying off the fruits.

There were no saguaro skeletons handy, but the trailer had a few mops and brooms. Also clothesline, which you rarely see nowadays. They tied enough mop and broom handles together to make a respectably long pole using a wooden ruler from one of the kids' schoolbags for a crosspiece, then started harvesting. The mother, who was surprisingly strong, was a real artist at it and would catch the fruits in a bucket as they fell. I tried it, and the fruits fell all over the place. It's a skill that must be learned. If the fruits are ripe, they taste like a mash of strawberry jam and kiwi fruit. You can eat them, dry them, make them into jam or wine, and so on. Saguaro brandy might be good, and I'm sure somebody has made it, but I've never tasted it.

An hour and a half later, the father and the Jeep guy returned, and we got the family on their way. My reward for helping was a bag of saguaro fruits, and they were excellent.

I won't say much about the geology on this drive because it's flat and mainly tertiary and quaternary surficial deposits of sand, clay, gravel, and so on. Boring stuff. They were mostly laid down when the climate here was cooler and wetter than it is now. I pass some low mountains of Cretaceous volcanics to the north of the highway, and then higher mountains of Jurassic granitoid stuff to the south. These are the Coyote and Quinlan Mountains, and to the south of them, the Baboquivari Mountains.

These mountains are Sky Islands—isolated mountain ranges that rise from the desert floor and are high enough to have a radically different climate. Pines and oaks instead of saguaro and creosote shrubs. Bears and mountain lions instead of snakes and scorpions. It's a different world. Most animals don't migrate north and south here. They migrate up and down, which is a better approach, in my opinion. If I were an animal, that's how I'd want to migrate. The Sky Islands have a few observatories for astronomers and a few peaks for technical climbers. Baboquivari Peak is where the Tohono O'odham say the creator lives. But south of there, few people go. There are other Sky Islands in the Madrean Archipelago, as we call it, mostly in Arizona and Northern Mexico, but some in New Mexico too.

At Sells, I head south on BIA 19 through some low rises of Jurassic rhyolite porphyry, then back onto quaternary surficial deposits. Don't pretend you care. It's all just rocks and dirt to you, and I'll say no more about it.

A mile north of Topawa, in one of those random, inexplicable turnoffs you find on these desert roads, I see Sordo standing next to his F-150. I pull over and get out.

"Nick!" Sordo shouts like he's on home plate and I'm deep in left field. This is how he greets people. Being an army retiree with some hearing loss may explain that. "How the hell are you? I haven't seen you since"—he gives me a big grin—"since you clued me and Frankie in on that special dirt. That's been, man, three years?"

We shake hands. Sordo is not a hugger. Neither is Frankie. I lean back on the fender of the F-150 and almost get a first-degree burn. He's been waiting here awhile for the truck to get that hot. It's only one hundred, but the Arizona sun is a scorcher at midday.

"Three years, almost to the day," I say. "Your girlfriend brought you a basket of saguaro fruit. Remember that? How is she?"

"She ran off and got married to some guy up north. Lives in Globe now."

"Sorry to hear that."

"It's for the best. She's twenty years younger than me anyway. I need someone closer to my own age. Say fifteen years younger."

That may sound rakish, but Sordo looks fifteen years younger than he is, so it kinda makes sense. It's physiological age that matters, in my book, for either a man or a woman.

"So what's the plan?" I say. "Frankie hasn't told me shit."

"We go to my place and rest, sleep if we can. We'll be traveling all night, and it's rough country. You need water?"

"I've got some."

"Then follow me," he says.

I follow Sordo for almost an hour on a road that gets worse and worse until it's a track, not a road—and if I weren't following Sordo, I wouldn't be sure it was a track.

Finally, we get to Sordo's spread. It looks just like it did three years ago. A single-wide trailer surrounded by a stable, a loafing shed where the horses loaf, a large steel machine shed, and a roofed pavilion with a dirt floor, maybe twenty-four by twenty-four feet, for parties. There's a flagpole by the pavilion, and it's flying Old Glory. A small shed covers a generator, but he doesn't use it much because he has solar panels. Another small shed covers a water storage tank and the wellhead of a very deep well. Sordo has a garden and gives the plants dappled shade in the summer with camouflage netting supported by a network of saguaro ribs. He's got it right, if the size of the tomato plants and melons is an indicator. The garden is fenced to keep the horses out, and the whole complex is fenced to keep the horses in.

Sordo gets out and opens the gate, and a big chocolate Lab runs up, paws his chest, and licks his face as he stoops to pet it. He points me to the machine shed. It's open, and I pull the Camry in there. He closes the gate and parks the F-150 in the shed behind me.

Before you form a mental picture of Sordo, I should just tell you about him. He's Black, or as Black as Frankie is Navajo, maybe half. He ended up here because an army buddy invited him to visit. He wanted to stay and got a part-time job coaching just about any sport played with a ball, except tennis.

Sordo doesn't shave but trims his beard closely. His hair and beard show only a little gray, so he looks a lot younger than his seventy-one years. At 178 pounds and six feet, he's a light heavyweight. That's close to my height, but I'm a cruiserweight or a heavyweight, depending on how much I've had for dinner. Sordo is lean, so the heat doesn't bother him much. It doesn't bother me either. It bothers Frankie because he has a hundred pounds on Sordo and is only three inches taller. Yeah, Frankie's overweight, but call him "fatty" and he'll rearrange your face. Call Sordo "scrawny" and he'll rearrange your face. Don't say you weren't warned.

Sordo amuses himself by roaming the desert on both sides of the border. Because it's remote, there's no border wall or fence here. Of course, there is some surveillance from the Integrated Fixed Towers and other contraptions, but Sordo is skilled at evasion, and I've advised him on how to really screw with seismic detectors. He occasionally runs into border patrol, but he shows them his retiree ID card and feigns a touch of senility, and they leave him alone. Nobody wants to look like an asshole by running in an old army guy and his horse. Sordo mines gold placers in the desert for fun and profit when it's cool, in the winter, which is how Frankie and I know him. "That special dirt" he mentioned was a real bonanza I found three years ago. An old alluvial deposit exposed by a recent landslip. He and Frankie made a lot of money on that one. It was on federal land, but I didn't see any injustice in having a Navajo and an old Black guy mining it on the sly.

So how do you slyly mine a desert placer with no water to run a sluice box or do panning? Good question. You use a dry washer, which looks and functions like a sluice box but works on air. It has a fan or bellows that blows air through a cloth membrane that covers the bottom of the box, under the riffles. The lighter sand and gravel get blown upward and migrate by gravity down and out the bottom of the box, while the heavier gold stays trapped against the riffles, exactly as in a water sluice box. Trick is that the gold-bearing sand and gravel need to be perfectly dry, but hey, in a desert, that's not a problem.

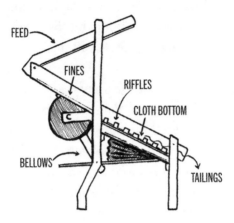

Despite the name, Sordo is not deaf. A little hard of hearing, but that's not unusual for someone who's seventy-one. Especially a veteran who served before people knew or cared about what small arms and an occasional blast can do to your hearing. The name comes from his ignoring what he thinks is idle chatter. Raise your voice a bit and speak only when you have something worth saying, and you'll get along fine with Sordo.

That is, if you're nice to his horses and dogs.

Speaking of dogs, I get pawed and sniffed by the two chocolate Labs, Dog One and Dog Two, on our way to the trailer. Which is very clean. Not tidy, clean. There's a difference. Sordo has stuff lying on every flat surface, but the place is not dusty or dirty. He says to relax while he fixes lunch.

Before I left Ashland, Frankie sent me an encrypted email that I haven't read yet, and it's on my laptop. I decrypt it and read it.

Sorry to spring this on you without notice, but it's necessary. I can't make the trip myself because the heat might kill me. If it didn't kill me, I'd end up dragged on a travois behind one of Sordo's horses, prostrate with heatstroke. Yes, I know I need to lose some weight.

Frankie's right. He can bench-press four hundred pounds, so he doesn't need resistance training, but he needs to drop some weight and start jogging or at least walking.

Sordo will take you to see the woman who owns the Emilio Rayón mine. She knows all that has happened there in the last century. We need to know how the ore ended up in track ballast in Arizona. It is important because without knowing that, I can't tell who the bad guys are here. Were Madero, Huerta, the railroad bull, and White Buns co-conspirators, and White Buns was just doing the usual thing of killing them off so he didn't need to share the loot? Killing them to conceal evidence of the conspiracy? Reacting to an attempt to cut him out? Or was he reacting to some other, legitimate grievance? I believe that Madero and Huerta caused the death of a railroad engineer by removing track ballast and causing the Rabid Horse Gulch derailment. But was White Buns a party to that? I do not know.

It sounds like Frankie knows White Buns's identity and is now on the final phase, which is determining what, if anything, he should do about it.

This phase is all about Frankie's personal moral code. Years ago, he swore an oath to support and defend the Constitution of the United States against all enemies, foreign and domestic, and to bear true faith and allegiance to the same. Every Marine does that. But he never swore an oath to support and defend the Constitution and laws of the State of Arizona. He's only interested in crimes if they offend his personal sense of justice. If he thought

Madero and Huerta had dishonored White Buns's daughter, sister, or wife, he'd say they got what they deserved, case closed, not wasting time on this. Now, Sheriff Pershing has sworn to support and defend the Constitution and laws of the State of Arizona, so he'd hound White Buns, whether he wanted to or not. That is how things are. Frankie understands Pershing, and Pershing understands Frankie.

You will travel at night with two horses to carry your gear. Tomorrow morning you will stop for the day and rest. Tomorrow night you will continue and reach the Emilio Rayón mine by sunrise. You will meet an exceptionally intelligent and attractive woman, Sra. Doña Esmeralda Fierro. Call her Doña Cartucho. It is a byname she inherited from her great-grandmother. She owns the mine and its surroundings. Throw away all bad thoughts. She is old enough to be your mother, almost. Her youngest daughter may be there. She is not a child, but young enough to be your daughter, almost. Throw away all bad thoughts about her even farther. You must show everyone in the household the greatest respect. Sordo knows Doña Cartucho well. She will not talk to you if she thinks you unworthy. Sordo has vouched for you, but she follows her own counsel.

Trust Sordo. Success in this matter is essential.

I don't like the sound of this. It's not so much what Frankie said but his tone. He's always serious, but this goes beyond that. I think he's genuinely perplexed. Not about the solution to this mystery but about something else. An ethical dilemma, possibly.

Lunch is corned beef hash and a very good garden salad. Then we sleep. That's not hard because I had only five hours last night. Sordo wakes me at 19:00 and tells me to gear up.

Nine hours later we're in rough terrain, crossing the spur of a desert mountain in chill starlight an hour before sunrise. I'm leading One Bit, a Thoroughbred/Quarter Horse cross. Big for the breeds, about sixteen hands. We're following Sordo, who's leading a purebred Quarter Horse. Consistently, he's named Two Bits. The slope is barren except for occasional cactus and creosote, but the horses have trouble with the loose rocks. They're saddled, but they're here to carry our gear, not to carry us. Except in an emergency.

For the first two hours of the trip, we had crescent moonlight, but the moon set around 22:00, and since then, we've been navigating without it. Which is not that hard in the desert. There are no artificial lights to blind you and no clouds, smog, haze, buildings, or trees to block the starlight.

And because of the clear sky, sunrise in the desert happens fast. The sun just explodes over the horizon. It's hard to explain if you haven't seen it. It's like what sometimes happens at sea, when the instant of sunrise is marked by a green flash.

Sordo stops and looks east. A yellow glow has been spreading low in the eastern sky. It gets exponentially brighter. I blink because my eyes are dry—it's a desert, folks—and the sun flashes red through my eyelids. Sunrise. Sordo stands there, motionless, looking at the sun until its lower limb clears the horizon. That happens faster than you might think. It's his ritual, and I participate.

We descend into a dry wash between mountain spurs. Here there is lots of vegetation. Dense brush and palo verde trees surround an open, sandy creek bed. It's easy on the horses, but we're leaving tracks a Cub Scout could follow. I mention this to Sordo, and he makes a gesture. Of course, he's right. We're leaving tracks, but we're out of sight, which is a lot more important.

The wash goes on for miles. When the climate here was wetter, landslides and erosion filled the bottom of the valley with soil and stones. Then the climate dried, and calcium carbonate cemented the soil and stones together to form a loose breccia. Over long ages, this seasonal stream made its own little canyon through that and hollowed out little caves and cavities in the walls that make comfortable dens for animals. Lots of coyote pups have been raised here, I bet. We had a real concert from them last night. They sound kind of like a tenor wolf, but with strange Lovecraftian yipping and shrieking thrown in, like the devil is pulling their mangy tails.

Two hours after sunrise, we come to a ledge that drops ten feet. When it rains, this would be a waterfall, and it has scoured out a depression at the bottom that's still full of clear water. A path to the left leads us downhill to the pool. The horses drink. Sordo fills their water bags.

"We in Mexico?" I ask.

Sordo snorts. "We were in Mexico before sunrise," he says.

Mexico, US, it's all just land. It was here before we came, and it will be here when we're gone. And the coyotes and the rabbits and the javelina won't remember we were ever here. Spend some time in the desert and you will think about deep time a lot.

Speaking of time, it's time I told you people something.

Don't do what Sordo and I are doing. It's illegal and it's dangerous. You'll be bitten by rattlesnakes. Scorpions will hide in your boots and sting your piggies in the morning. Cactus spines will pierce your eyeballs. If you're a guy, a Gila monster will gnaw off your schwanz while you sleep. You'll get sunstroke in the day and freeze blue at night. You won't find water because you're an idiot and don't know where to look. You'll end up crawling in the dirt with your blackened tongue lolling out, croaking, "Water! Water!" You'll probably die, and the vultures and javelinas and coyotes will pick your carcass clean. If you survive, which is unlikely, you'll be rescued by people who will think you're a complete fool and charge you for their effort. Then you'll write an article for *Outside* magazine, and they'll reject it because they don't publish articles by feckless twits.

And that's if you don't run into the criminals and drug smugglers. Or end up in a Mexican prison on weapons charges.

Got it?

We continue down the wash a few miles until it deltas out onto the plain. The palo verde trees have thinned out, and now it's just cactus, mesquite, and creosote shrubs. Sordo raises his left hand, and we stop. He points. A few hundred yards ahead, somebody is assaulting a barrel cactus. I pull out my binoculars for a better look.

"Some guy is stabbing a barrel cactus. No. No, he's trying to cut off the top," I say.

Sordo shakes his head. "He thinks there's water in there."

I keep watching the guy. He's learning that a barrel cactus is a lot tougher than it looks. Finally, he gets the top off. He looks inside, then kicks it.

We laugh. We both know there's nothing in there but firm green pulp. It tastes like a raw potato, more or less. With a lot of work, you can mash it and get a cup or two of juice.

Sordo waves forward ho, and we continue toward the cactus slayer. He's cut up some of the pulp and is chewing on it. When we're about fifty yards away, he sees us. He points his knife threateningly. Sordo grins. "Need some agua, amigo?" he says.

The cactus slayer throws down his knife. A wise move. He looks like a displaced hotel clerk. He's got a rat face, a feeble attempt at a mustache, skinny arms, a white short-sleeved, button-up shirt, and black chino pants. The only thing about him that makes sense out here is the hiking boots.

Sordo throws him a canteen, which he drains in a few gulps.

It's time for breakfast, and Sordo has said we won't cross the plain to the next range until evening. Partly the heat, partly not wanting to be seen. He leads to a rock outcrop, technically part of a horst, which is an uplift bounded by normal faults, if you care. It's about the size of a small house, faces north, and has an overhang that will give us good shade. And concealment to ensure we aren't visible from the plain or the air.

Neither of us has said anything to the hotel clerk, who follows us like a lost puppy. He has an archaic canvas backpack full of something. Not water, we know that. And not drugs. No narco would use this guy as a mule.

"So, what are you doing out here?" Sordo says.

Running away. The kid—I say kid, but he could be anywhere from twenty to thirty—was a cook in an upscale restaurant in Magdalena de Kino. He got friendly with one of the waitresses. He didn't get any, but that didn't keep a rival from thinking he had and then trying to kill him. So he bugged out. He's a little vague on how he ended up here, but it sounds like he was hitchhiking and pissed off his host, who kicked him out of the car on an unimproved road about ten miles south.

I'm unsaddling the horses while Sordo is prying this story out of the kid, who speaks English fairly well, but with a heavy accent. Sordo speaks fluent Spanish, but he knows mine is not so good. He's making the kid talk English so I can understand.

"You want breakfast?" Sordo says.

The kid nods.

"Then you cook it."

Now we see what's in his backpack. Cooking utensils, including an aluminum tortilla press. Tools of the trade. Not much food aside from a bag of masa harina and some bottled sauces I've never heard of. The kid starts to gather brush for a fire, but Sordo tells him to use our little mountain stove instead. I already unpacked it, along with the cookware and the food—powdered eggs, beans, and bacon. If I were running this expedition, I'd have screwed the cooking and brought pemmican. Best MRE ever invented: dried shredded meat and anhydrous fat in equal measures. It tastes like a fatty hamburger.

The kid walks off for ten minutes and comes back with some prickly pear pads. He fries some bacon and then cooks fry bread in the grease. He makes a big omelet with powdered eggs and diced prickly pear. The stove is a single burner, but the kid juggles the pans to keep the fry bread and the omelet cooking at the same time. And flips the omelet with a toss of the pan. He finishes and dishes the food onto our plates.

"Órale," Sordo mumbles, nodding approval.

"Good job, kid," I say. This establishes that the kid probably is a cook, though the rest of his story may be bushwa.

Sordo gives him a water bag and tells him to fill it at a tank a quarter mile away, up among some rocks. By "tank" I mean a large, deep crevice or depression where rainwater collects and remains, sometimes for months. There's a petroglyph behind me on the outcrop—a stick man pointing toward the tank, with wavy lines for water. It was probably drawn a thousand years ago, and the tank is still there.

"We can't just leave him here," I say when the kid's gone.

"No," says Sordo.

The kid returns with the water bag full, and Sordo puts him to work running it through the water filter into the clean water bag. This supposedly filters out just about everything, including viruses. But Sordo still adds a chlorine tablet to his canteen, and so do I.

Sordo and I play spades for an hour. He says he'll take the first watch, and I sack out for a long nap. I tell the kid to use the saddle blankets if he wants something to lie on. His name is Ricardo, by the way, but he goes by Rica.

25

LET'S YOU
AND HIM FIGHT

Around sunset, Rica makes us dinner. He put some black beans to soak after breakfast. There's an art to cooking beans, served pure and simple in their own thick gravy, and he's mastered it.

After dinner, Sordo asks the kid to repeat his story, which he does without any inconsistencies, but adding convincing details. Yolanda the waitress was an incorrigible tease, and Rica took her seriously. Unfortunately, so did Juan, the host and bouncer. Neither enjoyed her favors, but Juan suspected that Rica had, so he came at him with a knife. Stupidly, he did that in the kitchen, which is a gallery of knives, and Rica sliced his forearm with a chef's knife. This put Juan out of action, clutching a bloody towel to his arm and swearing revenge as he ran to the médico. The other cook asked Rica what it was about. When Rica told him, he smirked—because Yolanda was having an affair with the restaurant owner, and everybody in town knew it. Except Rica and Juan.

Rica says he might have stayed, but the médico reported the injury to the police, and Juan, not wanting to admit being bested by a cook, told the police Rica took him by surprise. The police liked Juan, and Rica didn't think he could rely on the other cook to support his story. So he fled.

Sordo looks at Rica with new respect, says he did the right thing defending himself, and he's a damn good cook who won't have any trouble finding work. And that he's well rid of Yolanda and Juan and Magdalena de Kino, which is a shithole. Rica knows this is true, but you can tell he's still hot on Yolanda anyway.

I climb up on the outcrop and scan the plain with my binoculars. I don't see anyone. We load up the horses and set out. I put Rica's pack on One Bit. He won't notice the difference. Rica asks Sordo where we're going. Sordo points at some distant mountains and says, "Over that range."

The plain is easy going—flat, mainly sand and gravel. A clear path, very old judging from how deeply it's beaten down, runs between the sparse shrubs and cactuses. Sordo follows it. The guy who did the petroglyph likely followed it too. I watch right, Sordo watches left, and Rica watches our rear.

It's past sunset, and we're into astronomical twilight with a crescent moon that will set in three hours. But like I said before, it's easy to navigate the desert at night, even in just starlight, and my night vision is very good.

We pass a four-wheel-drive-only road that would tear the bottom out of my 911, and I notice something white behind a big rock on the right. I tell Sordo. He stops, looks, comes back with a white canvas bag over his shoulder, and slings it over Two Bits. As we continue, he pulls bricks—kilogram cocaine packages—out of the canvas bag and heaves them into the desert to the left and right. The bag was probably ditched by smugglers for later retrieval when a patrol or other narcos approached.

Rica has been tagging along behind me. He jogs up and grabs my arm.

"Someone is following us. Hear?"

I stop and so does Sordo. It sounds like there's a car or truck on the path, probably a half mile away. The kid has good ears. Sordo can't hear it, and I can barely hear it, but I tell him that Rica's right. Sordo draws his rifle from the scabbard. It's a bolt action in 6.5 mm Creedmoor caliber, and he can hit a playing card at three hundred yards with it. Reliably. Anybody can hit a playing card at three hundred yards if he fires a thousand times.

Sordo looks at me. "Your piece loaded?"

"Yes."

"How many rounds?"

"Eight in the magazine, one in the pipe, and I've got two spare magazines." It's a Colt 1903 semi-automatic pistol in .32 ACP caliber that Sordo loaned me. It's a fine pistol, but underpowered. Sordo isn't a pistol guy and doesn't care. I care, but I left my Commander in the pistol safe I had installed in the 911's trunk.

"Okay. You and Rica take the horses over there," Sordo says, pointing down the trail about forty-five degrees left. "At least a hundred meters. Rica, you stay with the horses. Hold the reins—they won't bolt. Nick, come back and stay out of sight there," he says, pointing to a large creosote bush. "If things go south, give them some overhead fire. They'll cover, and I'll run back—over there, behind that bush. Confuse them with two targets. They'll see your muzzle flash, so move right or left after you shoot."

"What then?" I say. He didn't need to remind me about the muzzle flash, but he's used to commanding people.

"That's up to them. If they want a gunfight, we have to return fire. We can't run. They'll just follow us. There's nothing to stop their vehicle in this desert. Rica, you know how to lead a horse?"

"Yes."

"Take Two Bits. Go, go, go."

Rica and I hustle off between cactus and bushes at the angle Sordo told us to. We go what I judge to be the length of a football field. I leave Rica and run back, taking up my position behind the bush. I can see why Sordo wanted the horses where he did. They're not in the line of fire to our bushes. Yes, he knows what he's doing. He has enough ribbons on his uniform to decorate a Christmas tree.

The vehicle is a Jeep Wrangler, making a racket scraping against the bushes on either side of the trail. It'll need a paint job after this adventure. Of course, its lights are off. It stops about three car lengths from Sordo, who is standing in the middle of the trail with his rifle at port arms.

The driver yells at Sordo in Spanish. "What did you do with our talco?" Or something like that. Sordo says he didn't know it was theirs, thought it was his delivery. "Better give it back, old man," says the driver. Sordo says it's in camp, he'll go get it. He takes off toward the horses.

There are three guys in the Jeep. They argue over what to do if the old man doesn't come back, and what to do with him if he does come back. The driver asks the guy in the back what he thinks. He says *cuidado*, the tracks by the big rock showed three men and two horses. The old man leads one horse, a heavier guy follows him leading another horse, and a guy lighter than the old man tags along behind. All three have about the same stride and are about 180 to 190 centimeters tall. The light guy has new boots; the others have good but worn boots and may be hunters or prospectors. The men do not bear packs. The two horses are about the same size and newly shod. The horses have light packs, so the men have limited supplies and their destination is no more than a day away.

Wow. This guy's some tracker. I'd like to meet him.

The driver disagrees with the tracker for no good reason. He says Sordo is alone and they should shoot him. At least that's what it sounds like, but now they're arguing over each other, and like I said, my Spanish is a little weak.

If I move to intercept Sordo, they'll hear me. I could try the silent toes and fingers crawl, but there's not enough cover to conceal me anyway. The best I can do is fire if I see anyone getting ready to shoot.

I see Sordo jogging back. From a distance, he heaves the white bag onto the trail in front of the Jeep, then retreats to his bush. "Take it!" he shouts.

The guy riding shotgun gets out of the car and grabs the bag. They make a three-point turn, scraping off more paint and coming uncomfortably close to my bush, then race away. On this trail, racing away means about fifteen miles per hour. For about three minutes. Then I hear them turning around and coming back. I shout to Sordo.

Now Sordo is gravel-belly on the trail taking careful aim. He waits. The Jeep is closing fast. What is he waiting for? I'm drawing breath to shout, "Let's get outta here!" when Sordo fires. The Jeep stops, instantly. I hear the *chuga-chuga-chuga* of the starter, but it's no good. Sordo must have hit something important.

Sordo runs by me and I follow. We join Rica and start running with the horses. One Bit wants to canter, so I tell Sordo to slow down a little, and One Bit stays at a trot.

I expect Sordo to stop for a rest, but no, a quarter mile, a half mile, a mile, and he's still cranking. He should be in the Senior Olympics. Finally, he stops. He's breathing heavily, but no more than I am, the old coot. Rica looks at him in wonder.

I'm a little pissed off at Sordo for getting us into this. I know he wishes all drug dealers were dead. Or hard drug dealers, to be more precise. Fine with me if he wants to whack them, but I wish he wouldn't do it when I'm around.

Then I realize he held off *because* Rica and I are around.

Sordo looks back and has me look back with my binoculars. Nobody is following us.

I tell Sordo about the tracker. He says if the tracker is that smart, he isn't dumb enough to track an expert marksman at night. And that he's probably so pissed off at the driver he won't track us even if the driver asks, and the driver is such a jerk he won't ask anyway. Sordo also says we'll travel over terrain that will make tracking almost impossible, and tomorrow a forecasted monsoon downpour will obliterate most of our tracks anyway.

Sordo chooses a circuitous route to the mountains, and we continue onward in the dark.

26

DOÑA CARTUCHO

Dawn finds us on the western slope of a mountain overlooking the Emilio Rayón mine. Or what's left of it. The mine entrance is an adit, a horizontal entrance dug into the side of the mountain, which is what most people think a mine entrance looks like. But it's unusual—most mine entrances are shafts, which are vertical, with a hoist house covering the shaft; adits are photogenic, which is why Hollywood likes them. Down a gentle slope, on level ground maybe two hundred yards from the mine entrance, is a large building of gray weathered wood. It leans a bit, and part of the tin roof has caved in. It was probably used for ore crushing and processing. Close by, a rusty boiler and a stationary steam engine sit naked on a concrete pad. The engine must have powered a generator. The shed that covered it absconded, along with the generator. I see a few poles that supported electrical wires. Some insulators are still there but no wires. Another building, obviously the smelter, has stone walls and a large stone smokestack. Its roof is gone. The remaining structure, probably the change house, offices, dormitory, or all three, is weather-beaten but mostly intact, aside from broken windows and missing doors. Between the buildings lie remains of ore carts and the little tracks they ran on. An intact cart stands near the mine entrance.

But we're not going to the mine. We're headed for what looks like an old mission, about a mile from the mine. It looks vaguely like the Alamo but with a small bell tower that rises about twenty feet above the flat roof on one end. The place is obviously maintained and occupied, and from the tracks in front, it's clear that motor vehicles visit it. There appears to be a walled yard behind the building, but it's hard to see from this angle. Clearly, it's off the grid.

We're about a quarter mile away, on a gentle slope, when Sordo yanks his rifle from the scabbard and fires a round into the ground. That thing is loud. It makes my Commander sound like a party popper.

After a few minutes, we hear a shot fired from the mission, and Sordo waves us on. He tells Rica we're going to meet Doña Cartucho, a rich widow who deserves his highest respect. Sordo gives Rica the same advice Frankie gave me in that email, but in stronger and, as a diplomat might say, minatory terms.

As we get closer, I can see the mission is really a large house. It's adobe, not stone, and only one story. The entrance is a massive double doorway, and the wall above it is carried up to form a bell-shaped false front. There's an architectural term for that, but I forget what it is. Platykurtic is what I'd call it. The false front rises to the height of a second story at its apex. That's what makes it look like the Alamo. Despite being at least thirty yards wide, the front wall has only four windows, and they're barred.

We hitch the horses to a rail, and judging from the tracks, we aren't the only ones who have done so recently. Sordo knocks using the iron knocker. Given the size and mass of the doors, a knocker is probably necessary if you want anyone to hear you.

A barred Judas window in the right door opens. An old man looks out, sees Sordo, and slams it shut. Sordo says it's Bruno, the porter and butler. After a clanking and scraping of bolts being thrown and bars being lifted, the right door opens.

Sordo shakes hands with Bruno, who gives us a hint of a bow. In truth, he's a bit stooped over, so it's hard to tell whether it's a bow or not. We enter a wide central hallway. There's a long table in the middle, and chairs and bookcases line the walls—all heavy, dark wood—and the walls are paneled in the same. A crucifix stands near the head of the table. I don't get a good look at the books, but many are leather-bound and obviously quite old. It smells like an antique store in here. Terra-cotta tiles cover the floor. A chandelier provides electric light, so they have power, presumably solar.

Bruno leads us straight ahead, down the hall, through a less massive set of double doors, and into a courtyard. Now I see the house is U-shaped, with the base and the wings of equal length, each side about thirty yards in length. The U encloses a formal garden, maybe ten yards wide, covered by a pergola. High stone walls extend back from the wings to enclose a long, graveled yard containing a casita, a few sheds, and a large stable at the far end. A solid gate in the wall on the left is barred with two heavy timbers.

We walk through the garden to the casita. Bruno says that Juan (whoever he is) will attend to the horses.

"Different Juan," says Sordo, giving Rica a sly grin.

We're tired after traveling all night. There's no conversation. Sordo opens the door to the baño to show us where it is. I collapse into a single bed in a six-by-eight-foot bedroom that could be a monk's cell. Sordo and Rica do the same in other cells. As I'm drifting off, I hear someone setting food on the dining table. It smells like chicken. But I'm too tired to eat.

I wake around noon. I'm still tired, but I go to the baño and then get a drink of water from a pitcher on the dining table. There's a chafing dish with roast chicken. It's cold, but I eat a drumstick and a thigh.

Then back to my cell. I glance out the window and see Sordo talking with a woman in the garden. She's about his height and wears a sky-blue sleeveless sundress that shows her muscular arms to advantage. She looks more Spanish than Mexican. Her hair is intricately braided and must be very long. It's black with traces of gray. I can't see her face, but her profile looks distinguished, perhaps beautiful. In her fifties, I'd guess. She must be Doña Cartucho. I see all that within two seconds and then look away because I'm not here to spy on people. If I'd known they were there, I wouldn't have looked out the window at all. Of course, if people need to be spied on, that's different.

In five minutes, I'm asleep again.

It's late afternoon when I finally wake up for real. A young man is devouring the chicken. He's wearing khaki pants and a red silk shirt that's too big for him. Then I realize it's Rica. Bruno must have found him some clean clothes. He has washed, shaved, and combed his hair, and you know, he's not a rat-faced scarecrow at all. He's lean, but Sordo said that's what he looked like when he was twenty, so he'll fill out.

"It's a little overdone, but still very good," he says. "Try some."

"I like it this way," I say. "The skin is crispy."

"You can get that without overcooking it," he says.

Before I clean up, I go to the stable. Somebody has washed and combed One Bit and Two Bits. I pet One Bit for a few minutes. I try to leave, but he gives me that "Why have you stopped petting me?" look, so I continue. "Enough," says Sordo from the stable door. "You need to shower. He's got an excuse for smelling like a horse, but you don't."

The casita's baño is surprisingly modern, with lots of hot water, and the shower feels great.

When we're all cleaned up and ready to go, Bruno escorts us back through the garden, down the hall, and into a large sitting room. This is in the left wing of the house, if you're outside facing the front entrance. The walls are paneled in the same gloomy dark wood as the central hallway. It's sparsely furnished, obviously by design. On a Mexican Cubist rug are two orange Barcelona chairs facing a black leather sofa. Four chrome cylinders, about six inches in diameter and two feet high, stand by each chair and the corners of the sofa.

Doña Cartucho, now wearing a plain black sheath dress, is standing by one of the chairs. She's definitely a dish and just old enough to be my mother. But there's a look in her eyes that would frighten most people. It's that undefinable look of a fighting man. I've seen that look in women only a few times, and you don't want to know what the other ones were like.

Then I notice a bracelet on her right arm. It's silver, an exquisitely delicate Art Nouveau design, one of a series Frankie made twenty years ago, when he was developing his own style. He showed me photos. I don't mention it—that would be vulgar—but she smiles at me knowingly and gives a hint of a nod, as if I've passed some sort of test. Which I have. She can tell I take her excellent taste in furnishings, clothing, and jewelry for granted, and that's a compliment words cannot deliver. She can also tell I won't mention the bracelet is Frankie's work and have thrown away any "bad thoughts" of what it means between them.

Sordo introduces us. Rica bows. I nod. This is respect for her years and sex, not her social status, which I don't care about. She offers me her hand. But not Rica. She motions Sordo to the chair on her left and us to the sofa.

Bruno serves an apéritif, placing a glass on each of the four chrome cylinders. Doña Cartucho tastes it, closes her eyes, then nods.

"Good choice, Bruno. You had a glass or two yourself?"

Bruno is unperturbed. "Only a small taste to confirm it would please you, Doña Cartucho."

"You are abominably addicted to lying, Bruno. So, Mr. Cameron, what do you think of One Bit?"

This is the usual introductory small talk. Our horses, her horses, the weather. Turning to Sordo, she says Sigmund has banished rabbits from the vegetable garden, then explains to us that Sigmund is a German Shepherd. Sordo updates her on the health of his dogs. Rica and I listen attentively and say nothing.

Abruptly, she turns to Rica. "Señor Herrera, Sordo informs me you are an excellent cook."

"I am a cook, Doña Cartucho."

"And aside from cactus omelets, beans, and fry bread, what do you cook?"

"Many things, Doña Cartucho. I studied in Mexico City. In

Magdalena de Kino, my signature dishes were duck confit and *jambon persillé*. Though my *lentilles au jambon* was nearly as popular, which I found odd. *En effet, les goûts et les couleurs, cela ne se discute pas.*"

Doña Cartucho's jaw doesn't drop, but only because she is too well-bred for that. She is clearly astounded.

"Oui," she says, then looks at Sordo, who gives an imperceptible shrug.

Bruno is standing by, not having been dismissed. Doña Cartucho turns to him. "Bruno, would you please ask Lola to join us?" she says.

Bruno exits through a door in the paneling.

"We obtain some fresh poultry and lamb here, but unfortunately most of our meats and fish are frozen," she says.

Rica consoles her and says that frozen meats and seafood are often of better quality than fresh, if obtained from a reputable supplier.

Bruno enters with Lola, and now it's Rica's jaw that drops. She's gorgeous. Probably like Doña Cartucho at twenty. A real barn burner, hotter than the Lorenzo Pumice eruption at Popocatépetl. Sorry, Yolanda, you've been upstaged. We rise, but Doña Cartucho remains seated.

"Señores, my daughter Lola," Doña Cartucho says, then introduces us individually.

"Lola, Bruno, please show Señor Herrera the kitchen, pantries, and our modern conveniences. Note his observations and recommendations. He has extensive knowledge of the culinary arts. Especially cutlery, I am told. I have business to discuss with Misters Sordo and Cameron."

"Oh, Lola," she says as they are leaving, "you may address Señor Herrera en Français, if you wish."

Silence until they've left.

"Sordo says you want to know about the mine," Doña Cartucho says. "Why?"

"Some very rich ore from this mine has been found recently, scattered among railroad ballast in Northern Arizona," I say.

She looks intrigued but not surprised by this.

"And how do you know the ore came from this mine?"

"I'm a geologist. I've studied other samples from this mine in detail. And a geology professor I know surveyed the mine fifty years ago."

She smiles, looks up at the ceiling, then at me. "Was his name Bradford? With wavy ash-blond hair and very light eyes, a rather piercing gray?"

"Yes, Doña Cartucho. Charles Bradford, with piercing gray eyes but very little hair of any sort since I've known him."

She laughs. "I remember him," she says. "I was a little girl, five or six years old at the time. So you must know this mine was noted for the extreme richness of its ore, though not its quantity. But if you know the ore is from this mine, why ask me about it?"

"It may have been a motive for murder, Doña Cartucho."

She smiles. "And when was gold not a motive for murder?" she says. "Did not Polymestor slay Polydorus for his gold? Did not Pygmalion of Tyre slay Sychaeus, the husband of his sister Dido, in a vain attempt to obtain his gold?"

Whatever you say, ma'am. She takes a few sips of sherry, and Sordo and I follow suit. It's extremely dry and quite delicious. After a brief silence, she sets down her glass and continues.

"My grandmother and grandfather became caretakers at the mine after it shut down in 1938. They lived here, in the other wing, the servants' quarters. The company paid irregularly, and finally my grandfather threatened legal action. He had a contract and some important friends. In lieu of payment, the company deeded him the mine and the surrounding land, including this house, which, as you may have inferred, was the house Emilio Rayón occupied during his occasional visits to the mine."

She rises from her chair, walks to a very large rolltop desk against the inner wall, and raises the tambour, exposing a dozen or more small, framed photographs inside. She returns with two.

"This," she says, handing me one of them, "is Señor Emilio Rayón."

The portrait shows a handsome middle-aged man with a Verdi beard and carefully tended hair, wearing a white shirt with wing tip collar, a four-in-hand tie, and a vest and coat of, probably, dark gray wool. It's a black-and-white photograph, so any guess about colors is just that. He looks thoughtful, kind, and unaffectedly aristocratic.

I nod, rise, and pass the photo to Sordo.

"Doña Cartucho," I say, resuming my seat, "what perplexes us is how such a large quantity of exceptionally rich ore could have come recently from a mine that closed in 1938."

She smiles, then looks to Sordo. He nods.

"Well, then. My great-grandmother was the daughter of a miner here. She became a soldadera with Villa's División del Norte in 1913. She fought in many battles, first as an ammunition bearer, then on machine gun crews. She survived the Second Battle of Celaya, in April 1915, which, as you know, was a disaster for Villa. After that, Señor Rayón personally communicated to her through the lawyer Don Francisco Escudero, who was an advisor to Villa, begging her to take charge of the Rayón house as chatelaine and aid in organizing a defense against bands of marauders who were roving Northern Sonora at that time. The miners were brave but had no knowledge of military matters, and she did. Don Francisco explained to her that the situation in Sonora was worse than it had ever been, and she consented to return."

She falls silent, looking at the second photograph. She sips more sherry, then holds out the second photograph to me. I rise, take it, and resume my seat. It shows a tall woman who looks amazingly like her, wearing a white blouse, long skirt, and enormous sombrero. She's draped with machine gun cartridge belts and holds a rifle—I think a Mauser carbine—at order arms. This photo explains where the Lady Cartridge sobriquet came from.

"The mine had struck its richest vein in 1915," she continues, "but with the war, forced exactions, and marauders, it was not safe to hold even a small amount of gold or even the ore. Everyone wanted gold; the paper currencies were almost worthless. So the ore was concealed under coal piles by the engine house. Some was left out as a sop to any raiders, but the great bulk of it was hidden."

She goes to the desk again and returns with a slim photo album, which she hands me, and a few more photos, which she keeps. The album has photos of the mine with dates ranging from 1910 to 1925. The coal piles were between the engine house and the smelter, which makes sense. As I surmised, the steam engine powered a generator; a network of wires led from the engine house to other buildings and the mine entrance.

"I see," I say, and she resumes the story.

"My great-grandmother was loyal to Señor Rayón. He was a hacendado, but he treated his servants and the miners well. He had supported Maytorena, who was the Villista governor of Sonora, and therefore Carrancistas suspected him of radical sympathies. Because of that, and to gain control of the mine, they murdered him."

"Was justice done to the murderers?" I ask. I think I know the answer, and who meted it out.

"Yes," she says with a vague smile. "It was, though not by the courts. But my great-grandmother was also loyal to Villa, who desperately needed money to rebuild his army."

She offers me another photo, this one showing her great-grandmother standing by a watering trough with Pancho Villa on her right.

"So she sent a message to Villa about the hidden ore, thinking Señor Rayón would have approved of it going to an enemy of Carranza. Villa sent twenty men to take it. The miners fled when they heard Villistas were coming. They didn't fear for their lives, you understand. They were afraid the Villistas would make them work for nothing, so they left."

"Reasonable," says Sordo.

"After days of dirty work, the Villistas had six heavy wagons loaded up, about twelve tons, metric. They set out but came back within hours. Scouts told them the gringos were coming. Pardon me, no disrespect intended."

"None taken. I'm not a gringo," I say.

"Of course you are," she says. "And so is Sordo. Now, as you know, Villa raided your border towns for supplies, and your president, who supported Carranza, mobilized your National Guard and sent General Pershing with the regular army into Mexico to catch him. A hopeless task, but an understandable reaction. So the Villistas had their loaded wagons, and the cavalry was coming. What to do?"

She looks at me like she's expecting an answer. I give a slight shrug, and she continues. "Over that way," she says, pointing to her left, behind Sordo's chair, "the builders had excavated sand and clay to make this house, leaving a large pit. The Villistas dumped the ore into it, covered it up, erased their tracks, and fled. My great-grandmother saw this."

"Did the Villistas return?" I ask.

"No. My grandfather said my great-grandmother told him the gringos killed them all. So only she knew what happened to the ore. Or so we thought. She told no one. Her idea was that it must go to true revolutionaries. But the new owners of the mine were reactionary, and Villa's position was hopeless. So she kept the secret. Many years later, she wrote to Trotsky when he was in Mexico City. Two Russians and a Spaniard visited her, pretending to be Trotsky's men. But she could tell they were from Stalin."

Yeah, I think I know what happened to those guys. I just hope Sigmund doesn't dig deep holes in the vegetable garden.

She continues. "Great-grandmother remained here as chatelaine until the mine closed and Grandfather and Grandmother became caretakers. Then she went to live with a friend in Nogales. After the company deeded Grandfather the mine, she told him about the ore. He dug up some of it, processed it with the equipment that remained, and sold the gold. He invested the money luckily, and our family has lived comfortably on its income ever since. I like it here because it is where I spent my childhood. My children visit, but they do not want to live here. Lola may. She is more like me than any of my children."

"She favors you amazingly, Doña Cartucho," I say. "And what a wonderful story. I wish I could have met your great-grandmother."

She nods and rises. I guess this is the seventh-inning stretch, because she gathers up the album and photographs, returns them to the desk, then exits through the same door in the paneling that Bruno used. She clearly has more to say, so I think she's telling the cook to hold dinner for a few minutes. In the meantime, Sordo refills her sherry glass and his. I don't need a refill, but I could use a stretch. On the wall to the right of the desk is a large, framed mine map showing the layout of the Emilio Rayón mine, and I take a gander at it.

Doña Cartucho returns, we resume our seats, and she continues the story.

"And now to answer your question. Three years ago, or a little more, Bruno was up in the tower cleaning . . ." She looks at Sordo. "Cleaning, and he saw two men a kilometer east, at the pit where the ore was buried. They had shovels and a metal detector.

That is my land. Sordo was here and went to warn them off. They became belligerent and, well, Sordo, what did you do?"

"I smashed their metal detector and roughed them up," says Sordo. "They had a shitty Glock pistol, but I took it and unloaded it and smashed it between two rocks. Then I gave it back. Along with the pieces of the metal detector."

"That was very kind of you, Sordo. Then, two days later, my lawyer in Nogales called me—we have satellite telephone and Internet here, you know—and said some Americanos had a business proposition for me. Their obviously false names were Madero and Huerta. They wanted to meet. I took Sordo, and we met at a nice restaurant in Nogales. My son drove us in his truck. Of course, they were the same men Sordo had—what is that word you have, Sordo?"

"Biffed," says Sordo.

"The same men Sordo had biffed. We had dinner, and Sordo sat at the bar watching them closely while we talked. They apologized profusely for trespassing. A year before, they said, they'd met socially at a barbecue. They talked of their families and learned their great-grandfathers were Villistas who settled in Western Arizona in 1917, taking the names Madero and Huerta. They exchanged the thirdhand stories their fathers told them. Madero laughingly told the story of the hidden ore. Huerta nearly fainted. It was the same story he had heard from *his* father, even in its trivial details. He thought it was a fable, as did Madero. Now, they thought it was true."

"A bad assumption. I've heard lots of guys tell the same tall tale," says Sordo.

"True, but in this case, it was a true tale. Then they asked, very respectfully, if perchance I had any residual ore from the mine I might like to sell—how do you say *sub rosa* in English?"

"*Sub rosa*," I say.

"Well, then. Sell it to them *sub rosa* and cheat the tax man. I pondered this. Until Sordo chased them away, I hadn't thought of the ore for years. I didn't even know how much was truly there. I have far more money than I need and would scarcely notice an extra few million dollars on the pile. Besides, getting rid of it legally might technically be mining, and that would invoke incomprehensible regulations. Then I thought, why not share it out, to me, great-granddaughter of the soldadera, and to them, great-grandsons of her comrades? Share it three ways and close the book on that era. So they came, sampled it, assayed it, we agreed on a price, and they paid me for my one-third share in US dollars in an old American Tourister suitcase."

There's a loud knock on the panel door and Bruno enters the room with Lola and Rica. He's not letting them out of his sight. He may be a pathological liar, but he takes his job seriously. Doña Cartucho shakes her head and Bruno leads the pair back through the door. After they've left, she smiles.

"Well, that still left Madero and Huerta the problem of refining. They wanted to do it themselves since they owed much in taxes and wanted to conceal the income. Madero noticed the ore was of uniform size, like a coarse grade of crushed stone. This was because it was screened output from the second crushing operation, and the smaller pieces had been further crushed and refined. Madero must have read *The Purloined Letter* because he thought of hiding the ore in plain sight, among other crushed stone."

Here we discuss Poe's detective stories in detail, but I'm omitting the discussion as irrelevant to the matter at hand. I will say we agree the orangutan thing in *The Murders in the Rue Morgue* is pretty dumb.

"Then," Doña Cartucho continues, "they brought in heavy trucks and an excavator, mingled the ore with a much greater amount of crushed stone with a similar appearance, and took it away. I am reliably told they loaded it into a hopper car at Nogales and sent it north, declared as crushed stone for track ballast. It was to be delivered to Aguila, where they would unload it and deliver it to a discreet refiner. Even diluted, it was still far richer than the run of modern mines."

She stops, looks at me and Sordo, then takes more sherry.

"And that," she says, "is how it crossed the border. What happened after that, I do not know."

I have a photograph of Madero and Huerta that I printed from the Quartzrock Kiwanis website. I hand it to her, and Sordo leans over and looks too.

"Same guys," Sordo says, and Doña Cartucho nods.

"Thank you, Doña Cartucho. This is crucial information, and I won't forget the favor. But I am very sorry to tell you that Madero and Huerta are dead. They were murdered."

She looks at me, then at her sherry. "Justice delayed? Their great-grandfathers were the only survivors of the band. Perhaps they saved themselves by treachery. Perhaps, in God's view, their great-grandsons did not deserve to profit from it." She crosses herself. "Madero and Huerta must have been bad men. God does not punish good men for the sins of the fathers."

"They treated you fairly, Doña Cartucho, thanks to Sordo," I say. "But they were sometimes bad and sometimes good. As with General Villa, 'Blame and praise alike befall when a dauntless man's spirit is black-and-white-mixed like the magpie's plumage.'"

She looks at me the way she looked at Rica when he let loose in French. "Pardon my surprise, Mr. Cameron, but you must admit that is a rather obscure reference for a geologist."

I nod and continue. "But in their bad deeds, they weren't bold enough to be bandits like their great-grandfathers, so they engaged in secret crimes—fraud and peculation. And I'm informed they were responsible for the death of a railroad engineer, though not by direct violence."

"Then it was justice," she says. "Who killed them? Do you know?"

"I do not, Doña Cartucho, but I believe a friend knows."

"More to the point, do the police know?"

"No, Doña Cartucho, they do not."

"Then, Señor Cameron," she says, "it seems to me your friend has no moral obligation to reveal the killer to the police. They killed and suffered for it. That is justice."

"I completely agree, Doña Cartucho. But the authorities have accused an innocent woman of hiring the killer. We must show those accusations false."

"Then I hope what I told you will be of value."

"Of inestimable value, Doña Cartucho."

We sit in silence for a few minutes. I never thought of the Destroying Angel as a hobo, but why not? The Lord works indirectly through men. And if Madero and Huerta inherited assumed names from Mexican bandits, did Sheriff Pershing inherit an assumed name from a US Cavalry deserter? Did Frankie inherit an assumed name from a renegade? Did I inherit an assumed name from a Highland cattle thief?

I'm admiring the Cubist rug when I notice Doña Cartucho is looking at me the way older women sometimes look at younger men—not with lust (though some do that) but with a wistful appreciation and thoughts of their own youth.

"Did Frankie tell you he and I were lovers once?" she says.

I'd spit out my sherry, but at the moment there isn't any in my mouth. I'm not surprised at the news, just shocked that she said it. She smiles, and somehow, she looks twenty years younger.

From behind the gloomy paneling, a gong summons us.

27

FROM CHINA, WITH LOVE

Rica and Lola rejoin us for supper, chaperoned by Bruno. Rica offers to remain and ensure that Lola's birthday dinner next week is a memorable success. Lola says Maria, the cook, will be delighted to study under him. Pro forma, Doña Cartucho weighs the proposal carefully but consents. Not a surprise to me and Sordo. Given Doña Cartucho's lust for Rica's cooking and Rica's infatuation with Lola, it was obvious he'd be staying on.

When dessert is served—a delicate lime sorbet—Doña Cartucho drops a bombshell. Last week, she leased the Emilio Rayón mine to the Mexican subsidiary of a Chinese firm. Despite her telling them the mine was hopelessly worked out, they wouldn't take no for an answer. So she asked an absurd sum for a five-year lease, first year up front. To her surprise, they instantly consented, even when she stipulated they could do nothing but underground mining, with all processing and refining to be done elsewhere, tailings removed at least ten kilometers from the Rayón house, hours of operation restricted to 07:00 to 19:00, no machinery or equipment within a kilometer of the house, and noise level at the house kept below sixty decibels. Her attorney was dumbfounded.

I'm dumbfounded too, but I keep my poker face, and nobody can tell. That fable I fed Jing about the mine not being worked out? Somebody took it seriously. I could see the Ministry of State Security trying to confirm it, but rushing into a lease without confirming it? It's very odd. But this confirms Jing is a spook, not that I had doubts about that.

Everybody has coffee even though it's 21:00. There must be some Latin-Afro gene for caffeine tolerance. I didn't inherit it and decline the demitasse.

Then they all adjourn to the garden for a digestif by candle-light. I try to excuse myself, but Doña Cartucho raises her hand. "One moment, Señor Cameron," she says, and nods to Bruno. He quickly exits and returns a minute later with a small leather portfolio, which he hands to her. She rises and walks toward the casita. I see she expects me to follow, and I do.

When we are out of earshot of the others, she speaks. "When I said Señor Rayón was murdered by Carrancistas, what did you say?"

"I said, 'Was justice done to the murderers?'"

"And that is exactly what our friend Frankie said when I told him the story many years ago. You two have much in common. Do you read Spanish?"

"Un poco," I say.

"No matter," she says, handing me the leather portfolio. "This was written by my great-grandmother. The original is in her handwriting, and there is also an English translation. It is my own translation, so you may be sure it is a good one, but if you have doubts, consult the original. You may return this to Bruno tomorrow morning."

"Thank you, Doña Cartucho. I will read it carefully."

"I know you will. I may not see you before you leave tomorrow, but I hope to see more of you. I have a daughter your age who I would like you to meet."

"I would be enchanted, Doña Cartucho," I say. "Curious" would be more accurate. I'm sure her daughter is delightful, but would I fit in as Don Nicolás?

She says goodnight, and I retire to the casita. I strip and turn on the lamp at the head of the bed, which gives ample light. I open the portfolio and start reading.

How I Did Justice to the Murderers of Sr. Emilio I. Rayón

One afternoon in early 1916, a Monday and a wash day at the Rayón house, I was ironing three of Sr. Rayón's shirts. A woman from the mine did the laundry, but I insisted on ironing his shirts myself because they were costly, and a careless laundress had once ruined some of them. I was glad to iron his shirts. Sr. Rayón was a kind man who believed, as Villa did, that it was the job of the rich to relieve the poor of their misery.

We were expecting him to arrive before sunset that day, along with three hacendados who we interested in the mine's operations. I was in the courtyard, where we had a small portable firebox to heat the irons. Marco the stableman came to me and said a boy had important news for me.

The boy was no more than twelve or thirteen, but a robust lad with a repeating rifle. He told me he had been out hunting deer and saw four men on fine horses coming, he thought, from Sáric. One was Sr. Rayón. When they were four leagues south of us, the biggest man grabbed the reins of Rayón's horse, a second man shot him three times with a revolver, and a third man shot him three times as well. Rayón drew his pistol but fell forward in the saddle before he could fire it. The boy ran most of the way here to give me the news. Neither Marco nor anyone else heard the boy tell me this, and I told him to tell no one. His father was one of the miners. I told him to go to his father's cottage and stay there.

My grief was very great, but I could contain it. I had lost many friends since the revolution began in 1910. I resolved to pretend that I had not heard of the crime these men had done and to deal with them later as they had dealt with Sr. Rayón. There was no law here at that time. If I called on the miners to work justice, they might suffer reprisals later. If I did it myself, only I would suffer if my deed was discovered.

I went back to ironing as if nothing had happened. Two hours later, the men arrived. I recognized them as Don Agustín, Don Aurelio, and Don Porfirio. They were all rich men, but cunning and greedy. They had poor Sr. Rayón's body tied over the saddle. They said they were attacked by Villistas on the way from Sáric and repulsed them, but not before the villains had shot Sr. Rayón six times. The entire household turned out and wept.

Marco and Carlito the porter took the body and laid it on a long table in the central hallway. I could see he had indeed been shot six times, just as the boy had told me. We lighted lamps around the body, and Carlito and a maid stood watch over it. The scene horrified me. In the gloomy hallway with its dark walls, his body on the heavy table, surrounded by lamps, looked like a pagan sacrifice or a mummy in an Egyptian tomb. I hurried to my bedroom, where there was a prie-dieu with a large crucifix. I brought the crucifix back and set it at Sr. Rayón's head.

I showed the men into the drawing room and asked Carlito to bring them refreshments while I enquired on the progress of the dinner. In truth, I needed time to plan.

But first I needed to confirm the boy's story. This was easily done. A storeroom shares one wall with the drawing room, and on that wall, the wood paneling of the drawing room covers an old doorway. So instead of the thick adobe wall, there is only thin paneling, and a very small gap, low on the wall, created when the wood shrank as it dried in this desert, through which one can see and hear. I found this when I was a little girl helping my mother clean the house. I entered the storeroom and watched and listened. I could not believe how freely and callously they spoke of their crime. Their purpose, as I assumed, was to gain control of the mine after Sr. Rayón's death. They spoke as if it was already theirs. But that was not to happen.

The biggest and most dangerous of the three men was Don Aurelio. Though big, he had the sugar [diabetes] and was not very strong. He was a lustful man and abused the wives and daughters of his tenants. He also drank too much. Don Agustín was an old miser and envied anyone *younger than he. Don Porfirio was young, and in other times might have been a good man, but bad companions had twisted his weak will. I make no excuse for him; I say only that men of weak will can easily be bent to good or evil by their companions and by the times in which they live. Such men therefore cannot be trusted, however good they may seem at any one time.*

I took a decanter of spiced brandy from the sideboard in the dining room. In a windowless, locked room in the servant's wing, we kept a supply of medicines. Only I had the key. One of these medicines was a strong tincture of opium. I added a large dose of this to the brandy, then took the decanter and two glasses to my bedroom, placing them on a table near the bed.

I changed clothes, choosing a blouse that flattered my bosom and a skirt that did the same for my rump. I put on my best shoes. But more than that, I let my hair down. My hair did something to men. This is not true for all women, but my hair was long and a shining black, and it drove men mad with desire.

I returned to the drawing room and told them dinner would be served in the hour of ten. It was customary to dine at that hour in the Rayón house. The three men were playing cards. Don Agustín and Don Porfirio were intent on the game and scarcely noticed me. Don Aurelio looked at me with naked lust. I returned his look with a knowing smile and walked slowly to the doorway. He threw down his hand and came to me.

"If you would do what you are thinking, follow me," *I said. He followed me through the central hall, scarcely noticing the body of the man he had helped to murder, then into the servants' wing and into my bedroom. I locked the door, and he grinned. I had him sit down in a comfortable*

chair and removed his boots. I could see he was not yet aroused. His lust was undiminished, but the sugar illness hampered his performance, as it does in many men.

As I expected, he saw the decanter and asked for a drink. I poured him a large glass and took it to him, taking a sip myself to allay any suspicions, though he had none. Opium is bitter, but the spices in the brandy overwhelmed that. I told him the spices would increase his ardor, and he drained the glass in a few gulps.

I massaged his feet and engaged in flattery and light foreplay. Soon the drug had its effect. He fell into a deep sleep while sitting in the chair.

Before I could proceed with the rest of my plan, Don Agustín and Don Porfirio knocked at the door. "Aurelio," Don Agustín said, "we have waited long enough. You cannot leave the game when you have won so much from us."

Don Aurelio could not speak, of course, but I could. I began to make the sounds of passion. The two men laughed. "Join us when you have made an end, Aurelio," Don Agustín said.

I waited a short time, then left my bedroom by its side entrance and went to the stable. Marco was there, cleaning a stall. I told him to go to the mine comedor for dinner, telling the cook it was my orders. That was about a half league west of the Rayón house, a thirty-minute walk away. I charged him to tell no one that Sr. Rayón was dead. He understood I wanted to keep people away at such a time and announce the news tomorrow. He left.

I tossed my hair, making it convincingly disheveled, and gave my blouse and skirt a look of hasty dressing. Then I went to Sr. Rayón's bedroom and took a revolver and a handful of cartridges from his washstand. The revolver was loaded and of the same make, model, and caliber as *the guns of Don Agustín and Don Porfirio, which I had noted when they arrived. At that time, I could identify the make, model, and caliber of dozens of guns, even at a distance. I put the revolver in the waistband of my skirt, under my blouse. Then I went to the drawing room.*

"Pardon my intrusion, Dones," I said, "Don Aurelio will rejoin you soon. But the stableman says that Don Porfirio's black mare is lame."

"Lame? Not unless the fool has made her so," Don Porfirio said.

Don Agustín sighed. "These things happen, Porfirio. Let us go and see."

I had taken a lantern from the stable when Marco left, and I guided the two men there. All the way, they upbraided the absent Marco, whom they had never even met, saying that only a caballero truly knew how to care for a horse. This vicious talk made what I had to do next all the easier for me.

We entered the stable, and they walked to the stall where the mare was standing. I drew my revolver. They looked at the mare, saw no sign of lameness, then turned to me in anger. I shot each man three times. They were not strong men and fell where they stood. I have seen men fight on, briefly, after being shot in the heart. Not these two.

I put their revolvers in their hands to make it appear they had shot each other. Had they reloaded after shooting Sr. Rayón? I checked and they had, so I switched empty shells from my gun for the live ones in theirs, three empties in each gun. Nowadays, of course, such a fraud could be detected by science, but not then.

My precautions were unnecessary. Nobody came from the house or anywhere else. Marco had gone to the mine's mess hall. Carlito and the maid would not leave Sr. Rayón's body unattended, because of superstition, and the cook was attending to dinner. Also, they probably thought the shots came from somewhere outside the walls, perhaps from Marco shooting at coyotes or other pests, as he sometimes did.

I waited in the stable a long hour, until it was nearly ten. I could see that I would need Marco's help. He returned and found me. I told him I did not know what had happened, but the men had been arguing about something and must have shot each other. Marco said we must tell no one. The killing of two such prominent Carrancistas was sure to be blamed on us, given the known political sympathies of Sr. Rayón and his servants and miners. This was exactly the argument I had intended to make to him. Then he asked me about Don Aurelio. I told him Don Aurelio had wanted to ravish me, but I had given him opium in brandy, and he was in a deep sleep.

Marco wanted to dump all their bodies into a ventilation shaft that served a part of the mine long ago collapsed, but I said a shaft or well was the first place anyone would look if murder was suspected. I said we should take the bodies to an abandoned Indian settlement two leagues away and let the coyotes and vultures do the rest. This was far enough away that any connection to the mine would be unconvincing. The bones would be scattered and mistaken for those of bandits or their victims or for soldiers fallen in some unknown engagement.

Marco was a strong man. I kept watch while he carried Don Aurelio from my bedroom out through the back door of the servant's wing, by the privy, and into the stable. Don Aurelio was so heavy he was a load even for Marco. Marco remained in the stable, locking the doors from the inside.

I told the cook that the visitors had left, saying they would travel back to Sáric by night to avoid bandits and Villistas and pick up some food at the mine comedor on their way. She knew the cook there always kept some of his excellent gorditas on hand for travelers and late visitors, so this was believable. Gorditas are peasant food, but Sr. Rayón said these would be welcome at the French embassy in Mexico City.

An hour after midnight, Marco loaded the bodies onto the three horses the murderers had ridden, and we set out for the old pueblito. It was very cold, and the horses' breath made clouds that floated off into the desert, glowing in the moonlight as they went weaving between the chollas, which also glowed in the moonlight with their silky spines. I remember that for some reason. Also that it was very still, as if peace had come now that justice was being served.

We dumped the bodies at the old pueblito. I was surprised but not saddened that Don Aurelio had died on the way from too much opium. It saved me the trouble of shooting him. Marco cut off their clothes and threw them in a deep crevice. He had already taken their guns, boots, money, and other valuables. I never asked what he did with them. I knew he was a salteador when I hired him, but in those days, a salteador was what I needed, and he was always honest and loyal to me.

Marco took off the horses' tack, which he hid in a dry place among the rocks. I think he retrieved it later, kept the best, and sold the rest. But what to do with the horses? We knew they would likely follow us home, and their presence anywhere around the house or the mine would arouse suspicion. I could not bring myself to shoot them, and neither could Marco. Then he said, "If you order me in the name of Sr. Rayón, I will do it." But I could not do that and tried to think of another way.

Then we heard a sound like a cavalry troop approaching, galloping up the dry riverbed below us. We quickly took cover behind a high wall in the ruins, but we knew our position would be hopeless if they saw the bodies of the murderers.

But when the horses came into view, we saw they were riderless. It was a herd of wild horses. Marco jumped up, intending to drive the murderers' horses into the herd. But they needed no such encouragement. They were already running to join it.

On our way home, we could hear the coyotes yipping and howling in glee at the banquet we had brought them.

The next day, in the late afternoon, I climbed partway up the mountain above the mine and looked toward the old pueblito with Sr. Rayón's Swiss binoculars. I could see many vultures coming and going.

Nothing ever came of all this. In those days, it was common for men to disappear, and if anyone in the house or the mine suspected anything, they kept quiet. We gave Sr. Rayón a grand funeral, and the miners made him a monument near the chapel we used when a priest visited us, which alas was rarely. Years later, I had a large bronze plaque installed on the monument. It is still there. I burned the table on which we laid his body and had a new one made. It stands in the hallway today, with the crucifix.

And that is the story of how I, Magdalena Fierro, did justice to the murderers of Sr. Emilio I. Rayón, one of the few men I have ever truly loved.

I have made a full confession of these sins and my many others and have done the long penances prescribed for me. Now, as I approach my ninetieth year, I write this for my great-granddaughter. Esmeralda, I seal it and instruct it and other stories be given to you on your twenty-third birthday, which I know I will not live to see. I ask that you honor the memory of Sr. Rayón.

I return the documents to the portfolio, turn out the light, and immediately fall asleep. Around midnight, I wake for a drink of water. Sordo and Rica are absent. Sordo doesn't matter, but I'm worried about Rica getting himself in trouble with Lola. Not enough to lose sleep over, though.

I go back to sleep. I wake slowly, around 02:00, sensing someone is in the room. I'm lying on my back. I don't move and keep breathing slowly and rhythmically as if I'm sleeping. I don't hear anything and don't feel threatened. After a few minutes, I open my eyes very slightly. Someone is standing to my right, but in the bedroom with its single small window, it is too dark to see anything but a vaguely human shape. There is no motion. Five, ten, fifteen minutes later—I don't know exactly how long—whoever it is moves slowly through the open doorway into the kitchen. There is only starlight through the kitchen windows, but that's enough for me to see the outline of a tall woman in a long skirt or nightgown. She moves silently toward the exterior door, which isn't visible from my bed. I assume she leaves, though I don't hear the door open or close. I wait another ten minutes or so, then get up. There is nobody in the kitchen, and the exterior door is closed and locked. I go back to bed.

The next morning, it's just me and Sordo at breakfast in the casita. Sordo says Doña Cartucho gave Rica the old chatelaine's bedroom in the servants' wing.

"You want to see something?" Sordo asks.

Sure. We enter the servants' wing through a door in the garden and climb a steep staircase that leads to the roof, which is nearly flat, though sloped slightly for drainage, and mostly covered with solar panels and a few satellite dishes. None of this is visible from the outside because the exterior walls rise about four feet above roof level and much higher in the false front above the main door. As with most adobe buildings, the walls are thick, about two feet. And they have loopholes, very narrow on the outside but flared inward.

"It's up there," he says, pointing to the tower. There's a door into the bell tower, but the lintel is low, so we duck to enter. The thick walls make the interior surprisingly small, about eight by eight. Sordo takes a ladder up to the next level, and I follow, barely squeezing through the hole. Here the walls rise about waist height above the floor, and the rest is open, aside from the four corner columns supporting the roof, from which a bell is suspended. It would make a great belvedere. A tarp, tied down to cleats, covers something in the middle of the floor. Sordo removes the tarp.

It's an old, water-cooled machine gun. Clean and, from the smell, well-oiled. Mounted on a pedestal, not a tripod. Sordo demonstrates traverse and elevation.

"Wow. A blast from the past. Does it work?" I ask.

"Oh, you bet it works. A Maxim, MG 08. It runs like it just left the Spandau Arsenal. Part of Kaiser Bill's aid to Villa, thanks to the original Doña Cartucho. Our Doña Cartucho fires it twice a year to entertain the family. Tracers at zero hundred hours on Dia de la Revolución and May Day. It's quite a show. You should see her in cartridge belts and a long skirt."

I look up at the mention of the long skirt, and Sordo eyes me curiously. Then he grins and chuckles. "You've seen her, haven't you?"

"Seen who?"

"You know who I'm talking about. I've seen her too."

I let it pass. I'm not a superstitious person, but I'm also not the kind of person who fervently believes something doesn't exist solely because he lacks evidence that it does. I don't want to end up like the guys who denied the existence of rogue waves and continental drift. There's nothing wrong with saying, "I don't know." IDK. We should all say IDK a lot more than we do, especially we overeducated dipshits who think we know everything. Still, Occam's razor suggests my nocturnal visitor was Maria the cook looking for a good time or Doña Cartucho engaging in some cosplay. I just need to keep telling myself that.

"Is this a periscope?" I ask, pointing to what looks like a small stovepipe grafted onto the spade grips.

"Yes. See, you can sight through it and observe through it and still be protected by the walls. You don't even expose your hands because of this crazy trigger extension. But of course, if you fire it where it is, you'll shoot into the walls, right?"

"I was wondering about that."

"Watch this."

Sordo grabs a long cast-iron lever near the ladder hole. "Step back, laddie," he says. I step back, he throws the lever, and the pedestal rises two feet amid ratchet clicks.

"And now you're ready to rock 'n' roll. If you have a jam and need to open it up, you just lower the pedestal, and you're protected."

"Ingenious," I say.

"Yes. Some engineer from the mine designed it. A modern sharpshooter could disable the gun pretty easily, but when he came up with this contraption, there weren't a lot of modern sharpshooters around. Just crazy guys on horseback, howling and brandishing rifles. And I think this was intended to be used at long range, mainly for suppressing fire. Keep people away. That's how I'd use it, anyway."

I crouch down and look through the periscope. The gun points east into the desert, toward a small gravel pit. That must be where the ore was buried.

"How did you handle Madero and Huerta?" I ask. "Madero was a big guy."

Sordo laughs. "I punched him in the nuts. Felt like punching a bag of marbles. You should've seen the look on his face. His eyes were like this." Sordo circles his eyes with thumbs and forefingers. "Then I slapped Huerta and took away the pistol he was trying to pull out of his pants." Sordo fiddles with the Maxim's rear sight. "Looking back, I feel kind of sorry for them, even ashamed, like I hit a dog or something. They didn't even know how to fight. But how was I to know that? I asked them very politely what they were doing with the metal detector, and they got nasty. If they wanted to pull that machismo crap, you'd think they would've learned to fight first."

I shake my head. "You couldn't have known," I say. "And Huerta had a gun. And he was small, but he was slow." Sordo grins, and we go back to looking at the Maxim.

Sordo is an interesting guy. He has a passion for fairness. And he has a maxim (sorry, couldn't resist that): "Danger will destroy him who courts it, but he who avoids it will prevail." He heard that in a Baptist Sunday school when he was a kid. That was where he acquired his encyclopedic knowledge of the Old Testament, which he says was just about all they studied in that Sunday school. The Jesus guy was sort of an afterthought, he says. Maybe that was just his congregation, but my experience in a Presbyterian Sunday school was similar. I have a Muslim friend who argues that Presbyterians are a lot closer to Muslims and Jews than they are to Catholics. But that's a discussion for another day.

Anyway, some time ago I asked Sordo what his maxim really means. He had a very long and subtle explanation that sounded like something Thomas Aquinas would have come up with if he'd been a Baptist. He said it's not just something stupid about avoiding unnecessary risks, like not wandering around a bad part of Chicago at night. Of course, it means that. It also means questioning whether to engage what seems like clear and present danger but often is not. The danger may go away by itself if you simply decline to engage. The adversary may lose interest, chicken out, run out of resources, get soft and lazy, be defeated by another, and so on. Look at the Judeans in Babylon, he said. Cyrus the Great came along, kicked the Babylonians' asses, and told the Judeans to git along home. Or stay if they pleased, no skin off Cyrus's ass one way or the other. Or take the Cold War. The Soviets thought capitalism would collapse, and we thought their communist system would collapse, and we ended up being right, but nobody pressed the matter.

And if the adversary doesn't lose interest, chicken out, run out of resources, get soft and lazy, or get defeated by another, you've had lots of time to prepare and can choose to engage carefully and in limited ways, and only when you are reasonably sure of success.

There's more to it, but you need to ask Sordo if you want the full theory. Of course, if I asked him why he courted danger by screwing with the narcos, he'd have an answer. He can reason his way out of anything. He should have been a lawyer. Or a Baptist minister.

"This contraption isn't the main defense," Sordo says, putting the tarp back over the machine gun. "I'll tell you about that when we leave tonight."

Back in the house, Sordo shows me a windowless room near the kitchen. This must be the same windowless room where Magdalena got the opium tincture one hundred odd years ago. A big flat-screen monitor displays views from a dozen security cameras.

"Does anyone man this?" I ask.

"They don't need to. They can view it on their smartphones, and the cameras issue alerts, but it's usually a coyote. It's a local network, got nothing to do with the Internet. They're not under siege or anything, but the house is isolated, and they get hoboes coming around now and then."

"Hoboes?" I say.

"Bruno feeds them and sends them on their way. They'll steal things if you don't watch them, but they're pretty harmless."

Obviously, Sordo never met White Buns.

To the right of the monitor is a switch panel with a bunch of toggle switches and a key switch.

"That," says Sordo, "is the main defense."

He doesn't explain.

We walk toward the stable. One of the sheds is open.

"You need to see this too," Sordo says.

It's a potter's workshop, and Bruno is doing a sculpture. To his left on the workbench is a dog flamenco troupe. The dancer is a Chihuahua, the singer a bulldog, the guitarist a spaniel. They are finely detailed, and the dancer, despite being a dog, looks seductive. It takes a true artist to make a dog seductive, and I'm impressed.

"This is excellent, Bruno," I say. "Did you study art?"

Yes, he studied under Picasso. I guess he really is abominably addicted to lying. But who cares? I ask if he'll part with the flamenco dogs, and he agrees to a fair price. Theo will love them. Perfect companions for the frog mariachi band. I tell him I could sell his entire output in Quartzrock if he's interested. He says he'll think about it.

28

LESSEE'S REMORSE

Sordo is antsy to leave. Stated more accurately, Sordo is antsy to get me safely over the border so he can come back. He says we can leave around sunset and not wait for dark, so we gear up, say our goodbyes, and start out.

We head northwest, which is not the way we came, but it will take us past the mine. Now that Doña Cartucho has leased it out, we're curious. The mine isn't visible from the house—it's hidden by a ridge, which is the lower end of the mountain spur we descended when we arrived yesterday. We crest the ridge and see two Land Rovers parked near the mine entrance with two men in business attire standing by them. They must have come on the unimproved road—or rather, the trail—that goes south across the plain toward Sáric. A look through my binoculars tells me they're Asian, presumably Chinese since a Chinese company is leasing the mine, duh.

Sordo wants to keep clear of them, so he turns right, and we descend into the broad draw that separates the spur we just crossed from the spur the mine penetrates. The draw leads up the mountain to a saddle. Sordo is taking a different route going home than we took coming here, which is something anyone schooled in evasion would do.

We're a half mile up the draw when Sordo stops by a saguaro. "Some guys just came out of the adit. See what's going on."

I steady the binoculars on One Bit and look. "It's two guys in yellow hard hats . . . They're talking to each other as they walk to the cars . . . Now they're there . . . The shorter of the hard hats shakes his head . . . Now the two suits are talking to each other . . . Now they're talking to the hard hats . . . Both hard hats are shaking their heads and doing some weird thing like stroking their bellies."

"I think that means no, not interested, bite me, or something like that," says Sordo.

"Seems like a lot of 'no' or 'bite me' going on there. This could get physical."

"I vote for Southern Praying Mantis."

"From their movements so far, I vote for Fujian White Crane. Now the shorter hard hat has thrown something down, a bunch of papers . . . Now he's going to the Land Rover on the right . . . He's getting in . . . The other hard hat is following him, getting in on the driver's side . . . You see that? They spit gravel. Must be trying to piss the suits off. Got dust all over them . . . Now the suits are getting in their car . . . Look at that. They spun out, barely missed the ore cart."

"Too bad they left. With four guys, that could have been a great fight," says Sordo.

We resume our trek. It's early twilight when we look back at the Rayón house three miles away. Lights are glowing in the windows. It's not a last look for Sordo. He'll be back soon. But I may never see it again. And I'd like to see it again, even though there's something odd and unreal about it.

"She's quite a woman," I say.

"She sure is," he says.

I see wind stirring in the bushes far down the draw, below the mine. It looks like something is stroking a vast invisible brush over the creosote and ironwood. It moves up the draw in a wave. I watch, fascinated, as it sweeps past the mine, accelerating toward us. A minute later, it hits like a wall of Saran Wrap, smothering me, encircling me, then releasing me and continuing up the draw, leaving us in a dead calm. I take a deep breath, turn around, and see it reaching the saddle as a dying whirlwind. Sordo is watching it too.

"What the hell was that?" I say.

He hesitates. "Just the wind," he says.

I look back at the Rayón house again. "You said you'd explain the main defenses to me. What are they?"

"Mines. They're electrically fired from that switch panel in the house. I didn't tell you earlier because I thought you might pee your pants walking through a minefield."

Doubtful. First off, I hit the baño before we left. Second, I had to cross minefields in Africa, which was unpleasant but didn't cause involuntary urination, possibly because I had a guide. For various reasons, I won't tell Sordo about it. Third, like many geologists, I'm no stranger to high explosives. I tell Sordo that and he says, "Oh, yeah, seismic survey shit. I'm talking real explosives."

We continue up the draw toward the saddle. I've been thinking about Magdalena's story since we left the house—the horses carrying the bodies of the murderers to the abandoned pueblito—and believe we are following the same route. I infer this from her saying she climbed partway up the mountain above the mine and looked toward the pueblito. I can't see any reason for her to climb partway up the mountain to view the surrounding plain, which she could easily do from the elevation of the mine, and nobody would build a pueblito on the plain anyway, because there's no water. Therefore, the pueblito must be in the valley on the other side of the saddle we're climbing toward.

The draw was mostly scree lower down, but now we're into outcrops and boulders that have fallen from the cliffs on either side. The path between the rocks has narrowed, and the walls are steep. Sordo has slowed down because it's dark in here. But the moon is waxing, half full, and won't set until after midnight. No need for my night vision goggles, and their limited field of view would be undesirable anyway.

We're well into nautical twilight when we reach the saddle. Sordo pauses for a look ahead. In the valley far below us, I see a dry riverbed. This matches the description in Magdalena's story, and I can imagine her standing here, scanning the valley with Señor Rayón's Swiss binoculars, watching the vultures. There's a breeze coming over the saddle, and I feel a slight chill.

"Take a look with your Swars," Sordo says.

I pull out my binoculars, which are Swarovskis and Austrian, not Swiss. I can't see any sign of human or animal life anywhere in the valley. The riverbed is broad and sandy. I see several places that might qualify as the ruined pueblito but can't be sure which it is.

"Looks clear," I say.

We start our descent and must be walking within a few yards of the route Magdalena took more than one hundred years ago. It's June and not January, so I don't see the horses' breath glowing in the moonlight and swirling among the cholla as she did, but the silky cholla spines are glowing in the moonlight, as they did for her. And it is silent, as it was for her.

We've gone maybe 150 yards when I look back. In the deepening twilight, atop the saddle, exactly where we passed, I see the dark silhouette of a mountain lion. I stop. Sordo hears that and turns. I point.

Sordo looks at the cat, which remains motionless. Probably eyeing us, not that I could say for sure, given the distance. This is the third time I've seen a mountain lion in the wild. They are a rare sight, even if you spend a lot of time in the bush. They are secretive and prefer to hunt at night. This one is an adult, about two-and-a-half feet tall at the shoulders, I estimate. Males and females look a lot alike, but from its body shape, I think this one is female.

Sordo motions to me with his thumb and forefinger, which I assume means to have my pistol ready. He draws his rifle from the scabbard and slings it over his left shoulder European style, rifle in front, his left hand on the forestock. He can bring the rifle to aim in a half second from that hold. But he doesn't seem concerned and continues down the draw. The cat slinks into the shadows behind a boulder the size of a Stonehenge sarsen.

I watch the rear, spending half my time walking sideways or backwards. The cat reappears now and then, always high in the rocks and clearly following us, but mostly lurking unseen in the shadows. That's the usual pattern. Hikers attacked by mountain lions rarely see them. They just feel claws on their back and fangs in their neck.

This continues, the cat disappearing among the boulders and then reappearing on them, as if she's playing a game with us, which I suppose she is. After a half hour of this, she disappears for ten minutes. I think she's left us, but she emerges from the shadows, now maybe a hundred yards away. After another ten-minute disappearance, she emerges again, a little closer, maybe seventy-five yards away.

The cat maintains this distance until the draw ends at the broad, dry riverbed. It's very easy going, with a safe distance between us and the dense brush on the banks. The moonlight is bright on the sand. I look back. She's standing in the middle of the riverbed, no more than fifty yards behind us. I stop. Sordo stops and looks. She walks slowly into the brush, somehow doing so in complete silence. Sordo turns and we continue.

She keeps appearing on the riverbed and then disappearing in the brush, coming slightly closer each time, with occasional flashes of eyeshine. This continues for another half hour, until we come to a sandy shelf on the left bank, only a few feet above the riverbed. Piles of stones cover it—the remains of unmortared stone walls—and a mostly intact wall, about seven feet high, stands behind the ruins. This must be the abandoned pueblito in the story, and the wall must be the one Magdalena and Marco hid behind when they thought a cavalry troop was coming. I half expect to see three naked bodies white in the moonlight, though I don't.

But I see the cat sitting on the wall.

I whistle softly. Sordo looks where I point. She's about thirty yards away, staring at us, her eyes shimmering in the moonlight. Sordo turns, returns his rifle to the scabbard—God knows why—and continues down the riverbed. I follow, watching the cat, which remains motionless on the wall, staring. A quarter mile later, we round a bend and I lose sight of her.

Sordo stops to rest, sitting on a boulder. I join him and drink from my canteen.

"Well, I guess we know who that was," he says.

I don't reply. I know what Sordo is thinking. He knows Doña Cartucho gave me Magdalena's story. He knows I've been thinking about it—who wouldn't? And he thinks this summoned the spirit of Magdalena in the form, appropriately, of a mountain lion. He must have picked the idea up from Frankie, who believes this can happen if you think too much about a dead person, though of course the animal won't necessarily be a mountain lion. There's probably a set of Navajo rules that determine the animal. If you think even more about a dead person, especially in grief or remorse, their spirit can attach itself to you as a sort of innocent parasite, draining your life force and making you ill. This is Ghost Sickness, and it's not the same as the hokey spirit possession you see in old Vincent Price movies at Halloween. You're no more possessed by the ghost than a salmon is possessed by a lamprey. I admit I don't understand it fully, any more than Frankie understands the Five Points of Calvinism fully. Anyway, Ghost Sickness is curable, but best to avoid it by not thinking too much about dead people in the first place. This seems like good advice for everyone. I agree with the recommendation, if not the reasoning.

Sordo rises, heads off with Two Bits, and starts singing "Louie Louie." He's one of the few people in the world who knows the words. Something about a sailor and his girl. I don't know the words but can handle the *do do do* riff. And to this tune, in Sordo's cover of the Richard Berry version, we start truckin' on down the wash. I see what Sordo is doing. Nothing like an earworm to take your thoughts off dead people, right? That damn song spins through my head all night.

Around 02:00, we cross a low ridge and descend onto the plain where we met the narcos. Sordo calls a halt and we eat some gorditas that Maria the cook packed for us. They're excellent, and not just because we're hungry. Bet I know where the recipe came from.

Sordo leans back against a rock and looks up. The moon is down, and we're far from light pollution. More impressive than the bright stars is the intense blackness between them. It's ghastly. Overhead, the Milky Way covers that blackness with a thin gray mist. Sordo studies it. "When Esmeralda lets her hair down," he says, pointing straight up, "that is what it looks like."

I have a fleeting impression, what Grandma Cameron would have called a second sight. I'm standing behind Theo, who is looking out a window at the ocean. It's near sunset. Her hair, once dark, is streaked with gray. I raise my right hand to stroke her hair and see the veins on my hand are standing out as veins do on the hands of an old man.

There's just a hint of dawn when we pass the dead Jeep. Despite taking a different route coming back, Sordo couldn't resist getting close enough to see if the Jeep was still there. "Those boys are in deep shit," he says. "Not only did they lose most of the shipment, they lost their ride."

"It wasn't really their fault, though. You took their shipment and shot their Jeep. Jeep killer."

"I did them a favor. You think Señor Narco will believe that some old Black guy snatched their shipment, swiped ten kilos, and then tossed them back the sack with two kilos on top and a ten-kilo bag of masa harina on the bottom? And then shot their Jeep? And then made off on horseback like, what, Django Unchained? No, he'll think they stole ten kilos and the Jeep too. They know that. Their only option is to run away and start with a clean slate. And live to see their grandchildren. I did them a favor."

"Whatever you say, He-Kills-Jeeps."

Sordo doesn't want to stop at the same rock shelter we used before, and he knows of another one a half mile away on the opposite side of the wash. We head for it. It's an outcrop the size of a small house, like the other, and it faces north like the other, so we can't see inside because we're approaching from the south.

We're almost there when I hear something. A sharp crackling, like someone is unwrapping a candy bar. Sordo doesn't hear it, but he hears me stop and looks back. I cup my ear and point to the rock shelter. Sordo nods. He draws his rifle from the scabbard. He points with his thumb and forefinger to one end of the outcrop. He wants me to cover that end. I draw my pistol.

Very slowly, Sordo moves toward the other end. I lose sight of him as he rounds the far side. Then someone shouts, "¡No dispares!" A minute later, Sordo shouts, "It's okay, laddie!"

I'm not stupid, so I stay a few yards back from my end of the outcrop—no narco is jumping this Highlander—and then ease around the corner, pistol at low ready. Sordo is sitting on the ground next to a Latino kid.

It's the tracker. Ferny by name, and he speaks unaccented English because he's from Tularosa. After Sordo whacked the Jeep, the driver and the guy riding shotgun lost their heads, being in the middle of nowhere at night with nothing but salted snacks, bottled water, and a GMRS radio that was out of range of anything. Also guns, which were no use at all.

But Ferny kept his head, said he would track the old man, and went off into the bush with his day pack full of water bottles, a jumbo bag of M&M's, and a flashlight. He said he'd signal back. Of course, he just wanted to ditch his idiot companions. He walked a mile into the desert, then walked back parallel to the trail. At dawn, he followed our tracks and came to the rock shelter where we rested the first day.

He figured we were making a round trip, smuggling the guy with the new boots, and would return in a day or two. He was wrong about the smuggling but right about the round trip. And he figured we'd return by a different route and avoid using the same shelter again, which was right too. So he looked for other shelters near the wash and found this one. He says he's done with narcos and wants to go home to Tularosa, and the narcos won't find him because they think he's from Tucson.

"You'll never see them again, kid," says Sordo.

Ferny already knows where the tank is—he doesn't miss anything—so Sordo sends him for water.

"Okay, Sordo," I say after the kid's gone. "You said we wouldn't meet anybody on this trip. So far, we've picked up a Mexican French chef, had a run-in with amateur narcos, witnessed the start of a Tong War, and almost been surprised by some renegado Boy Scout working on his tenth tracking merit badge or whatever he is. So what gives?"

Sordo is trimming his fingernails with his pocketknife. He doesn't look up. "Yes, it's been quite a trip," he says.

29

DANIEL, THE SOLE JEWISH RESIDENT OF QUARTZROCK

We rest until sundown and then continue our trek home, with Ferny in tow. I tell Ferny he could become a hunting guide, but he says he doesn't like killing animals, and I agree. I suggest the border patrol, but he doesn't like that idea either. Okay, how about getting a degree in forestry? Good, he likes that idea. He has visions of tracking miscreants for the Mounties in the Yukon.

We arrive at Sordo's place soon after sunrise. His house sitter is in the pavilion with a cup of coffee and a cigar. He takes the horses. Breakfast is ready but needs to be heated up in the microwave. We eat and then sleep.

I wake around 13:00, then compose and encrypt a long trip report for Frankie. I'll send it when I break radio silence in Tucson. The mystery of how the incredibly rich ore from the Emilio Rayón mine got mixed in with track ballast is solved. The remaining question is how the mix ended up in five different places on spur tracks in Northern Arizona and how White Buns and the railroad bull got involved. The plan, as Doña Cartucho said, was to have it delivered to Aguila, about sixty miles northwest of Phoenix, loaded into trucks, and delivered to a shady refiner. What happened? Have at it, Frankie.

I exclude the bit about Doña Cartucho leasing the mine to a

Chinese firm and the bullshit story I fed Jing that explains it. I'll tell Frankie about it later, but it's unrelated to the murder mystery and would just muddy things at this point.

At 14:30, Ferny is still sleeping, but Sordo stirs forth. We talk for a while, then I gather my stuff and we head out. Sordo leads in his F-150 until we hit BIA 19, where he waves and peels off.

When I hit Tucson, I stop for lunch at a Scottish restaurant. McDonald's. While I'm eating, I check emails and send Frankie my trip report. I loiter for a half hour, reading the *Wall Street Journal* online. I'm enjoying the excellent McDonald's French fries when Frankie calls.

"Whadda you want?" I say.

"You need anything?"

"Yes, my car. Where is it?"

"It's in Tucson. Somebody will swap cars with you. You'll get a call in the next hour."

"Cool," I say. Rodolfo must know how to pull strings if he can get the car to Tucson that fast.

"That was a great report you did, Nick. Very detailed. Did you take notes?"

"No, of course not."

"You'd make a great spy."

"Not interested," I say. Fact is, I was in the espionage racket for a year, sleuthing rare-earth mineral sources. Industrial espionage, like what Jing is doing, which explains how I spotted her right away. Takes one to know one. I wrote a novel about my experience, *Quantum of Monazite*. The editor loved it but wanted to change all occurrences of "monazite" to "nerve gas." I told him you don't mine nerve gas, but he said most people don't know that.

"You know Daniel Rosen?" Frankie says.

"Of course I know him, he's hired me as an expert witness a dozen times."

"It was a rhetorical question intended to introduce a subject of conversation. Sure, you know him. So do I, but he won't talk to me. He's got a grudge with me because I warned the Council about Scrotelli."

That's a long story not worth going into, but it involved a violation of the Indian Arts and Crafts Act of 1990 that stuck one of Daniel's clients with a $250K fine. Frankie probably would have told Dan before going to the Council if he'd known Scrotelli was Dan's client. But he didn't know.

"And? You want me to arrange a bygones-be-bygones session or what?"

"No, I want you to ask him about Revolutionary Rocks. It was a company Madero and Huerta set up to import rocks from Mexico. Chesney found some records of it when he and that forensic accountant were going through Madero's stuff."

"They were his clients. Rosen won't discuss it," I say.

"You aren't asking him about confidential communications. Revolutionary Rocks sued 'the railroad' over something. Chesney doesn't know what railroad or what it was about. I'm thinking it had something to do with that hopper car of 'track ballast' they shipped north. Clearly, something weird happened with it. Question is, what? Daniel should know. The case must be a matter of public record. Get him to tell you about it. He's in Scottsdale for the next few days. Ask him to lunch."

"Okay. Time I checked in at home anyway. It's been weeks."

"See ya."

I finish my Quarter Pounder and go downtown to pay my respects at the Pancho Villa statue, which has acquired new meaning for me. The very white guy in camouflage pants and a Miller Lite T-shirt is there—he's persistent, I'll say that for him—and has an updated screed for me. This one is even better, with another long tirade from Salvador Alvarado. Excerpt:

He [Pancho Villa] is the bandit Doroteo Arango who hides in the uniform of a chief of the Northern Division; he is the minister of Cain and Caco, as his countenance betrays: he is the caveman who nourishes himself upon bones and raw flesh and the roots of trees.

Wow. This sounds like MSN babbling about Donald Trump or Fox News babbling about Joe Biden. I tell Camouflage Pants I can't wait for the next installment.

While I'm there, I get a call from a guy who tells me to meet him at "that place," which I assume means the RV dealership where I got the Camry. We swap cars in the cathedral garage there, and I head north to Scottsdale in my 911.

When I say I'm checking in at home, I mean I'm spending the night at my townhouse in the Scottsdale Backspin Club. How I inherited it will explain a lot of things, so here's the story.

When I was thirteen, I spent a month at my Grandpa Cameron's cottage on Mackinac Island. Grandpa went to Cleveland for an angioplasty and left me with my aunts. Boring. Then I found his stash of 1950s detective novels. They had lurid covers with studly detectives in trench coats and shapely women in pointy bras. What thirteen-year-old could resist? A week later Grandpa returned, found me alone in the cottage, and asked where the aunts were. I replied, "The dames are at the pancake joint." Then I said I wanted to learn "the noble art" (boxing) and asked when I'd be old enough to "pack a roscoe." Grandpa grinned joyfully. After that, we'd do tough guy talk whenever we were alone. I became his favorite grandson, an accolade I treasured even though I was his only grandson. Every summer, I'd visit him on Mackinac Island, and in the winter, unless I was out of the country, we'd meet almost every week in Scottsdale for dinner at Andretti's.

Fifteen years later, Grandpa called me, sounding oddly joyful. He said he had made a new will, and when he "cashed in"—his words, not mine—I would inherit his cottage on Mackinac Island, his townhouse in the Scottsdale Backspin Club, and a tidy pile of "dough." I thanked him and said it would be a long time before that happened. He didn't reply. That's when I knew he was going to die. Two hours later, I got the call.

By then I had already made a tidy pile of dough through stock options at an oil exploration company, so I decided to retire and spend my spare time on the Arizona rock show scene while I developed a process for hydrogen wells that would make me even more dough. I could feel Grandpa Cameron nodding his approval.

Now, far as I know, Daniel Rosen is Quartzrock's only permanent Jewish resident. Lots of Jews lived there in the nineteenth century, when it was a boomtown. Merchants and craftsmen and whatnot. Same thing in other boomtowns. There's a Jewish cemetery at Boot Hill in Tombstone, believe it or not.

When I'm halfway to Phoenix, I call Dan's cell and ask if he wants to have lunch at Goldwasser's Deli tomorrow. I tell him it's rocks business. He's okay with that, and we agree on 12:30.

The next day, I get to Goldwasser's around noon. The food is great, and it's all kosher, which means it's wholesome and therefore repulsive to most Arizonans. It's not a hole in the wall, but modern, big—must seat 150 at least—and always busy. But you don't say, "Is there a doctor in the house?" in this joint. You need to be specific, like, "Is there a cardiologist in the house, preferably one who specializes in arrhythmogenic right ventricular dysplasia?" Sure, it's a stereotype, but if you do your research, you'll see it's an accurate stereotype. It's reversed for farmers and foresters. Ever meet a Jewish forester? Yes, different ethnic and religious groups have different occupational preferences. Deal with it.

I get a table and start checking prices on the Paris Rock Bourse. There's little movement. Agate futures are up a bit; amethyst geodes for August delivery are down. I've got a straddle on lapis lazuli, and it looks like I'll turn a tidy profit on it.

I look up from my phone, and there's Dan. Twelve thirty on the nose. Punctual, for a lawyer. We greet each other as "Dr. Rosen" and "Dr. Cameron." It's a joke—he's a JD and I'm a PhD—but it turns the heads of the dames at the next table.

I ask him about the grandkids, and we dispute the relative merits of sending a nine-year-old girl to Talmud Torah school versus public school versus some private academy I never heard of. He's surprised when I argue for Talmud Torah. I say she'll learn to define things, draw distinctions, spot issues, and so on. A critical thinking curriculum for fourth graders.

Dan defers a decision on the school thing. He'll let his daughter decide, if he knows what's good for him.

"Say, Nick, could you do me a favor?" he says. "I think I've been unfair to your friend Frankie."

"Really?"

"Yes. That thing with Scrotelli. There's no way he could have known Scrotelli was my client because he wasn't my client when Frankie told the Council about him. I didn't understand the chronology until recently. Besides, Frankie wasn't the only one who reported him. So give him my apologies and ask him if he wants to do breakfast sometime."

"He gets up at oh-four-hundred."

"Lunch then. Or dinner."

"Will do. Speaking of Frankie, he wanted me to ask you about something. Nothing to do with Scrotelli."

"Sure, anything I can do."

"Okay. It's about Revolutionary Rocks suing a railroad."

Dan rolls his eyes. He takes off his gig lamps, sets them on the table, and rubs his peepers. He doesn't look Jewish. He looks French. Put him in a striped shirt and a beret and give him a pack of Gauloises, a pencil mustache, and an accordion, and he'll be at home in a sleazy Lyon café.

"Ah, yes. Revolutionary Rocks against Cholla Railroad, Inc. Creosote County case number something-or-other. Revolutionary Rocks was Madero and Huerta's company. But you know that. Set it up to import rocks from Mexico. You know that too. I thought they'd be bringing in onyx lamps and amethyst geodes, but their first shipment was a carload of crushed stone for track ballast."

"That seems strange."

"No kidding. Importing crushed stone to Arizona? That's like carrying coal to Newcastle. So the car was in the yard at Winslow, headed for Aguila. I know that seems odd, but you can't have each car in a train turn off here and there and continue on its own way. You split them up in a yard. Anyway, Cholla Railroad, which is a small-time operator, somehow hooked it up with some other cars of track ballast, and a contractor who was doing track bed maintenance for them used it up, along with five other carloads. They went into CYA mode and pointed fingers. It was one of those deals where people tell you it's impossible something happened even when it indisputably happened."

Coffee arrives, and Dan stirs in some creamer. "So I had to file the complaint to get their attention. It never went to trial. Stuff like that never does."

"That's it? So Cholla Railroad settled?"

"Indeed they did, and they even paid more than a carload of number three crushed stone was worth. But that didn't satisfy Madero and Huerta. Oh, no. They wanted to know where the stuff was used. That was quite irrelevant to their claim, but I tried to find out. I felt like a fool asking about it. It's not like the rocks had barcodes or something."

"Why did they care where it was used?"

"Believe me, I wondered about that and asked but never got a good answer. It's not like you'd try to disguise drugs as crushed stone, though I wouldn't have put it past those two to try. Now that they're dead I can say that. Or maybe the rocks were a lot more valuable than declared on the manifest, but that's hard to believe. It was very strange. They acted like they'd lost a Wells Fargo gold shipment."

I'd love to tell Dan how right he is, but that will need to wait.

"Did you ever find out where it went?" I ask.

"Possibly. After spending six hours of billable time, I finally found a guy in Winslow who said he heard it was used on some branch line near Albuquerque."

"What did the guy look like?"

Dan shrugs. "No idea. I talked to him on the phone. Some private security guy. I forget his name. It would be in the file, but confidential. He insisted I keep his name out of it. He said he could be fired for talking to me, which might be true."

"Was his company Wilt-Garner?"

"That's a company?"

"Yes. Wilt-Garner Railroad Security. Hyphen between Wilt and Garner."

Dan looks up from stirring his coffee. "That's it, I remember now. He told me his *name* was Wilt Garner. So I guess I don't know his name. Damn gandy dancer."

"Did the guy talk like an NYC shamus?" I say.

"Shamus. Where do you get this stuff? Yes, like an NYC shamus, except he was dropping his *r*'s, like 'the cah went to Albakuhkey.' I poked fun at his accent when I told Madero and Huerta. But they seemed satisfied, and that was an end to it. So why is Frankie interested in this?"

I knew he'd ask that and I'm ready. "He bought Madero's compound, and there's a big pile of crushed stone in there with a sign for Hermosos Paisajes Landscapes on it. He says it smells like track ballast."

Dan smiles. "Frankie the bloodhound. Yes, that was another of their shady companies. But I doubt the things are related. Reclaimed track ballast is widely used by shoddy landscapers. It's not my business, anyway."

We move on to baseball and a triple play the White Sox had a few weeks ago. The Diamondbacks are playing in DC tomorrow, and Dan suggests we watch the game at his favorite sports bar. He assures me it's a dive, so I'm okay with it.

I tell Dan the last time I was in a dive sports bar, there was a big police raid across the street. He asks where and I tell him it was some lawyer's office in Ashland, Wisconsin.

"You saw that? I thought you were down here," he says.

"No, I was up in Ashland. How did you hear about it? It's not national news."

"I was talking with an old friend in Duluth, and he told me about it. When a lawyer gets busted for stealing from clients, there's unseemly schadenfreude." Dan rubs his hands and grins in mock gloating. "We love to discuss it."

"What are the charges?"

"Oh, a laundry list including, appropriately, money laundering. Plundering the Metaxas Trust. Tax fraud, of course. The weird thing is that he's also charged with arson for torching some oddball museum in Chicago."

Well, that ices the shortbread. "It wouldn't by any chance be a radio museum?" I say.

"Yes, that's what Hoffler said, a radio museum. So you've heard of this?"

"I heard about the radio museum burning down on WLS."

Dan keeps talking, but I get distracted thinking about how Theo might be doing. I still don't see how Frankie plans to clear her. I mentally rejoin Dan.

". . . So besides the federal and Wisconsin stuff, there's a UFAP warrant out for him on the arson charge," Dan says. (That's Unlawful Flight to Avoid Prosecution. It lets the Feds help catch fugitives from state charges.)

"Where do you think he's gone?" I say.

"Who knows? Gulf coast, sailing to Trinidad? Or maybe he'll hole up in the woods for a few months until the heat dies down, then make his move."

We finish lunch, and I go back to my townhouse.

I spend an hour drafting a very precise email detailing what Dan told me at lunch. I encrypt it and send it. Then I start inspecting my smoke and carbon monoxide alarms, leak detectors, cameras, and so on. My joint is an IoT showroom.

A leak detector is shrieking when Frankie calls.

30

OH, SWEET MYSTERY OF BALLAST, AT LAST I'VE FOUND YOU

"**W**hadda you want?" I say.

"You need anything, like earplugs, for example?"

"No, that was a leak detector. I'm testing the audible alarms."

Frankie asks why I care about audible alarms when I'm never there and get alerts on my phone and a robotic arm shuts off the main water if a leak is detected anyway. I tell him I'm the kind of person who likes everything to work. Then I tell him I sent an encrypted email, even though there was nothing sensitive in it worth encrypting, and he should read it. But he wants me to brief him on Dan's info dump anyway. I do that and then start summing up.

"So Dan's source was obviously our railroad bull of happy memory who was lying about the stuff being used on the Albuquerque line. He gave Madero and Huerta a bum steer."

"Okay, stop. Dan talked to the guy three years ago. What makes you think his bull and our bull are the same person?"

I have the answer. "From the looks of the bull's disgusting shed and revolting house, I'd say the guy had lived there a long time. Supporting that, cops called the guy 'Arley' or 'old Arley,' which would be an odd way to describe a stranger or recent acquaintance. And I heard the firedawgs call the cyanide shed

'Arley's shed,' which suggests they knew him; otherwise, they would have just called it 'the shed.' This broad familiarity tends to corroborate long residence."

Frankie lapses into one of his long silences. I look out the front window. A real tomato in a tennis skirt is walking a bichon. I'd like to have a dog, but I travel so much that it would be unfair to the dog. Great way to meet dames, though. Maybe I could just walk dogs for old people. Same result, with a good deed thrown in.

"Okay," Frankie says. "So let's say he was there three years ago and was working as a private railroad security guy, instead of working at Burger King and switching jobs later. How do you know there wasn't another guy with a Newark accent doing the same thing at the same time?"

I have an answer for that too. "Well, Sew-crates, I'm not making a dumb argument that the probability of two different Wilt-Garner security guys with a Newark accent ending up in Winslow is astoundingly remote. The only one we know of had a Newark accent, so it would make more sense to think a Newark accent is the most likely scenario. Wilt-Garner might recruit heavily in Newark, for example. Even if Wilt-Garner just randomly drafted people and randomly assigned them to Winslow, the chance of getting another one with a Newark accent would be the same, almost, as the chance of getting the first, and would not cause us doltish wonder. But the people aren't recruited and assigned randomly. Wilt-Garner specializes in protecting high-value cargo, and they want everybody watching everybody. So they don't want two people who might know each other at the same site. Especially when they come from New Jersey. I got that information from the Wilt-Garner reviews on Glassdoor.com. The Wilt-Garner website was not very helpful."

Another one of Frankie's ten-second time-outs. I mute the phone and test the leak detector in the laundry room. It's done shrieking by the time Frankie responds.

"That's not bad. I had the guy checked out, and you're right. So yes, Dan's bull and our bull are the same guy. Now for the second part. You're assuming the bull knew from the start the ballast was valuable, else why the bum steer? But did he? Or did he find out later? Maybe he or White Buns just stumbled on a place where it was used. So maybe he was truthfully repeating what someone told him about the ballast being used on the Albuquerque line. He didn't say it *was* used there, just that he *heard* it was."

"No," I say, moving from the laundry to the powder room. "I think he knew from the start. Somebody rigged things so Cholla Railroad took Madero and Huerta's car along with the others. It's extremely unlikely that would happen by accident. Railroads aren't stupid. Whoever rigged it needed a motive for risking discipline, possible termination, or even criminal prosecution. The only motive strong enough was getting the gold. And we know the bull got the gold. But obviously, he'd want to conceal the wealth to avoid a very searching investigation by Wilt-Garner until he was ready to bug out for Honduras or wherever. Now sure, somebody else might have done it and then on his deathbed told the bull about it, and so on, but let's take the most parsimonious explanation here."

"Agreed. The bull rigged things so Cholla took the car. And then he or an accomplice, say a hobo, monitored the maintenance operation and saw where the ballast was used."

"Yes."

Another ten-second time-out. I test the leak detector under the powder room sink.

"And none was used on the Albuquerque line," Frankie says. "The guys tell me the entire hopper car is accounted for in the five spur sites they found between Gallup and Flagstaff. Not only that, they found evidence of ballast being removed in several places, besides the site of the Rabid Horse Gulch derailment. Not picked over, removed. And in other places, the ratio of ore to plain rock was far lower than expected, indicating it had been picked over. So not a case of their stumbling on one site by accident."

"Yes, and I think we can rule out third parties stumbling on those sites by chance. So the bull was giving them a bum steer."

"Yes. And how do you think he knew what was in the car?"

"Hmm," I say, eyeing the leak detector under the refrigerator. "Let me see. What kind of person would be rooting around in a hopper car of track ballast? Gimme an H!"

"H."

"Gimme an O!"

"O."

"Gimme a B!"

"B."

"Gimme another O!"

"O."

"Hobo. Hobo. Hobo."

I hear Frankie using his SodaStream and seize the chance to test the leak detector under the refrigerator.

"Yes," he resumes. "So the bull and White Buns were partners. White Buns told the bull, the bull rigged things so Cholla took the car, White Buns watched where it was used, White Buns gradually gathered it up, and the bull refined it. And just to confirm, you are absolutely sure Dan said he mocked the bull's accent when he told Madero and Huerta?"

"He said 'poked fun at,' not 'mocked.' Poking fun is good-natured. Mocking is nasty."

"Thanks for the diction lesson. Point is, Madero and Huerta wouldn't have had much trouble tracking down the one guy in Winslow with a Newark accent, right?"

I'm removing screws on the dishwasher kick panel to get at the leak detector under there.

"Might be more than one," I say, "but only one who was a Wilt-Garner railroad bull."

"Okay. Somehow Madero and Huerta got to the bull and made him talk. They probably found out he was dealing opiates and blackmailed him into telling them where the ballast was used. So that explains the pile of ballast at Madero's place. Not the first load either, of course. And I think I know who they hired to find the bull."

"That's on you to sleuth out, my fine feathered friend. One thing, though. This means White Buns savvy rocks. It's unco rich ore, but a layman wouldn't see that, especially mingled with other rocks."

Frankie agrees. Then we talk about the ethics of the case. This makes me pause on the leak detectors because I need to construct a formal argument. At first, I'd thought White Buns and the railroad bull were bad boys for stealing Madero and Huerta's gold. But not if you put yourself in their shoes. I give Frankie my opinion:

1. White Buns and the railroad bull thought whoever owned the carload believed it was just number three crushed stone. That was what it said on the manifest, right?
2. Cholla Railroad needed track ballast and got a carload of track ballast.
3. Cholla Railroad paid Madero and Huerta more than fair value for the load of ballast. Admittedly after being sued, but all's well that ends well, right?
4. If there was an aggrieved party, it was Cholla, who maybe lost five or ten thousand in legal fees and paid a little extra for the ballast. But that was their fault for not just admitting they got the ballast and paying for it when Rosen first asked.
5. Therefore, I see no grave sin in White Buns and the railroad bull diddling with the car's routing. It's like they just stepped in and brokered a sale.

6.   White Buns picked over the ballast, taking only pieces of the gold-bearing quartzite. Based on the reports from Frankie's guys, it sounds like White Buns replaced what he took with other crushed stone.
7.   In comparison, Madero and Huerta removed large quantities of ballast with no concern for the result. That was extremely reckless and likely to cause serious injury or death.

"I agree," Frankie says, "and now it's time to wrap this up. I want you in Winslow on Friday."

"How about I leave tomorrow? After the Diamondbacks game? I'm watching it at a dive sports bar with Dan."

Brief pause. I test the leak detector under the dishwasher.

"Okay, but you need to be in Winslow at sunrise Friday. Meet Ambrose and Isaac in the parking lot at La Piazza."

"Never met 'em. How will I know who they are?" I say.

"If you see more than one pickup truck in the parking lot at sunrise with two Navajo in it, call me and I'll disambiguate."

"When is sunrise?" I ask. Stupid question. I could just check my phone, but I'm reinstalling the dishwasher kickplate.

"Oh-five-ten. And one thing. This is the risky part. Condition orange. Keep your haggis handy, laddie."

"I think you mean claymore. But they're both deadly in their own way."

"Whatever. Just remember White Buns thinks you have something to do with this. He thinks you're as guilty as Madero and Huerta and the railroad bull."

"Guilty of what?"

"Guilty of killing the railroad engineer who died in the Rabid Horse Gulch derailment, idiot. White Buns is the sword of justice. That's his motive. It all makes sense now."

It does. Like Magdalena whacking Señor Rayón's killers. I'd

OH, SWEET MYSTERY OF BALLAST, AT LAST I'VE FOUND YOU

rather see miscreants tried and dealt with according to the law. But, as Calvin observes, regardless of what the civil authorities may do, God sometimes sends avengers of his own choosing.

"And one more thing," Frankie says. "We need White Buns alive if you want to get your lady friend off the hook. If you see him, don't engage. Steer clear. Run away if you have to. Use deadly force only to avoid death. Did you hear that? I didn't say 'death or great bodily harm,' I said 'death.' Let him break your legs if he wants. Capisci?"

"Aye."

31

GRAB A BALLAST FORK, BOYS

I'm testing the smoke and carbon monoxide alarms when my neighbor Elena comes over to see if my house is on fire. She's a widow, eighty-two, with a small dog. I ask if she'd like me to walk her dog tomorrow morning. She's delighted.

The next morning, I find a West Highland Terrier really does attract dames of all ages. I tell Elena I'll be glad to walk Bruiser whenever I'm in town. I catch up on emails and financial stuff and meet Dan around noon for the Diamondbacks game. They win 5–0. Some lucky guy at the next table has a date who, like Trixie, is driven into a sexual frenzy when her team wins.

I tell Dan I'll see him the next time I'm in Quartzrock, then leave for Winslow. I take the back way, Highway 87, because I really dislike the freeway route, which goes through Flagstaff with all those damn trees. Actually, the back way has more trees, but it's a national forest so they have a good excuse for being there.

I have dinner on the way and check in at La Piazza around 21:30. I wake at 04:30 and watch the parking lot from my room on the second floor. At 05:08, an F-150 pulls up in the circular drive and stops by the front entrance. Right at sunrise, like Frankie said. Two guys are in the cab. The passenger is big, like Frankie, the driver small. Maybe it's a biased sample, but in my experience, Navajo come mainly in two sizes, with nothing much in the middle. Somebody told me Sardinians are the same way.

I hustle downstairs and approach the truck on the passenger side. A magnetic sign on the door says:

Revolutionary Rocks
Quartzrock, Arizona
928-555-0199

It's Madero's truck. I'd know it even without the sign.

The big guy rolls down the window. Yes, it's a hand-crank window. Madero was a cheapskate. Skin a flea for its hide and tallow. "Ambrose?" I say.

He shakes his head and nods toward the driver. "He's Ambrose. I'm Isaac," he says.

"What's goin' on? This is Madero's truck."

Isaac gets out. "Frankie bought it. Bought Madero's compound too."

He looks scornfully at my sweatshirt. It's fifty-five degrees and he's in a T-shirt. If he were Frankie, I'd say, "Hey, you're used to just a loincloth," but you don't joke like that with strangers. It's okay with Frankie. He calls my kilt a loincloth. And he calls the Highland Games the Flintstones Olympics.

We stand there for a minute. I guess he wants me to sit in the middle, so I do.

Some writer observed that three men in a pickup truck look like the Three Stooges going to paint some old lady's house. He was right. You feel like a stooge too.

Ambrose drives us west, north, then west again through the high plain. There are no trees, just grass, sage, and yucca. And an occasional prickly pear. The road gets worse until we're on a neglected trail that hasn't been graded for years, if ever. Ambrose slows down, dodging rocks. I still have a cell signal, which makes sense because it's so damn flat. They've got KTNN playing country music. Not my fave, but it's the right music for three guys in a pickup truck with wheelbarrows in the bed. Some ads in Navajo, and Ambrose responds by saying something to Isaac in Navajo. Isaac nods.

I would ask where we're going, but from the ballast forks, shovels, and two wheelbarrows in the bed, it's obvious. We're off to steal White Buns's cache. Frankie said that Ambrose found it when he was following antelope tracks, so he obviously knows where it is. And not only will we steal White Buns's cache, but we'll also make sure White Buns knows we're doing it because his trail camera is watching. And we'll really piss him off when he sees the Revolutionary Rocks sign on the truck.

By my reckoning, we've gone about thirty miles, which is nothing in this country, when we come to a low mesa that's extensive but elevated only twenty feet above the surrounding terrain, with very gentle slopes. I know this rock. It's the Holbrook Member of the Moenkopi Formation, Lower Triassic. Reddish-brown, slope-forming, alternating sequence of claystone, siltstone, and sandstone. Low-life rock, good for nothing but getting eroded into soil.

Ambrose follows the trail northward, skirting the bottom of the slope. Ahead is a railroad track. The trail turns west again, running about fifty yards south of the track. Ambrose stops. To the left, the ground rises, about a 10 percent grade, up to a low outcrop that rims the top of the mesa.

"Here," says Ambrose, looking left. We get out. I lower the tailgate. Ambrose climbs into the bed and starts handing stuff to me and Isaac. The wheelbarrows are heavy. Big pneumatic tires, stout hickory handles, and thick steel beds. Two of them and two shovels. And two ballast forks, which Ambrose hands to me, grinning. I look at Isaac, and he's grinning too. These guys know the whole tale, that's obvious. I check the tines for blood stains.

For all I know, spearing people with ballast forks may be a local tradition.

It looks like Ambrose, or should I say Moe, is in charge of the operation. So I (Larry) put the ballast forks in one wheelbarrow, Isaac (Curly) puts the shovels in the other wheelbarrow, and we follow Ambrose up the slope.

Ambrose stops. There it is, behind some sagebrush. A bit less than a cubic yard, but about a short ton, I'd say. It must have taken White Buns a long time to collect it. Even the railroad bull, may he rest in peace, could have gotten a half million in gold from this pile.

I grab a ballast fork and start filling my wheelbarrow. If you're wondering why you use a ballast fork instead of a shovel, try pushing a shovel into a pile of number three crushed stone. Go ahead, try. Let me know how that works for you. The narrow tines of the fork, on the other hand, neatly find their way between the stones.

Ambrose and Isaac climb up over the outcrop and onto the top of the mesa. Why, I have no idea. I keep loading. When my wheelbarrow is half full, I take it down to the truck and pitch the ore into the bed. This stuff is heavy, and a full barrow would be hard to manage on this rough ground. I make another trip.

Ambrose and Isaac return with a cooler full of beer and sandwiches. We have one of each. There's no ice in the cooler, but it's still cold from last night's chill. It's okay to drink a little in the morning if you're fishing, hunting, or doing any kind of heavy manual labor.

"Is there a convenience store up there?" I ask, looking at the mesa.

Ambrose shakes his head. "I've been watching this pile for two weeks. Had my camp up there."

"Sounds lonely."

"It's not so bad. You see things." Ambrose looks at the pile.

"You guys take care of this. I need to get the rest of my gear."

I take off my sweatshirt—now I'm down to a T-shirt—and Isaac nods. I'm buff, it's true. We load all the ore in less than an hour. Then we sit down on the tailgate for another beer. I look at the railroad tracks. It's obvious they haven't been used in a while. They're getting overrun with grass and sage. This spur went to a mine, but that must have closed recently.

Eventually, Ambrose shows up with a canvas pack almost as big as he is. He throws it in the truck, then goes back to where the ore pile was. A few yards away, he picks up a big rock, then throws it down. He comes back.

"Smashed his camera," he says. "Just rubbing it in."

The truck rides better with a ton of rocks in the back. A ton is above the rated payload for this low-end model, but if I mention that, the guys will think I'm a total wuss. Weirdly, I can tell they know I'm thinking that.

But the soft ride doesn't last long. We've gone maybe five miles when Ambrose backs the truck up a few hundred yards into a side trail, then off the trail maybe twenty yards. He shuts down and we get out.

"Frankie says to unload here," Ambrose says.

This doesn't make sense to me, but Frankie always has a reason. We unload and leave. Back on the side trail, Ambrose stops the truck but leaves it running. He and Isaac cut some sage and erase our tracks. When we get back to the main trail, they do the same. This must be something they do a lot because it doesn't take long.

Back at La Piazza, Ambrose parks, and we all get out. He walks over and holds out the truck keys with his right hand.

"Your keys?" he says, extending his left hand, palm up.

"What?"

"Frankie says you're taking the truck to Quartzrock. We need your ride. We can't walk home."

I give him my key and pull my gear out of the 911 while Ambrose gets his gear from the truck. It won't fit in the 911's trunk, so he crams it into the back seat.

"It burns premium," I say.

"Good luck," says Ambrose. "And thank Frankie for us."

We all shake hands. They spend a few minutes adjusting the mirrors and seats. I can tell Isaac wonders if he'll fit, but the car's made for Germans, so there's no problem. In the front, that is. The rear seat is made for Nibelungs. When they leave, Ambrose drives like a ground sloth. Once he's out of sight, who knows what will happen.

Frankie is facing an ethical dilemma. His moral code tells him White Buns did the right thing in whacking Madero and Huerta. So he doesn't want to turn him in. But if he doesn't turn him in, the blame will continue to fall on Theo, who is innocent.

It's a bad situation. Even if Frankie was willing to give the county attorney all the evidence of this convoluted tale, starting with a feral soldadera and ending with a railroad bull *en brochette*, it would only be a fantastic theory without conclusive proof. The county attorney and DPS would stick with their theory about the radio museum and the Metaxas Trust. If history has taught us anything, it's that once people have a darling theory, they will prefer it over others, even if they need to keep piling on ad hoc hypotheses to save it.

I don't know what Frankie is planning. If he wanted me to know, he would have told me. But he hasn't, so he doesn't. Clearly, he's luring White Buns back to Quartzrock, with me as bait. What happens after that, I have no idea.

On my way out of town, I stop at Walmart and get a tarp and some paracord to cover the wheelbarrows, ballast forks, and shovels. Not that anybody would care about what's in there, but I don't want stuff falling out. Arizona is terrible for that, especially in the south. Rain is rare, so people just throw junk in trucks and trailers with no cover, and of course it blows out. Furniture, yard waste, building materials, you name it. They never learn.

I'm south of Flagstaff when Frankie calls.

"Ambrose wants to buy your car," he says.

"Does he know what that car is worth?" I say.

"So he's a grubby Indian and can't afford it?"

"Oh, cut the bullshit. I'd say the same if he were a white guy."

"I know that, but you think Ambrose would? You're a damn sensitive guy. Start showing it."

I think Frankie's full of shit on this one. Ambrose struck me as an astute guy. He would likely respond with, "Sure I know what it's worth, I checked Kelley Blue Book." Besides, Ambrose wasn't grubby. He was surprisingly clean and tidy for someone who just spent two weeks hanging out with coyotes on a godforsaken mesa. I've been a lot dirtier after two weeks of scratching and stomping in the Northwoods. That said, Frankie has a point, but like everybody else, he stereotypes now and then.

"Okay," I say. "Tell him I'll consider an offer. Now what the hell do I do with this truck?"

"Drive it to Madero's compound. Park it conspicuously in front of his shop. Then check in at his trailer. The door will be open."

"It's a shithole. I don't want to stay there."

"I had Leonard's crew clean it after the CSI guys were done. There's still some of that good old Madero smell, but it's not filthy."

I'm not looking forward to this. "Okay, look, I get your plan. I'm hobo bait. I wait in Madero's pit until White Buns shows up to whack me. I get it. What do I do until he shows up? How about I have Janie come over?"

"No, lover boy. I'll be there. In fact, I'm there right now. I've got it stocked with food and that Kentucky rotgut you like. We stay there until White Buns drops in."

"What if he doesn't drop in?"

"He will, laddie. Two things I know for sure. The sun will set, and White Buns will come for you tonight with blood in his eye."

32

NICK GETS DISQUALIFIED

I hit Quartzrock around 16:00 and stop at the Flying Mulewhip for coffee. Janie's there, looking hotter than a pyroclastic bomb in the Lupanar of Pompeii. She asks if I'm cured of whatever diseases I picked up from the little chippy, whether I've registered with Sheriff Pershing, and so on. Then she asks what I'm doing tonight. Damn you, Frankie. I tell her I'm delivering a hijacked cigarette truck but I'm free tomorrow night. She's delighted.

I key in the gate code at Madero's compound and do what Frankie told me. I carefully park the truck in front of the shop. The crushed stone pile is still by the gate. I take my gear and go to Madero's trailer. The door is open like Frankie said. I go in. I know the layout because I've played cards here, but you don't know it, so here's the floor plan:

- *All countertops Formica.*
- *Living room, bedrooms, and radio room carpeted in a lime-green nylon loop carpeting. All other rooms lino-leum (vinyl sheet flooring) pretending to be tile.*
- *Beer kegerator holds two kegs.*

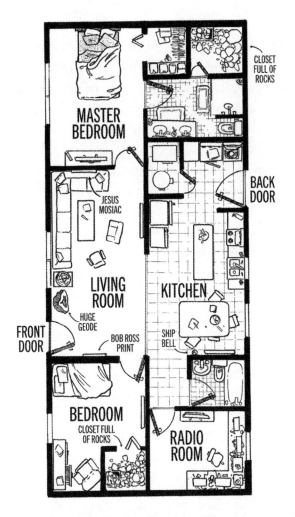

Frankie is sitting at the dining table making a wax model for a ring. He looks up. I point to the left, to the master bedroom. Frankie nods and continues his work. I take my gear in there. Frankie's right. They cleaned the place well. Carpet clean as new, dresser dusted, bedding smells fresh.

First thing is a shower. Of course, it's a beige plastic surround with a plastic drain pan and two valves with transparent, jeweled plastic knobs. I turn on the hot first. It doesn't get hot.

"Hey, Frankie!" I shout. "Is the water heater turned off?"

"Try the right valve. And no more shouting," he says.

Sure enough, Madero hooked the valves up backwards. Right is hot, left is cold. But maybe that's how it is in some parts of the world. Sardinia, for example. It's an arbitrary standard anyway.

The valve thing is a minor nuisance, but the adhesive rubber flowers on the drain pan are worse. And pointless because the drain pan is corrugated for traction anyway, so the flowers are loose at the edges and form both a petri dish and a tripping hazard.

I dry off, change clothes, and join Frankie in the kitchen. I test the kitchen sink. It's hooked up right.

"It's only the master shower," Frankie says. "But he screwed up some of the wall outlets. He didn't know hot from neutral. Leonard fixed them."

There's a pot on the stove. Mutton stew. I smelled it when I came in. That's how I met Frankie. He brought mutton stew to a Kiwanis picnic. It's a Navajo thing, but it's also a Scottish thing. My grandmother made it. He saw I was the only person eating it, and that's how we met.

Frankie sees me looking at the pot. "Help yourself," he says. "That's what it's there for."

And I do.

"What's the plan?" I say.

"We wait here. You wait in the living room, over there." He points to the sectional sofa. "I closed the blinds but they're cheap junk, and he can see around the edges. I'll be in the second bedroom. He'll come, trust me."

"I don't want to squirrel your plan, but what if he has a roscoe? He could plug me through the wall if he can see where I am."

"He won't. That's not his signature. He likes to make the punishment fit the victim. He drowned Madero in a rock tumbler, squashed Huerta under a geode, speared the railroad bull with a ballast fork, and tried to brain you with a baseball bat. Maybe this time he'll club you with Porsche special tool #223232 or something."

I look at the sofa. There's a rain stick stuffed between the corner cushions.

"I put it there," Frankie says. "Use it if you need to."

Frankie stows his wax model and tools in a hard-shell case and sets them aside.

"Looks like the railroad bull killed himself," he says. "ICD Code T65.0X2. Cause of death, toxic effect of cyanides. Manner of death, intentional self-harm: suicide. He wrote a note: 'If I don't do it, he will.' Then he got good and drunk and made himself an old-fashioned with a dash of sodium cyanide. So he was dead when White Buns arrived. But White Buns probably thought the guy had just passed out on the floor. For the bull, that behavior was not unusual, as investigators have noted."

Frankie goes to the refrigerator and gets a bottle of water. "The medical examiner hasn't released the report yet, by the way."

"My lips are sealed."

Frankie pulls a cribbage board from a kitchen cupboard. We cut for the deal.

"Ambrose and Isaac think you're a brother," Frankie says.

"It's mutual. I'd work with them any day," I say.

We play until sunset, when Frankie throws down his hand.

"I'm going to the bedroom," he says.

"Huh?"

"I didn't say I was going to sleep. I'll be awake, lights off. Stay in the living room. When he comes, I'll back you up if you need it."

"Is it okay for me to watch TV?"

"Sure. Just turn off the sound. I'll hear him before you see him."

Frankie retires and I look around. Madero was eclectic. There's a Bob Ross print on the east wall of the living room. A mountain, a lake, trees. On the opposite wall is a Jesus mosaic in the style of a Byzantine icon, very skillfully done. I wonder if Madero did it. Despite his incompetence as a handyman, he was a damn good lapidary. Of course there's a bisected amethyst geode on a pedestal by the front door. Every lapidary has one. This one's big, about three feet high, but not like the seven-footer that squashed Huerta. Then there's a ship's bell on the kitchen wall. Somebody must have given him that. He was no sailor, though he might have done barrel duty at one time or another.

I can't see anything that White Buns might fittingly assault me with, so I assume he'll bring it, whatever it is.

I turn on the TV. To clarify, that's the living room TV. There's a TV in every room of the house, bathrooms and closets excepted.

And lo, besides the usual streaming services, there's a Bob Ross channel. I turn it on. Fascinating. Bob Ross, if you don't know, was a guy who did complete landscape paintings in thirty minutes on a TV show in the 1980s and 1990s. His show has been rebroadcast ever since, but he croaked a long time ago. I think his paintings are dorky, but you can't question his skill.

Bob has done a mountain lake, a forest brook, another mountain lake, and northern lights over a mountain and is starting on a seascape when White Buns smashes in the back door with a big rock.

I jump up and grab the rain stick. White Buns runs through the kitchen and comes at me with a rock pick. I dodge behind a chair. He swings the pick, but I block it, and it gets stuck in the rain stick. I push back and twist and throw the rain stick with its embedded pick over the kitchen table.

This guy is pissed. He closes, throwing punches at me from fifty different angles. He's short, but he's got a long reach. I cover up and then barely connect with a right hook and go to the body. I dodge a few jabs and backpedal around the chairs until I'm facing the kitchen.

And there's Frankie watching us like we're an exhibition bout at the MGM Grand.

This makes me lose concentration for an instant, and White Buns nearly connects with a short jab. I backpedal again. Then I see Frankie reach for the ship's bell.

DING DING DING.

Startled, White Buns jerks left and I connect with a solid overhand. He goes down into one of Madero's cheap chairs, which falls backwards, and there he is on the floor, looking up in a daze at Frankie.

"You," says Frankie, pointing at me, "are disqualified."

Then he grabs White Buns's right hand. "The winner!" he says.

He's right. I threw the punch after the bell.

33

WHITE BUNS WANTS A REMATCH

hite Buns takes a good look at Frankie and knows the game is over. He's lost the scruffy beard he had when he whacked Madero and Huerta, and he looks like he's lost some weight too. I recognize him in his new look, but most people wouldn't.

"Call 911," Frankie says.

I wasn't expecting this. I'm not sure what I was expecting, but it sure wasn't delivering White Buns to the cops.

"What?" I say.

"Call 911 and tell them we have a home invasion," Frankie says. "But tell them I've got things under control."

I look at him, and he looks back at me with a nod.

"Open the gate," he says, "and stay outside so they know where we are."

The front door has one of those kick-down doorstops. Madero used it when hauling rocks in and out. I open the door and kick it down so I can hear Frankie if he needs me. That's unlikely, but why take a chance?

I call 911 and tell them we have a home invasion at Madero's old place but Frankie has restrained the culprit. The dispatcher wants me to stay on the line. I walk over and open the gate, then go back and stand outside the double-wide.

It's quiet. It seems like I can hear Frankie and White Buns talking, but I can't hear what they're saying, if they're talking at all. It's a pleasant night, about sixty-five degrees, and the stars are bright. There's little light pollution, so you can see the Milky Way, just as in the deep desert.

My phone bings. It's a text from Jing: *PCM*. I text back, *Busy. TTYL*. She responds, *KK*.

The first vehicle to arrive is Sheriff Pershing's Explorer, lights flashing but no siren. Pershing brought his comical side-kick, Deputy Tuco Serrucho. Serrucho, who looks amazingly like Ricardo Montalban, likes the role and plays it well. He'll be the next sheriff, or I miss my guess. Pershing waves me back toward the Explorer. There's lots of chatter on their portables. They both have their gats drawn.

"Hey, Frankie, you okay?" Pershing shouts.

"Fine, thank you. Please come in and join us, Sheriff."

Pershing shakes his head and tells Serrucho to go around to the back door. They enter at the same time. I told 911 that Frankie has White Buns under control, but they need to assume that White Buns might be holding a gun to Frankie's head or something. I stay outside.

The ambulance arrives next, followed by more deputies. The paramedics can't find anything obviously wrong with White Buns except that he's sweaty and really stinks, but I guess you expect that in a hobo. He has a slight bruise on the forehead, but he doesn't have a concussion, far as they can tell, and his vitals are normal. He says he feels fine. I need to up my game. I tell them I'm okay, but they insist on checking me out too. I pass.

Bob Ross is still painting away, distracting everybody in the room, especially Deputy Serrucho, who seems mesmerized by him. Pershing tells Frankie to turn it off and he does.

They stuff White Buns into Pershing's Explorer and head to the sheriff's office. By now, more cops have arrived to take photos and collect evidence and so on. That includes a photo of me showing a slight bruise on my right cheekbone, the only visible evidence of White Buns's ferocious assault. And the rain stick with embedded rock pick. And the big rock used to smash the back door. I say as little as possible. Clearly, Frankie has something up his sleeve, but I have no idea what it is, so the less I say, the better.

Frankie and I repeat the home invasion tale to the guy who's doing the report, which doesn't take long because the whole thing lasted less than a minute. I realize that in a movie, the fight would have lasted ten minutes and entailed complete destruction of Paco's trailer. Not that it would be hard to destroy the trailer, but in the real world, fights don't last long enough to do that. Sure, boxers keep it up, but they do their road work, are used to getting hit, dodge most punches, wear padded gloves, and get a one-minute rest every three minutes.

Next, we go to the sheriff's joint. We stand outside.

Pershing comes out. "Hey, Nick, you have Rosen's cell number? The guy wants to make a statement, but I want him to talk with counsel first. I told him he should just wait for the initial appearance and get a public defender, but he says he can afford his own and wants, and I quote, 'a Jew attorney.'"

"Always an advisable choice in attorneys," I say, "and he's come to the right place."

Rosen should be in town since he was leaving for Quartzrock after the Diamondbacks game yesterday. I call and hand Pershing my phone. It's 21:40, but Rosen is a night owl. He avoids criminal cases unless somebody is already his client, but he'll take this one. Best to stay on the good side of the sheriff, and Pershing knows how to return a favor. He arrives ten minutes later.

It's 22:30 when they go to the interview room and start the video recording. Of course we aren't invited, but Pershing has called Frankie on his private phone and stuffed it in his pocket, so even though we can't see what's going on, we can hear it. We walk across the street to a decrepit town park and sit down on a splintery bench under a palo verde tree that has lost most of its branches in a windstorm. Don't plant one as a shade tree. Frankie puts the phone on speaker, volume low.

Sheriff Pershing: Good evening. I'm John Pershing, sheriff of Creosote County. It's 22:32 Arizona time on 14 June. I am in the interview room at the sheriff's office here in Quartzrock. Four other people are with me in the interview room. To my left, could you identify yourself, please?

Detective Magyrak: I'm Detective Roman Magyrak of the Arizona Department of Public Safety. R-O-M-A-N M-A-G-Y-R-A-K.

Sheriff Pershing: Thank you, Detective. And to my right, off camera, could you identify yourself, please?

Deputy Serrucho: I'm Deputy Tuco Serrucho, Creosote County Sheriff's Department.

Sheriff Pershing: Thank you, Deputy. And across the table, to my right, could you identify yourself, please?

Attorney Rosen: Yes. I am Attorney Daniel Rosen, counsel to the interviewee.

Sheriff Pershing: Thank you, Counselor. And across the table, to my left, could you identify yourself, please?

"Philo Tape," whispers Frankie.

Philo Tape: Sure. I'm Philo Tape. P-H-I-L-O T-A-P-E. Papa Hotel India Lima Oscar, Tango Alpha Papa Echo.

I look at Frankie. He smiles.

Sheriff Pershing: Thank you, Mr. Tape. Now, Mr. Tape, you have said you want to tell us some things. Do you understand that you have the right to remain silent and that anything you say in this interview can and will be used against you in a court of law? And do you understand that you may end this interview at any time you please, for any reason or for no reason at all?

Philo Tape: Duh.

Sheriff Pershing: No offense, Mr. Tape. Just doing my job. So, may we take that as a "yes" to both questions?

Philo Tape: Duh.

Attorney Rosen: Sheriff, I'd like to say that I have counseled Mr. Tape against making any statements of any sort at this time. I have explained to him that he has a constitutional right to remain silent and that anything he says in this interview can and will be used against him in a court of law, that he may terminate this interview at any time he wishes, that he has the right to the assistance of counsel for his defense in the instant matter and in any other criminal matters of which he may be accused, that if he cannot afford an attorney one will be appointed for him by the court, that he has the right to a speedy and public trial by an impartial jury, that he has a right to be informed of the charges against him and to confront the witnesses against him, and that he may use compulsory process for obtaining evidence and witnesses in his favor. Having been thus fully informed and advised, Mr. Tape nevertheless insists on this interview.

Sheriff Pershing: Thank you, Counselor. Mr. Tape, is what Attorney Rosen said correct?

Philo Tape: Sure, four-eyes here told me all that.

Sheriff Pershing: There's no need for disrespect, Mr. Tape.

Attorney Rosen: It's his manner, Sheriff. I think it's hobo talk. He calls you "the walrus" because of your mustache.

Sheriff Pershing: I've been called worse, Counselor. Mr. Tape, for the rest of the interview, could we please dispense with hobo talk and call each other Mr. Tape, Sheriff, Counselor, Detective, and Deputy? Is that okay?

Philo Tape: Sure, Sheriff.

Sheriff Pershing: Thank you, Mr. Tape. So, you understood all that your counselor here told you?

Philo Tape: Yes.

Sheriff Pershing: Thank you, Mr. Tape. Has anyone promised you anything, threatened anything, or pressured you in any way?

Philo Tape: Oh, for Chrissake, no. Can we just get on with this?

Sheriff Pershing: Just doing my job, Mr. Tape. So, then, Mr. Tape, what, if anything, would you like to tell us this evening?

Philo Tape: I want a rematch.

Sheriff Pershing: What do you mean, Mr. Tape?

Philo Tape: I want a rematch with that Nick Cameron hunk.

Sheriff Pershing: Mr. Cameron says you broke down the back door of the trailer and came at him with a rock pick. Do you have anything to say about that, Mr. Tape?

Philo Tape: Damn right I did, and I would have beaten the crap out of him if that big Indian hadn't rung the bell.

[Silence for about ten seconds.]

Sheriff Pershing: Counselor? Okay. Is that all you wanted to say, Mr. Tape?

Philo Tape: I killed Madero and Huerta.

[Silence for about five seconds.]

Sheriff Pershing: And who are, or were, Madero and Huerta, Mr. Tape?

Philo Tape: Oh, cut the bullshit. You know who they were. Paco Madero was the big fat-assed guy I knocked on the head with a pipe wrench in that shitty workshop of his across from the dump where you found me tonight. That stunned him, and I shoved his head into that big bowl of mud and rocks and held it there until he was dead.

"You didn't notice he'd been knocked on the head, with his head being covered in mud and all. But he was," says Frankie. "And that is not public knowledge."

Sheriff Pershing: Did you intend to kill Mr. Madero, Mr. Tape?

Philo Tape: Duh. No shit, Sherlock. Huerta was easier. I just punched him in the nose, threw him on the floor, and tipped that big geode on top of him. And I sat on it until he stopped breathing, the sneaky shit.

"Consistent with the autopsy. Broken nose and profuse bleeding," says Frankie. "Again, not public knowledge."

Sheriff Pershing: Did you intend to kill Mr. Huerta, Mr. Tape?

Philo Tape: Oh, duh. No, I just wanted to play. Of course I wanted to kill him.

Sheriff Pershing: Thank you, Mr. Tape. May I ask why you wanted to kill Madero and Huerta?

Philo Tape: They killed my friend.

[Silence for five seconds.]

Philo Tape: Last spring. The Rabid Horse Gulch derailment.

Sheriff Pershing: I remember that derailment, Mr. Tape. I read the NTSB report. A locomotive engineer was killed. Are you saying Madero and Huerta caused the derailment?

Philo Tape: Damn right they did. They took out ballast and destabilized the track bed.

Sheriff Pershing: The NTSB report attributed that to heavy rains and an unstable subgrade.

Philo Tape: Are you calling me a liar?

Sheriff Pershing: Certainly not, Mr. Tape. I think you may believe what you said is true. I'm just telling you what the report said.

Philo Tape: And I'm telling you Madero and Huerta took out ballast and destabilized the track bed.

Sheriff Pershing: And why would they do that, Mr. Tape?

Philo Tape: Because the ballast was ten percent super high-grade gold-bearing quartzite. Worth close to a million, at least.

[Silence for five seconds.]

Philo Tape: Okay, don't take my word for it. Take a close look at that pile of rocks by the gate to Madero's compound.

Sheriff Pershing: We shall, Mr. Tape, we shall. Deputy Serrucho, Nick Cameron is standing around outside somewhere, or he was. Find him and have him look at that rock pile Mr. Tape is talking about. Also tell him for me that Mr. Tape wants a rematch.

I amble over toward the cop shop, leaving Frankie on the bench. Serrucho comes out.

"Hey, Sheriff says to tell you the hobo wants a rematch," Serrucho says.

"Yeah, I bet he does. If Pershing can arrange it, I'll be there."

"And the sheriff wants you to take a look at a pile of rocks in Madero's compound."

"Why?"

"The hobo says there's gold stuff in it."

"Maybe there is. I looked at it the day Madero was killed and thought I noticed something odd about it." This is true, and it's all I can truly say. I haven't looked closely at the pile, so at this stage, anything I say about it would be a guess. I could mention Frankie's opinion, but he's not an expert anyway, so no point in it.

Serrucho drives me to the compound and up to the rock pile. I tell him to turn on his takedown lights and put his spotlight on the pile.

I really do need to look closely, especially in the bad light. I find a few pieces of the gold-bearing quartzite, take out my lighted loupe, and inspect.

"Interesting. Very fine grains, but definitely gold and a high concentration. I'd say hundreds of ounces per ton, but extraction would require some pretty fine comminution." I grab a piece of the plain ballast and hand it to Serrucho, along with my lighted loupe.

"Okay, look at that, and now look at this." I hand him a piece of the gold-bearing quartzite. "See the difference?"

"I think so. Okay, let's get back."

Serrucho drives us back and returns to the interview room with the rocks. I rejoin Frankie. I've missed a half hour of the interview, but Frankie can fill me in later.

Sheriff Pershing: Deputy Serrucho has rejoined us. Please report, Deputy.

Deputy Serrucho: I drove Mr. Nick Cameron to the compound formerly owned by Paco Madero, now owned by Francesco Benally. By the gate to the compound is a pile of crushed stone, about ten cubic yards, in my layman's estimate. The headlights of my vehicle were pointed at the pile, and at Mr. Cameron's request, I turned on the takedown lights and directed my spotlight at the pile. Mr. Cameron inspected the pile and found pieces of rock he identified with his magnifier as gold-bearing quartzite. He provided me with these samples of that, and with these samples of the base material, which he identified as other quartzite superficially resembling the gold-bearing quartzite. Mr. Cameron estimated the gold-bearing quartzite would yield hundreds of ounces of gold per ton but said because of the fine grain, gold extraction would require very fine communition.

Philo Tape: Comminution.

Sheriff Pershing: Thank you for that excellent report, Deputy Serrucho, and thank you for the correction, Mr. Tape. Deputy Serrucho, did Mr. Cameron estimate what percentage of the pile might be gold-bearing quartzite?

Deputy Serrucho: I asked him that on the drive back, Sheriff, and he said that judging from the surface layer, ten percent by volume might be a reasonable estimate. But he also said that without sectioning the pile any estimate would be speculative.

Philo Tape: I told you so.

Sheriff Pershing: I did not contradict you, Mr. Tape, I simply sought confirmation. Mr. Cameron has a PhD in geology from the University of Arizona and is qualified to provide that confirmation.

Philo Tape: Could I have more water?

Sheriff Pershing: We could all use a break. Five minutes. I'll leave the cameras running. Deputy Serrucho, could you please ask someone in dispatch to bring us five bottles of water?

Frankie grins. "You missed the DPS guy asking about the radio museum and the Metaxas girl. It was great. His whole theory of the case dissolving before his eyes. White Buns was baffled. Obviously, he had never heard of the radio museum, and he didn't connect your lady friend with the Metaxas name. Why would he, right? Anyway, the Magyrak guy kept at it, and finally White Buns said, 'Just shut your damn piehole. I don't know anything about your Greek prostitute and her dumbassed radio museum.' Then Pershing—good old Gentlemen John—said there was no reason to call Miss Metaxas a prostitute, and White Buns apologized."

Oh, man. First Lou from Winnipeg and now White Buns.

"Hey, Frankie," I say, "I haven't been spending much time online. Have I missed something? Are Greek prostitutes a thing now?"

Frankie looks up, thoughtfully, then fiddles with his phone doing Google searches and counting results. "'Greek prostitutes' seems an anomalously common reference, and notably so, if you adjust for the small population of Greece compared to other countries," he says. "But I think it results primarily from the abundance of Greek historical sources, especially from the classical period."

A sound hypothesis, in my opinion. I do my own googling and don't see a notable spike in search frequency on the term. But references to "Greek prostitutes" outnumber references to "Scottish prostitutes" four to one. Time to change the subject.

"Did White Buns say anything about the railroad bull?" I say.

"Oh, yes. He told the whole story about finding the gold-bearing quartzite in the hopper car, getting the bull to fudge the routing, watching where it was used, harvesting, refining, blah blah blah. Just as we inferred. He said he was always careful to replace every piece of quartzite he took with a piece of granite. His friend was an engineer, so he didn't want to compromise the track bed. Take a rock, leave a rock."

Frankie drinks from his water bottle. "He said Madero and Huerta found out the bull was dealing opiates and threatened to tell the cops if he didn't cooperate. So the bull told Madero and Huerta where the ballast was used. They went crazy removing it, which led to the derailment. In White Buns's view, that made the bull as guilty as Madero and Huerta."

I'm curious about why White Buns would gratuitously skewer the railroad bull with a ballast fork when he was already dead. I ask about it.

"He said he went there to kill him and thought he was dead drunk, but once he speared him, it was obvious he was just dead. No reflex action and little blood. Again, details not known publicly, further corroborating his story."

I'm wondering if Rosen said anything about *Revolutionary*

Rocks v. Cholla Railroad Inc. He did. Frankie says he must have raised his hand or something because Pershing said, "Counselor?" and then Rosen said he had handled a civil case involving a carload of railroad ballast owned by one of Madero and Huerta's companies that was misrouted in Winslow and delivered by Cholla Railroad to a contractor who was doing track bed maintenance for them. But that the case did not touch on how the misrouting occurred or the precise nature of the crushed stone the car contained or whether the contractor used it, and if so where, and various other disclaimers that went on and on until you weren't completely sure the car existed in the first place. And then Rosen said maybe Madero and Huerta imported another car of crushed stone that got misrouted in Winslow too, and the civil case had nothing to do with the car White Buns was talking about. Eventually, Pershing stopped him and said, "Let's talk about this later, Counselor."

I still don't get why White Buns was after me and Theo, so I ask about that too. Turns out he'd seen me at rock shows with Madero, and when he saw me at Madero's compound looking at the ballast pile, he figured I was in on it. But when Pershing and Serrucho were taking him out the front door of the trailer tonight, he saw the ballast pile was still there. Then he knew I wasn't in on it, otherwise I would have gotten it out of there. So he's sorry about the rock pick, but he still wants a rematch. As for Theo, he didn't mention her at all. Frankie thinks he thought we were a couple, so he could find me wherever he found her, which is why he put a tracker on her car. He didn't say anything about following us to Superior and Bayfield, but why confess to being thwarted, right? And he didn't mention anything about me and Ambrose and Isaac taking his stash.

The next question is why Frankie had us take White Buns's stash and then unload it five miles away. As always, Frankie has an answer.

"To keep it on the rez. See, the railroad deeded that right-of-way to the nation after they decommissioned the spur last year. So the ballast might be tribal property. Interesting legal question, though. A lawyer might argue it's really property of the estates of Madero and Huerta, given they were deprived of it by fraud, but then they settled the lawsuit about it, so maybe not. I don't know who legally owns it, but I know I don't. And the point was just to lure White Buns, not to steal his stash."

Sheriff Pershing: Are we ready to continue?

Philo Tape: Is it hot in here?

Sheriff Pershing: Doesn't seem hot to me, but we can make it cooler. Deputy Serrucho, could you please do that?"

Deputy Serrucho: Yes, sir.

Philo Tape: I think I need something to eat. I feel queasy.

Sheriff Pershing: Are you having trouble breathing, Mr. Tape?

Philo Tape: A little, maybe. I think it's just heartburn. Got some Tums?

Sheriff Pershing: Serrucho, run over and get the paramedics. [*Shouting after Serrucho*] And tell them we need to get Mr. Tape to the clinic immediately!

We see Serrucho bolt to the fire station next door.

Philo Tape: I feel a little better. I think it's just heartburn. I'll be okay.

Sheriff Pershing: You don't look okay, Mr. Tape. You need to see a doctor. Owing to a possible medical emergency, we are ending the interview at 23:27.

"Is he having a heart attack?" I say.
"That would be my guess," says Frankie, "but a mild one. I'm sure he'll be all right."

34

THE PATIENT
IS RESTING COMFORTABLY

They have White Buns on his way to the clinic in four minutes. They call it a clinic, but it's really a clinic with a ten-bed hospital grafted on. We're a hundred miles from the nearest real hospital.

"I need coffee," says Frankie. Usually, Frankie doesn't drink coffee in the evening, but this isn't a normal evening.

We drive to the Flying Mulewhip, which is open twenty-four hours. The amateur mule portraits have been sold, amazingly, including the mule apotheosis I was sitting under when we started this crazy-assed story. Now the eponymous mulewhips are everywhere, flanking posters of Ronald Reagan in his role as host of *Death Valley Days*, shilling for 20 Mule Team Borax. Not to knock borax. Aside from laundry, it's very useful for artisanal gold extraction. If the railroad bull had used it instead of mercury, he wouldn't have been drooling like a dachshund when I met him.

Frankie wants more than coffee and orders the chicken-fried steak. Oddly for him, he flirts a little with the waitress, who is quite a dish. Lisa is her name, if you're interested.

The first thing I do is text Trixie. *How's fishing?* This was our prearranged all-clear code for Theo. The county attorney still

hasn't taken her case to the grand jury, and after tonight's reve-
lations, he won't. I don't expect Trixie to respond until morning,
given the late hour.

Next, I step outside and call Jing. It's close to 02:00 if she's in
Chicago but my time if she's in Los Angeles, PDT being the same
as MST, which Arizona, being smart, remains on year-round.

She's in Denver and says she's coming to Phoenix on Sunday
and wants to see me. Why not? I tell her I can meet at Andretti's
restaurant in Scottsdale for dinner at 17:30. It's a short drive from
there to my townhouse in the Scottsdale Backspin Club, which
Jing will surely want to see.

So now is the time to tell Frankie about my fooling Jing and
the Ministry of State Security into thinking the Emilio Rayón
mine wasn't worked out. And I do.

"Well, that would explain the mine lease and the drama at the
mine," says Frankie.

I expect him to launch his usual barrage of questions, but he
doesn't. He goes back to his double helping of chicken-fried steak.
A few minutes later, he starts the barrage. This goes very fast, so
you'll get the effect better if I write it as a Q&A.

Q: You knew the ore was from the Emilio Rayón mine,
but you asked Jing for an analysis anyway. Why?

A: Because I thought she was a spook, and how she
answered might confirm that.

Q: When she told you the guys at Tsinghua said it came
from the Ocotillo Mines, why did you think they were
lying instead of mistaken?

A: Tsinghua is the best university in Asia. They wouldn't
make that mistake. There's a chance they might not

identify it as from the Emilio Rayón mine, but they couldn't possibly think it came from the Ocotillo Mines. It's like mistaking an elk for a beaver.

Q: Therefore, you concluded they were lying and trying to send you on a snipe hunt?

A: Yes. So I decided to send them on a snipe hunt. I told Jing a guy told me the ore came from a Mexican mine people thought was worked out but really wasn't, and he wanted me to bankroll him leasing the mine.

Q: And you knew Jing had seen the ore in the railroad bull's shed, and that the sample you gave her looked like the same stuff, correct?

A: Yes.

Q: And you knew she would think you got the ore from the shed, right?

A: Yes. I didn't tell her where I got it, and where else would she think I got it? She wouldn't think I picked it up on a railroad track.

Q: Exactly. And did you know Jing would think the railroad bull was the imaginary pitchman who wanted you to bankroll the mine lease?

A: Yes, probably, anyway.

Q: And that Jing would think if the railroad bull was pitching the story to a PhD geologist, the story was likely

true—or at least something the bull believed was true—
because a PhD geologist would be the last person he'd try
to scam with a bogus mine story?

A: I didn't think of that, but yes, good point.

Q: And that Jing would take the presence of an ample
quantity of ore in the bull's shed as convincing evidence
the mine really was not worked out, corroborating your
fable?

A: Yes.

Q: And did you think Jing would infer you harpooned
the railroad bull to keep the mine all to your pinchfist,
lickpenny Scottish self?

A: Possibly. No, probably. She seemed to know a lot about
Scotland.

Frankie goes silent. He flags down Lisa for a refill on his coffee. Then he looks at me with his poker face, which is the face he
wears about 99 percent of the time. I have no idea what he's thinking, but then I rarely do, and if I do, it's some sort of telepathy.

"It's the completest thing, Nick," Frankie says. "I'm seriously
impressed. In twenty-five words or less, you convinced one of the
smartest intelligence agencies in the world that gold would gush
from a worthless mine. Then for a kicker, you convinced them
you are a ruthless PhD assassin who calmly aids police at the
scene of his heinous crimes. And they can't do anything about
any of it."

"Can't they? They don't know the railroad bull killed himself,
so they might try blackmail, not that it would work."

"No. Jing is the source for all their information, and they know you know that. They think you'd just whack her if they tried blackmail, and she's not a throwaway. Even if you didn't whack her, would the MSS want their agent testifying in an American court? And they probably think you recorded your calls with Jing, which I'm sure you did. You know she's a spook, and you could spill the beans on her any time you please. So even if they were completely sure you killed the railroad bull, they still would not try blackmail. I bet they think you have something fiendish going on, and they want Jing to find out what it is. You're holding a full house, and they have a pair of deuces."

Silence for a minute. Frankie expects me to say something.

"Okay," I say, "but for all that, it would take a real gomeril of an intelligence analyst to recommend spilling a big wad on a mine lease without a survey."

"We don't know what the MSS recommended. Likely the information got forwarded on to some mining company, and they went crazy with it. And Doña Cartucho telling them the mine was hopelessly worked out and refusing to lease it at first? That probably just convinced them she had another offer pending, say from your imaginary pitchman, and your story was true. Greedy people would never think she was being honest and honorable."

Frankie sips on his coffee, then resumes.

"And now Joyful Cow Mining, or whoever it is, does a cursory survey, finds no evidence of unmined gold, and whines to the MSS. And they will reply, 'We said it was credible and plausible, but we also said we could not confirm it, so this is on you, sucker.' Unless Joyful Cow Mining has an in with the State Council, in which case there will be some serious groveling at the MSS."

Frankie sips more coffee and becomes pensive. After a few minutes, we talk about what comes next at the mine. We conclude the MSS and Joyful Cow won't give up. They'll think there's an undetected exploration shaft or something like that. Seriously, what other explanation can they think of? That all the ore in the bull's shed came from a stash hidden by Villistas a hundred years ago, mixed with track ballast, and gleaned by a hobo? Doña Cartucho won't tell them anything, that's for sure.

And they won't find out about White Buns's confession either. Pershing and the DPS will not publicly announce that incredibly rich gold ore can be picked up on spur tracks between Gallup and Flagstaff. They can see the headlines:

Gold Rush Halts Rail Traffic
Supply Chain Breaks
Railroads Blame Arizona Police
National Guard Activated

Once they've gone over the site of the Rabid Horse Gulch derailment and the other four sites, and after Cholla Railroad has cleaned them up, they might talk. Probably not even then. The good thing is that Frankie already knows what sites need to be cleaned up, thanks to Ambrose and Isaac, who, I bet, have helped themselves along the way, which is why Ambrose wants my 911. He probably has the bills in a paper bag waiting for me.

It's 01:30 when Frankie orders two slices of pie.

I notice flashing lights, lots of them, over at the clinic. I can't see them directly, but I can see their reflections on the clinic walls. Frankie has his back to the window and can't see them at all.

"Hey, take a look over there," I say.

Frankie looks. "Hmm. Maybe bringing in people from an accident on I-10 or something."

"Want to go take a look?"

"No. I don't know about you, but once I finish this pie, I'm ready for bed."

Lisa brings the check, and Frankie flirts a bit. Oddly for him, he pays with his debit card. Usually, he pays in cash. We drive to his place. I imagine the cops are done at Madero's old double-wide, but Frankie's place is nicer anyway. I'd prefer my garbage truck, but I'm not getting Leonard out of bed at 02:00.

I conk out as soon as I hit the bed. But I don't sleep well. Around 03:00 there's a helicopter flying around. Maybe evacuating White Buns to Phoenix. I go back to sleep. The sun is well up when I wake at 07:00.

I pick up my phone from the nightstand and google *Quartz-rock news*. The first thing that pops up is ABC15 in Phoenix: "Alleged Murderer Escapes Hospital in Quartzrock."

"Frankie!" I shout. "White Buns escaped."

"Yeah, I read it already. Pershing called me at oh-five-hun-dred and told me about it too."

"He'll take a lot of heat for this."

"Not at all. He handed White Buns off to the DPS guys. They were waiting for an okay to transport him to a hospital in Phoenix. He escaped from their custody."

"So Pershing gets credit for the arrest and the confession, and the DPS gets blamed for the escape?"

"You got it."

There's something suspicious about this. I join Frankie in the kitchen. He's unloading the dishwasher, and I thank him for waiting until I was awake to do that. "How did it happen?" I ask.

It's a strange story, Frankie says. They took White Buns to the clinic, and an EKG suggested inferior myocardial infarction. They gave him a troponin I test, and it was high, supporting that diagnosis. But he seemed okay, blood pressure and pulse and oxygen level and so on all good.

They had him in a little room by the emergency entrance. A tall, dark woman with a doctor's badge came in and kicked out the DPS detective. She accused him of touching her improperly. The detective says she brushed against him. She was a dish, possibly a barn burner, but older. But the detective was older too.

The detective stayed in the hall with two other DPS guys. He was terrified of being accused of sexual assault. After five minutes, he tried the door, and it wouldn't open. A wedge cam was glued under the door with cyanoacrylate. They broke down the door, the window was open, and White Buns and the doctor were gone. No outside camera watches that area. Just trees and lantana bushes there. It's like White Buns and the doctor, or whoever she was, just vanished.

"They must have something to go on," I say. I take a cup from the dishwasher and put it in the Keurig, which happens to lack water, and he's moved the coffee too.

"Not much," Frankie says. "The orderly at the emergency entrance said he saw an old Black guy walking across the parking lot but didn't get a good look at him. He was wearing a MAGA hat and carrying a spaghetti squash, believe it or not. Aside from that, and a pretty poor description of the woman, who had a slight French accent, nothing. She was wearing nitrile gloves, by the way. Not unusual for a doctor."

Frankie sees I'm confused and points to a cupboard over the microwave. There's the coffee.

"Didn't they have a cop posted outside?" I say.

"They did, patrolling the west side of the building, but he walked over to the parking lot to check out the old Black guy. Thought he was trying to steal a BMW. But when he got to the BMW, all he found was the spaghetti squash with 'Sucker!' written on it with a Sharpie. They think they'll find prints or DNA or something on it, but I doubt that. If they do, it will be prints and DNA from the produce guys at Fry's."

"And the helicopter I heard last night?"

"Searching for them with super-duper night vision stuff. Unsuccessfully."

The Keurig says *descale*, but Frankie can deal with that later. Like I said before, he drinks coffee rarely, and he's probably never had the descale warning come on before.

"Pershing must have asked you if you had any ideas about this, right?" I say.

"Of course. I told him the EKG result could happen if leads were misplaced, likely V1 and/or V2. Maybe White Buns moved them. Cardiologists get referrals from those screwups all the time. A PA or a GP could easily be confused by that, especially at 00:30 in the morning, and especially given the troponin I test."

My coffee finally stops dribbling. This thing really does need a descale. "Kind of hard to fake the troponin test, though, right?" I say.

"True, but maybe he didn't fake it."

"He really did have a heart attack?"

"Or maybe he ran fifteen miles before he showed up at the trailer. Remember how sweaty and smelly he was? Say he ran most of the way from Hope. You said the guy is a distance runner, remember? Endurance running notably elevates cardiac troponins I and T, NT-proBNP, and creatine kinase-MB. There's an article about that in one of the AHA journals, December 2018, as I recall."

"Okay," I say, throwing the used Keurig cup in the garbage. "Why would he get himself busted; confess to two murders, burglary, aggravated assault, and despoiling a corpse or whatever they call it; and then execute a carefully planned escape?"

"To show how smart he is. To flout the law. And to reveal who caused the Rabid Horse Gulch derailment."

"And coincidentally, to clear Theo?"

Frankie shrugs, then goes to the refrigerator, gets bacon, and puts six strips in the frying pan.

I think Frankie planned it all. That long midnight supper at the Flying Mulewhip, designed to give him an irrefutable alibi if anyone suggested he had anything to do with the escape? If he hadn't overdone it with the coffee and the flirting and the debit card, he might have fooled me too.

And this explains what Frankie and White Buns were talking about while I was outside waiting for the cops to arrive. It also explains why White Buns didn't mention our stealing his stash. Frankie told him not to. Because Frankie had us move it far from tracks that will soon be crawling with law enforcement agents to a place where White Buns can remove it at his leisure.

But I'm glad Frankie kept me in the dark. Even now, I don't have any real evidence he planned it. I just think he did. Only one thing bugs me. I've got a damn good idea of who the escape artists were. And I'd really like to know how he managed to make them and White Buns disappear. But I can't ask him.

35

CONFIDENTIAL TO THE READER (BY FRANKIE)

THIS IS FRANKIE

Yes, I planned the escape. And I kept Nick in the dark to protect him in the extremely unlikely event this blows up. He's suspicious, but he's suspicious because of clues that mean something to him and would be laughable to anyone else.

As you know from Nick's able summary about the radio museum, even if we revealed all the facts about the conspiracy to the cops—and there is still plenty they don't know, even after the Scrool bust—it would just give Ms. Metaxas an even stronger reason for wanting Madero and Huerta whacked. Nothing I discovered would help her.

I know what you're wondering. After I figured out the real motive, why not go to Sheriff Pershing and give him the facts? Great question. But what would I tell Pershing? "There was this soldadera who makes Wonder Woman look like Little Miss Muffet, and she tips off Pancho Villa about some high-grade gold ore and the Villistas come to get it, but the US Cavalry also comes, so the Villistas bury it and some of them escape, and then their great-grandsons go to get it, but soldadera's great-granddaughter's boyfriend kicks their asses because she was having her hair braided and couldn't personally kick their asses, and then soldadera's great-granddaughter splits the loot with them, and they mix it with crushed stone and import it, but a hobo finds it and a railroad bull reroutes the car and . . ."

That dog won't hunt, as Sheriff Pershing would say. It would take me all day to convince Pershing, let alone anyone else. I don't have time for that. Once I've figured something out, I want to move on. I don't do this for profit, you know. I do it for fun.

The easiest way to conclude the case quickly was for White Buns to confess—and with a confession that could be given only by the true murderer. But that would leave me with a problem. As you know, I don't think White Buns deserves to rot in prison for whacking Madero and Huerta.

So the obvious solution was confession followed by escape.

It was easy to lure White Buns. I knew he would come, and I knew he would run the distance from Hope. I knew I would have at least ten minutes with him after I sent Nick outside to call 911. That was plenty of time to explain the escape plan, which I knew would work because my research told me White Buns was trained as an Air Force medic and could play his part perfectly.

And you know who the escape artists were. I told Sordo the MAGA hat and the spaghetti squash were over-the-top, but he thought it was a good joke and might confound the police. It may. I hear they're thinking the old Black guy in the MAGA hat is probably a vegan.

I said I don't do this for profit, and I don't. But I told White Buns I'm out of pocket about $20K on this case. He said he'd make good on that. And I know he will.

And no, I'm not telling you how I made everybody disappear. Trade secrets, as Nick would say.

That's all until next time, and thanks for reading.

BACK TO NICK

36

THE PATIENT IS STILL RESTING COMFORTABLY

"There's something that didn't come out in the interview but will come out when they delve into White Buns's past," Frankie says. "The engineer was White Buns's partner, not just his friend. And not like 'howdy, pardner.' Like 'significant other' pardner. I picked that up from the engineer's obituary. It's online. You had to read between the lines, but if you did, it was obvious. I confirmed it with other research."

"That explains a lot. The ferocity of the attacks, in particular. So White Buns is gay?"

"Does it matter? If someone kills your true love, it's natural to take revenge. Excusable, in my worldview, regardless of what the law says."

Maybe. Seems to me there's a risk of mistakenly taking revenge on an innocent party. For example, White Buns trying to take revenge on me. But I understand where Frankie's coming from. He's half Italian, after all. Not that a Highlander would think differently.

"He may be AC/DC," Frankie continues. "I don't have any evidence to confirm or refute that, and I don't care. But he's not exclusively gay."

"How do you know that?"

Frankie leans forward, both hands on the kitchen counter, and raises his eyes to heaven.

"Beware of statistical syllogisms, Nick. Leave them to dumbassed lawyers and profilers. I know White Buns is not exclusively gay because his lover the locomotive engineer was a woman."

I feel like I've been dealt a trick question, but yes, female locomotive engineers exist, and I should have thought of that.

Frankie continues. "The obituary was also where I found out that White Buns was Philo Tape. A former mining engineer, interestingly. Why former, I don't know. Maybe he just got tired of it and preferred the life of a hobo."

Could be. I've seen people walk away from careers for all kinds of reasons or for no reason at all. Funny thing is that it usually works out for the best.

Frankie removes the bacon and breaks six eggs into the hot grease.

Jing calls.

"Is that Jing?" says Frankie.

I nod as I pick up and put the phone on speaker. "Hey, Jing. What's happening?"

"I'm still on schedule to leave Denver today, so I'll be in Phoenix Sunday."

"We still on for dinner?"

"Yes, and I'd love to see your place in the Backspin Club."

Frankie grins. This is the 1 percent of the time when he cracks his poker face.

"I think you'll like it. It's very upscale."

"I would expect no less from you, Nick. And have you talked with that person who tried to scam you on the mine deal?"

Frankie's grin widens.

"No, he's been very quiet lately."

Frankie is quaking with suppressed laughter.

"And he never mentioned the name of the mine?"

"Oh, yes, he did, I remember now. Nylon or Rayon or something like that. But he said the mine was in Mexico. He said it petered out and was abandoned, but years later, somebody sunk some boreholes and found an isolated part of the lode, detached by faulting when the region was structurally active. But of course the guy died before he could exploit it."

I've never seen Frankie so close to cracking up.

"That sounds like quite a tale," Jing says.

"Jing, you would not believe how many bogus mine stories are floating around out there. It's usually some old prospector who dies in total squalor but gasps out vague clues to the location of a fabulously rich mine with his last words. Or scrawls the clues in an old ledger and his great-great-grandson finds them. These scammers can't even come up with a new plot. At least this Nylon/Rayon mine story was refreshingly believable. Except for the dying part. That was trite."

"Well, I'll see you at Andretti's at 17:30 tomorrow. I'd love to hear more about your dissertation on hydrogen wells. At least that's something real. I need to run now."

"Okay. Call me when you get to Phoenix. See ya."

Frankie has recovered and reverted to his poker face. He rolls his eyes.

"That was quite a performance, Nick," he says. "I predict Joyful Cow Mining will have a drill team on its way within twenty-four hours. But I also think the Ministry of State Security views the mine as a sideshow. The MSS is after big stuff. Like, for example, unlimited clean energy from hydrogen wells. It's you they're after, laddie. Only one thing worries me about this."

"What?"

"You. Because, let's face it, you like women and could fall prey to Jing's . . . uh . . ."

"Strumpety stratagems."

"Very good," Frankie says, nodding. "I was worried you'd say 'wiles.' I predict that at dinner, she will talk only briefly about your dissertation, then rush you into a bout of unbridled strumpetry. After that, and it may take awhile, she will occasionally act troubled but will keep a happy face. More strumpetry will occur. This could go on for weeks or months. It might wear out even you. Eventually, you will ask what is troubling her, and she will tell you she is under pressure from MSS, that they are threatening her or her family, and she needs to come up with useful information, or else. It's an old one, but it often works. She won't offer you money for secrets because she knows you don't need money."

"What do you suggest?"

"At dinner, talk about an imaginary fiancée. Model her on some woman you know to keep your story straight, just don't use her real name. Call her Catriona MacGregor. Must be thousands of them. Now, if Jing makes a strumpety sortie, tell her you are engaged to this mythical Catriona and will not be unfaithful. Tell her it would cause a clan war or something. You could spin that yarn all night. And you didn't act like a horndog in Winslow, right? So she might believe you. I'm not sure what she would do next, though. I'll need to think more about this."

Why not send the MSS on another snipe hunt? I can come up with a process for increasing the hydrogen output of natural geochemical reactors that won't work but sounds plausible enough to waste lots of time and money. I'll noodle on this while Frankie is noodling on his scheme.

Now Chanda calls. Again, on speaker.

"Nick, where are you?" she says.

Frankie grins.

"Chanda, my yoga princess! I'm in Quartzrock. I had some business here."

"Is that where the murderer escaped? It was on NPR."

"Alleged murderer. Yes. Yes, he definitely escaped. Gave them the slip. Hightailed it. Absquatulated. Went on the lam."

"I love how you talk. When are you coming back? My mother wants to meet you."

"Things are a little confused here right now. Maybe in a week or two."

"I finished the Car of Juggernaut."

"Excellent. I love that thing," I say. It's true, I think it's very cool. "Can't wait to see it. Send me a photo. We could turn it into a robot. Say, Chanda, I'm with a friend, Frankie. You talked with him, right?"

"Yes, say hello for me."

"We're sitting down to breakfast. Could I call you in an hour?"

"Sure, Nick."

Chanda likes to talk, so that could have gone on for at least an hour.

We eat.

I'm cleaning up the dishes—Frankie does it if I cook, I do it if he cooks—when Trixie calls.

"Trixie, my Viking princess, how are you?" I say.

Frankie shakes his head and rolls his eyes.

"I'm fine. You're in Quartzrock, right? Did you hear about that murderer escaping? It was on ABC."

"Alleged murderer. Yes, I heard something about it."

"Sounds fab. Anyway, I drove down to Damp Lake and told Theodora everything's okay, but she wants to stay there. Something about a hobo on the loose."

"That's silly. A hobo was after me, but we're all copacetic with the hobo now. She can go home."

"I'll tell her. But I think she likes it there. She wants to buy the cabin."

"Well, that's between you two. How's fishing?"

"It's great! Most profitable week I've had in three years. When are you coming back?"

"Things are a little confused here right now. Maybe in a week or two."

"Okay, let me know. It'll be good to have you back."

I didn't know Theo's real name was Theodora. Wasn't the Empress Theodora a Greek prostitute before she married Justinian?

My phone rings. It's Theo. Frankie nods repeatedly.

"Theo, my love. Where are you?" I say.

"Damp Lake. I have a Verizon cell signal. There must be a new tower."

"That's great! Say, things are all cleared up with White Buns. He was never after you anyway."

"Really?"

"Yes. It's all taken care of. So, when can I see you again?"

Brief silence.

"I wanted to ask you if you could come and stay a week at our cabin on Madeline Island," she says.

"You couldn't keep me away. It'll be a week or two before I can get back there, though."

"That's fine. Just let me know a few days in advance so I can get things opened up. It's still winterized."

"Will do. Say, I picked up something I know you'll like. A small ceramic group, done by a guy who studied under Picasso."

"Really?"

"He says he studied under Picasso, but I think he's lying. The dogs are great, though."

"Dogs?"

"Yes, it's a dog flamenco troupe. The singer is a bulldog, the guitarist is a spaniel, and the dancer is a Chihuahua. I'll text you a photo."

We talk for a few minutes, and I say I'll call her tomorrow.

Frankie is sitting at the dining table, his head buried in his hands. He straightens up and looks out the sliding door toward the mountains.

"Nick," he says, "why are you continuing this ridiculous four-way crane dance? Why can't you just tell Chanda and Trixie and Jing you're not interested? You've made your decision. You're red-hot on Theo or Siobhan or Theodora or whatever she calls herself, and she's obviously white-hot on you."

"When the time is right," I say. Frankie doesn't know that I have a hard rule, ten on the Mohs Hardness Scale, that I don't end relationships, even incipient ones, over the phone or with text messages, email, WhatsApp, and so on. I do it in person, over a good meal in a nice restaurant. Finding a nice restaurant will pose a challenge in Ashland and Superior, but we can make do.

Frankie can't let it go. He gives me advice like I'm his younger brother. "Remember that thing I've told you a thousand times?" he says.

"Avoid the damsel in distress?"

"No, the other thing I've told you a thousand times."

Frankie has told me dozens of proverbs thousands of times, but from context, I take a guess.

"It is well that we should be kind to women in the strength of our manhood, for we lie in their hands at both ends of our lives."

"That's the one. Think about it."

"Okay," I say.

"And I mean think seriously about it, Nick. Tonight we'll talk more about Jing. Right now, I need to work."

"Could I borrow your truck?" I say. "Leonard wants me to check out some selenite lamps with him. He wants to give the Truck Stop a rocks motif."

"Sure. Go ahead. If you're near Fry's, pick up a spaghetti squash."

BOOTY AND DJIBOUTI

Frankie keeps his keys on a hook by the door. I get in the truck and start it up, but the accelerator won't budge. I take a gander. Something is crammed under the pedal.

It's a gold bar, unmarked mill bullion, about twenty troy ounces, with a Post-it Note attached: *Tell Nick I'll be at Marcello's boxing gym in Melrose Park on July 27. I'll get that Dumas manuscript for you. Give me a month.*

I don't like this. I'm okay sparring with White Buns, and I'll be at Marcello's on the twenty-seventh. But the Dumas manuscript concerns me, and I'll tell you why.

Way back at the beginning of this crazy tale I told the cops about La Pierre de la Chienne, or Dogstone. Told it the way Frankie told it to me years ago. Jesuit missionaries from New France presented an exquisite Petoskey stone to Louis XIV, and he had it set in the bejeweled collar of his favorite dog, Bonne, who admired it for hours each day in the Hall of Mirrors. It fascinated her, and because of that, it fascinated Louis, giving rise to unwholesome rumors about him and the dog. But I digress. Louis and Bonne were long dead in 1792 when rioting revolutionaries ransacked the royal treasury and stole the Dogstone along with the rest of the French crown jewels. Most of the jewels were later recovered, but not the Dogstone. Frankie says all this is attested in reliable sources from the seventeenth and eighteenth centuries.

Everybody knows that story, or at least everybody who cares about the bijouterie of Louis XIV's dogs. But there's more to it.

Frankie picked up the rest of the story in the early '00s when he was at Camp Lemonnier in Djibouti. He was drinking mineral water at a café in Djibouti City. I think that was his job, to hang out in cafés and observe. He must have stood out like the Hound of the Baskervilles crashing the Westminster Dog Show, but maybe that was intentional. If people take a good look at you, you get a good look at them, right? Anyway, he was ready to leave when an old guy walked up and addressed him in French, which—unusual as it is for a Navajo or anyone else from Arizona—Frankie knows pretty well. The guy was a Foreign Legion retiree with badly fitting dentures that migrated around his mouth and he happened to be drunk, so Frankie had trouble understanding him. He thought Frankie was from Laos, and if you saw Frankie, you'd understand how he could be mistaken for a supersized Laotian. Of course, Frankie didn't correct him because the waiter and others in the café overheard the drunken legionary and thereafter assumed Frankie was indeed Laotian. The guy spent hours telling Frankie his life story and eventually mentioned that his father was a jeweler and *un lapidaire*. So Frankie asked him if he'd heard of the Dogstone.

The legionary must have been a soulmate because he fell into Frankie-like total silence for a minute. Then he looked around. The crowd in the café had thinned out, so he drew his chair close to Frankie, ordered another drink, and spilled his beans.

The Dogstone was never lost. One of the revolutionaries who pillaged the royal treasury in 1792 was a dog lover who hid the Dogstone and formed a secret cult—Les Gardiens de la Pierre de la Chienne—that has guarded it ever since. Charles de Gaulle, a noted dog lover, was allegedly grand master of the cult from 1940 until his death in 1970.

Frankie asked the legionary where he heard the story. He had a credible explanation. He heard it from two aged Vichy fugitives who had been ordered by Marshal Pétain to find the Dogstone but failed. They fled France in 1944, relentlessly pursued by ferocious Gardiens, partisans, the British Special Operations Executive, the OSS, and of course a few Germans. They ended up in Eritrea, where the legionary ran into them in a gambling den in the early 1990s, still watching their backs.

Fast-forward to 2018. Paco Madero and Joey Huerta had an exceptionally beautiful, iridescent Petoskey stone, so beautiful they gave it a name: the "Charlevoix Blue." But nobody would offer them more than a few thousand for it. Then they heard a shady French collector was obsessed with the Dogstone, so they cooked up a story to make him think the Charlevoix Blue was it. They told him Charles de Gaulle spirited the Dogstone out of France in 1940 and pledged it as security for a Mexican loan to the Free French. Madero's grandpa (or Huerta's, depending on who told the tale) snitched it from a diplomatic bag in Veracruz before it could get to Mexico City. Long story short, Paco and Joey played stupid, pretending they didn't know the actual Dogstone would be worth twenty or thirty million, and accepted the collector's offer of $800K. The collector couldn't resist taking advantage of these Mexican yokels and hopped a plane to CDG gloating over his triumph while Paco and Joey declared open bar at the Mulewhip Roadhouse.

And that's the story I told the cops at the start of this tale.

Fast-backward to Djibouti City in the early '00s. Intrigued by the legionary's story, Frankie bought him drinks to keep him talking, and although the upper plate of his dentures fell out at one point, the old guy continued telling the tale until he passed out. Frankie arranged his transport home, delivering the old man's comatose carcass along with his dentures wrapped in a bar towel to his unappreciative wife who, interestingly, was Laotian.

But before he passed out, Beau Geste, or whatever his name

was, told Frankie about the Dumas manuscript. Apparently, Alexandre Dumas owed a big gambling debt to a Belgian coal baron who was a fan of his, and the guy agreed to accept a short novel as payment. The result was *The Son of D'Artagnan and the Dogstone* (or *Le fils de D'Artagnan et la Pierre de la Chienne*, as Frankie would say it), which Dumas knocked out in a week. He told the coal baron the story contained cryptic clues to where the Dogstone was hidden. The few French scholars who have read the manuscript say it's embarrassingly bad work that would have ruined Dumas's literary reputation if published. They think he made up the thing about the clues so the coal baron would keep the manuscript secret and spend the rest of his life trying to figure it out. But nobody knows for sure, and it remains unpublished, occasionally inspected, and under heavy guard by cryptographers who find nothing but can't rule out the possibility there's something there. Today it sits in the collection of Ben Weidner, a Francophile fitness mogul in Los Angeles.

Now Frankie wants to crack it. He says he's decrypted the fourth message on that dorky Kryptos sculpture at CIA headquarters and a fifth one that nobody knows about yet, so he may succeed with *The Son of D'Artagnan and the Dogstone*. I hope he does. But if I'm not careful, he'll have me crawling through the sewers of Paris looking for the Dogstone while he eats truffled foie gras at the Hôtel de Crillon.

The gold bar I yanked from under the accelerator pedal is stained with railroad grease, so I clean it with a dashboard wipe. It looks about 920 fine, consistent with the Emilio Rayón ore assay, and it's crudely cast, so it must be the railroad bull's handiwork, grant him eternal peace. I shove the clean bar under the driver's seat, crumple White Buns's Post-it Note, toss it into my mouth, and chew. It tastes like boxcar.

I'll brief Frankie later.

$$\vdash$$

REFERENCES

Nick always gives credit to his sources, but he can be a real prick about not giving citations for his sources. Therefore, I, his unappreciated author, have prepared these citations for him, at my usual hourly rate. Hey, Nick, bite me.

Screeds by Alvaro Obregón and Salvador Alvarado against Pancho Villa.

Guzmán, Martin Luis. *Memoirs of Pancho Villa*. Translated by Virginia H. Taylor. Austin: University of Texas Press, 1965. Book 4, Chapter 24.

"Blame and praise alike befall when a dauntless man's spirit is black-and-white-mixed like the magpie's plumage."

Nick is quoting Wolfram von Eschenbach.

Von Eschenbach, Wolfram. *Parzival: A Romance of the Middle Ages*. Translated by Helen M. Mustard and Charles E. Passage. New York: Vintage Books, 1961.

"quasi pannus menstruatæ"

Pershing is quoting the Vulgate version of Isaiah 64:6, *"et facti sumus ut inmundus omnes nos quasi pannus menstruatæ universæ iustitiæ nostræ . . ."* (And we are all become as one unclean, and all our justices like the rag of a menstruous woman . . .)

"It is well that we should be kind to women in the strength of our manhood, for we lie in their hands at both ends of our lives."

Nick is quoting Frankie's paraphrase of an aphorism attributed to Chief He-Dog (Lakota Sioux).

"For the Bayesians here, this means that if a prosecutor goes to trial, there's a high prior probability of guilt, maybe 90 percent, so if the jury is right only 90 percent of the time, a conviction will be right about 99 percent of the time."

Nick says this is a trivial application of Bayes' Theorem using point estimates and is mentioned only to observe that accuracy of guilt determination in the criminal justice system depends on many things, not just the trial process. He cautions that even if, at trial, the overall average of the prior probability of guilt is 90 percent, you would be a fool to assume that the point estimate is accurate in any particular jurisdiction or case. Subject to those disclaimers, he explains that in the example given, 81 percent (0.9×0.9) of guilty people are convicted, and 1 percent (0.1×0.1) of innocent people are convicted, meaning that the chance of a convicted person being guilty is $81 / (81 + 1) = 98.78$ percent, or "about 99 percent." On the other hand, in the same example, he says the chance of an acquitted person being innocent is only 50 percent. He also says that in practice, most Bayesian analyses, including this one, are based on unverified or unverifiable assumptions.

ACKNOWLEDGMENTS

After final editing, I presented the manuscript of this book to Nick Cameron and Frankie Benally over lunch at the Flying Mulewhip. I asked if they had a dedication or acknowledgment. Nick made a vulgar gesture. Frankie didn't look up from his Sudoku.

A few days later I got an email from Nick saying he wanted to thank several women whose names will not, for liability reasons, be listed here.

I wish to thank beta readers who suggested many improvements to the story. Jeannie, Jen, Mike, Lloyd, Rick, John, Nancy, and Chris, just wait until I read your manuscripts.

Facts matter. Many thanks to S F, DEng; J G, MD, FACC; W A, PhD; C A, JD, Esq; and M B, MSc for engineering, medical, geological, legal, and computer science fact checks, respectively. Remaining errors, if any, are the author's.

Special thanks to K M, PhD, enrolled tribal member, for Native American sensitivity reading. Any remaining insensitivity should be blamed on the author.

And very special thanks to Liz, who endured many readings and offered excellent advice.

And sincere thanks to SparkPress for being crazy enough to publish this.

And finally, everlasting gratitude to Jodi Fodor, MFA, without whose excellent editorial guidance the book would have been way worse than it is.

ABOUT THE AUTHOR

Logan Terret grew up in Northern Michigan but has lived in the Southwest for the last twenty years. Formerly the chief software architect for one of America's largest financial firms, he is now retired and devotes himself to desert wanderings, mystery novels, machine learning, dog walking, and other pursuits. He is an inventor and licensed attorney. He lives in Phoenix, Arizona.

Looking for your next great read?

We can help!

Visit www.gosparkpress.com/next-read
or scan the QR code below for a list
of our recommended titles.

SparkPress is an independent boutique publisher
delivering high-quality, entertaining, and engaging
content that enhances readers' lives, with a special
focus on commercial and genre fiction.